# THE
# FIRST
# LADY

## JAMES PATTERSON

### & BRENDAN DuBOIS

CENTURY

Century is part of the Penguin Random House group of companies
whose addresses can be found at global.penguinrandomhouse.com.

Penguin
Random House
UK

First published by Century in 2018

www.penguin.co.uk

A CIP catalogue record for this book is available from the British Library.

ISBN 9781780899770
ISBN 9781780899787 (trade paperback edition)

Printed and bound in Great Britain by Clays Ltd, Elcograf S.p.A.

Penguin Random House is committed to a sustainable future
for our business, our readers and our planet. This book is made
from Forest Stewardship Council® certified paper.

MIX
Paper from
responsible sources
FSC® C018179

# THE
# FIRST
# LADY

# CHAPTER 1

TWENTY-ONE MINUTES before the ambush, Harrison Tucker—former state senator, former Ohio governor, President of the United States, leader of the free world, and a month away from being re-elected in a landslide to a second term—is lying on his chest on a king-size bed in an Atlanta hotel room, feet toward the headboard, chin resting on a pillow, watching a retrospective documentary on the TV series *House of Cards* with the love of his life.

A breakfast cart with the remains of two meals has been pushed to one side of the small but adequate room, and he sighs with pleasure as his companion, Tammy Doyle, straddling his back, gives him a thorough and deep post-coital back rub.

"Look," he says, watching the fictional president slither his way across the screen, "writers have to fictionalize politics and deal-making, like on *The West Wing* or *Madam Secretary*, but there's no way Frank Underwood could be elected president in real life. You know why?"

Tammy lowers her head, purrs in his ear. Prior to this they were both clothed, while he was giving a fund-raising speech and she was watching from a distant table that had cost her lobbying firm ten thousand dollars, but now they were both nude, the room filled with the scent of perspiration, coffee, and sex.

"Is it because he wears a toupee?" she whispers. "Or because what's-his-name was fired in disgrace?"

"Hell, no," Harrison replies. "It's because he strangled that dog in the first episode. Remember? Most voters own cats or dogs. They have a sixth sense when it comes to someone who doesn't like animals. They would have felt that from Frank. No one would vote for him. Trust me."

She kisses his right ear. "Have I ever not trusted you?"

"If you didn't you've kept it quiet... which is a nice change of pace."

Tammy laughs—a sound that still thrills him—and she really digs her warm fingers into his back and says, "Your state campaign director here in Georgia, Congressman Vickers."

He closes his eyes. Only his Tammy talks politics after lovemaking. "I'd rather not think about him right now," Harrison says.

"You should," Tammy says in her soft, low voice. "The setup for the rally was a disaster. A jumble of people couldn't get in the door because they didn't have the right tickets. That means the wheels are coming off the field operation here."

"I thought the speech went well."

Tammy leans forward again, rubs her nose against his thick hair, like a loving cat, rubbing up for attention. "Harry, the speech went well because the people love you. After years of conflict and shouting, you've calmed things down, you've gotten the country moving again, and because your opponent, the honorable governor from California, is a fruitcake. But there should have been more people there, and the ticket fiasco pissed off some of your supporters for no good reason. It all goes back to Congressman Vickers. Sack him."

Harrison shifts a bit from her weight. "Tammy . . . the election's four weeks away. Wouldn't that be seen as a sign of weakness? Besides, the latest polls in Georgia have us up by six percent."

"Five point six," she replies. "And no, it won't be seen as a sign of weakness. It'll show that once again, you have the balls to make the tough decisions when you need to do the right thing. Vickers is a drag on the campaign. Kick his butt to the curb— it'll energize your supporters and volunteers."

"Good point," he admits. "I'll think about it."

Tammy laughs again and reaches down to his shoulders, rolls him over onto his back, and her full curvy body is now on top of him. He wraps his strong arms around her and gives her a hug he wishes would last forever. Smiling and with her thick brown hair cascading down the side of her beautiful face, Tammy says, "You know what?"

"What?"

"I do love you, even if you're a power-mad, patriarchy-supporting President of these evil United States."

He gives her a firm squeeze around her waist. "And I do love you, even if you're a corrupt, money-hungry lobbyist that degrades the political process."

Another kiss, fully sweet and pleasurable, only disturbed by Harrison's thought of what his wife, Grace Fuller Tucker, First Lady of the United States, might be doing at this very moment in the District of Columbia, hundreds of miles away.

Showered and dressed once more in the gray Brooks Brothers suit that Tammy Doyle had stripped off of him a few hours earlier, Harrison Tucker leaves his hotel room exactly one minute ahead of schedule, with Tammy behind him. Outside the room, standing calmly on the Oriental-style carpeted floor, Jackson Thiel, the lead agent on his PPD—personal protective detail— nods. "Good morning, Mister President."

"Good morning, Jackson," he says.

His Secret Service agent—a tall, bulky African-American with short hair and the traditional curly Motorola radio wire running out of his ear—also says, "Morning, ma'am," and the acknowledgment of Tammy pleases Harrison. He knows he has put the Secret Service in an awkward position with his relationship— he loves this woman and refuses to call it an affair. But he has spent his last four years building trust with his agents, listening to their security recommendations, remembering their birthdays, and ensuring they are treated well. In return, they have treated him with respect, affection, and . . . understanding.

Harrison falls in line behind the business-suited Jackson as he heads to the near bank of elevators. Jackson brings up his coat sleeve and murmurs into the microphone, "CANAL is on the move," CANAL being his Secret Service code name.

As they get to the elevator, the door slides open, revealing another Secret Service agent and a quiet military man dressed in civilian clothes, holding two very thick and bulky briefcases. The only time in his presidency Harrison ever felt unready was the day he was briefed on the horrible power and responsibility belonging to him in that briefcase, carrying the codes and communications devices to launch nuclear weapons.

Harrison goes in, followed by Jackson, and then Tammy. She smiles at all of them and lingers for a moment next to Harrison, and he knows it sounds like he's reverted back to high school, but that bright smile just lifts him off his feet. Even the man holding the keys to nuclear Armageddon doesn't seem as frightening.

It's crowded in the small elevator, and Tammy is standing right next to him. He lowers his right hand, slips it into her left hand, gives it a squeeze. He knows deep inside he's doing wrong, that he shouldn't be having this relationship with Tammy, but she makes him happy. That's all. Gives him love and affection and makes him happy, and for all the late nights, the compromises, the hard decisions, and the bone-weary responsibilities of being what the Secret Service calls "the Man"... well, doesn't he deserve some happiness?

The elevator comes to a halt, and in seconds there's a procession moving quickly through an underground tunnel. Atlanta is honeycombed with tunnels and steam pipelines and old passageways, and this one leads to the sub-basement of the hotel where he was supposedly spending the night alone.

Another elevator, another agent already pre-positioned. Into the elevator, and Tammy leans in and whispers, "All right. When we get out I'll swing around out front, catch a cab. When will I see you again?"

He turns, kisses her ear through her thick hair, whispers back, "How about New Hampshire? In three days I'm speaking at Hart's Location, one of the places where they cast the first votes in the nation."

Tammy says, "Only for you. I hate that state. They think they're God's chosen in picking the next president."

He moves his lips away from her. "They picked me, didn't they?"

Tammy laughs. "Even a broken clock is right twice a day."

The elevator door opens up, other Secret Service agents are waiting for him, and he follows their lead as they go through a storage area with plastic shrink-wrapped goods on wooden pallets, past rolled-up metal doors, a loading dock next to a wide alleyway. It's barely dawn, and Atlanta's morning air feels refreshing and his arm is around Tammy's shoulders.

When he turns to say good-bye to Tammy is when it happens.

The first thing he notices are the bright flashes of light, and he half-expects to hear gunshots follow, and there are people now, coming out of a doorway, coming at him, more flashes of light and it's—

Camera flashes.

Spotlights on television cameras.

About a dozen of them, moving toward him, some charging, baying beast demanding to be fed, demanding to be answered, shouting at him, pushing ahead—

"Mister President!"

"Mister President!"

"Mister President!"

# CHAPTER 2

GRACE FULLER TUCKER, First Lady of the United States, takes her time walking through the offices of the East Wing, saying good morning and hello to her young staff members. Her Secret Service detail of two men and one woman spread out behind her as she walks forward past her young charges, who are referred to by the news media as "the First Lady's children." She always smiles at the joke but never lets on that the little phrase digs at her, a constant reminder she and Harrison will always be childless.

She may be First Lady, a guest on *Ellen*, a popular subject on the covers of *People* and *Good Housekeeping,* and patron of a number of children's charities, but fate and her husband's political career have conspired to ensure that she will never, ever be a mother.

Some days, like this one, she almost believes it's been worth it.

"Morning, ma'am."

"Good morning, Mrs. Tucker."

"Lookin' fine, Mrs. T."

She laughs, touches folks on their arms or shoulders as she passes through, thinking, *Yes, it's been a good day so far.* This morning she attended a breakfast meeting at a homeless shelter for kids in Anacostia. There had been plenty of press there, plenty of attention to the overcrowding and lack of funding, and also—unfortunately—plenty of wide-eyed children sitting on mats on the floor, looking up at all of the adult activity, children who have never had a bed or a place to call their own.

Yes, a good meeting and photo op, although she was tempted to tell the assembled news media it was still a national disgrace that a country as wealthy and as smart as the United States hasn't solved the homeless problem for children, but in the end she kept that opinion to herself. Once, she could have said that to Harry, but he'd stopped listening to her a long time ago.

The offices on the second floor of the East Wing used to be tiny and cramped, off one long, narrow hallway, but the previous First Lady had replaced them with a collection of open-plan cubicles. The only private offices belong to her and her chief of staff.

One of her staff members, Nikki Blue, comes forward, carrying a coffee cup emblazoned with a caricature of the First Lady with a halo and angel's wings—originally from an Internet blog site that hated her and her husband.

"Thanks, Nikki," she says, accepting the cup gratefully and taking a small sip. "If Patty could bring me my schedule and—"

Something is wrong.

Something is very wrong.

The talk and chattering is finished. There are whispers and sighs, and this little warren of cubicles is now deadly quiet.

She turns, sees where everyone is looking.

To a trio of television screens, hanging from the ceiling behind her, all tuned to one of the cable news channels.

Someone whispers, "Oh, that son of a bitch."

Up on the screens is a video of her husband stepping out in an alley somewhere in Atlanta, looking shocked, like a deer at night surprised by a spotlight, his arm around another woman...

Another woman.

Grace stands stock-still, forcing her legs not to tremble.

The video runs again and again, like some damn marital Zapruder film, Harry being tossed into the back of an SUV by the Secret Service, the woman—fairly attractive, a cold and logical part of Grace admits—being chased into a hotel building, through a kitchen, out to the lobby, and then to the front, where she manages to get into a taxi, the camera work jerky and bouncing as they keep pace with her.

The cab, though, is stuck trying to get into traffic, and the woman—now named as Tammy Doyle, a lobbyist with a K Street firm here in DC—is shown turning her head away from the cameras, microphones, and shouting.

Now the video is back to showing the President being ambushed, being pushed into the SUV, being driven away, and now the talking heads are spouting off their views, theories, and deep thoughts—even though this news has just broken minutes ago—and she gasps as hot coffee is spilled on her shaking hand.

Grace brings up the coffee cup.

Oh, she is so tempted to toss it at the nearest television screen.

She turns, forces out a smile to her children.

"I'll be in my office," she says. "And can someone answer that darn phone? Let's get back to work, people."

Grace goes into her office, softly closing the door behind her and locking it. Her hand is still shaking as she puts the coffee cup down on her desk.

She turns off all the lights, hugs herself, and leans back against the closed and locked door.

She will not cry.

She will not cry.

She won't give her husband the satisfaction, even if he's hundreds of miles away from her.

Grace jumps as a phone rings on her desk, and from its tone, she knows it's her private line and she knows who's on the other end.

Never in her life has a ringing phone frightened her so.

# CHAPTER 3

WHEN HE HAD been running for the state senate back in Ohio, years ago, Harrison Tucker recalled reading a story about Air Force One on 9/11, and how its pilots—desperate to get the President off the ground from Sarasota, Florida—had taken off at high speed, forcing passengers back into their seats, nearly crawling vertically in the air to gain altitude and safety.

Now, as President, Harrison sits in his well-equipped and comfortable office on Air Force One's main deck, next to his forward suite, wishing this massive and expensive aircraft could fly him somewhere to safety and isolation.

But that's not possible.

There is no safe haven from what has happened in Atlanta, and the news will get worse with every passing minute. His allies up on Capitol Hill will hesitate to expend political capital on his behalf. The influential columnists and bloggers will re-evaluate their support as Election Day draws near. The governor of California will see a chance to turn the race around in his favor. And all of Harrison's plans and dreams to help those millions down there in the wide expanse of this country...are now in jeopardy.

Sitting on the other side of his wide and polished desk is Parker Hoyt, his chief of staff, the man who has been behind the scenes for years—making the deals, pulling the strings, putting out the fires that took him from the Ohio State House to 1600 Pennsylvania Avenue. His dark blue eyes are solemn, his gray-white hair crew cut, and he has a hawklike nose mocked by political cartoonists from coast to coast.

Parker gives him a sympathetic glance. "I told you that you'd eventually get caught."

"I know."

"I told you that the most-photographed, most-watched man in the world couldn't get away with having an affair forever."

"I know."

"I told you—"

Harrison holds up his right hand. "Damn it, Parker, no more I-told-you-so's, all right? Give me a plan, a blueprint, something to get me out in front of this story, to get me…out of this mess."

Parker says, "Well, speaking of this story, we have about a dozen members of the press in the rear of this aircraft waiting for a statement."

"Let them wait." Harrison shifts in his seat, looks out the row of five windows, the drape hanging to the left, seeing the empty, wooded landscape of southeast America pass underneath. So much open space in this country…and he has a brief moment of envy, of men his age living down there in small towns, with small homes and even smaller problems.

He swivels his chair back and says, "Parker…"

His chief of staff crisply nods. "All right. We're going to need to come clean about your relationship with Tammy Doyle."

A hard, cold feeling settles into his chest. "Can't we just say she's . . . well, a friend? A travel companion? Someone to keep me company on these long trips?"

A brutal shake of the head. "Mister President, with all due respect, grow up. You've tossed a huge piece of raw meat to the press four weeks before the election. They're going to chase down her background, her travel records, her relationship with you. They'll match up your campaign stops with trips she's made to check on her lobbyist clients. That's step one. Step two, they'll start talking to people, and people love to talk. All it'll take is one chambermaid, one room service clerk, one loose-lipped person looking for his or her fifteen minutes of fame, to verify that the two of you spent the night together somewhere, in New Orleans, or LA, or Chicago."

Harrison sighs. "Never Chicago."

"Lucky you," Parker says. "So we need to get ahead of the story, and that means following a script. And fair warning, you're going to hate it."

The cold feeling in his chest is still there, but he knows from experience to trust Parker Hoyt. His chief of staff not only knows where the bodies are buried, but also had a hand in putting them there in the first place. Harrison likes to think of himself as a realist—something he told the voters four years ago during his first run for the White House—and knows he wouldn't be sitting here without Parker's advice and counsel.

"All right," Harrison says. "What's the script?"

Parker nods with satisfaction. "It starts with the phone call to your wife, then a day or two at a retreat, an apology, and then a photo of you walking hand in hand across the South Lawn as you take Marine One to Camp David. Maybe get a prominent religious figure to come spend some time to counsel you. Then some carefully placed leaks to the news media that the First Lady is furious with you, is making you sleep on a couch or in the White House bomb shelter, but that she is open to forgiveness and eventual reconciliation."

Harrison rubs at his face. "What about Tammy?"

Parker utters an obscenity. "You forget about her, right now, right this minute."

"But she—"

"I don't care if she's Mother Teresa on the outside, the world's greatest lover on the inside, a political genius, and gourmet cook as well—she's out of the picture. You've got to worry about your re-election, worry about the First Lady. Besides being angry and hurt, she's now in the mood to cut off your manhood and toss it into the Potomac. And there'll be a large section of the population . . . voters, Mister President . . . who would cheer her on. We can't have that."

Harrison stays quiet. The interior of Air Force One is so insulated and well built that the sound of the powerful jet engines is just a distant whisper.

He says, "Is there any other way?"

"No."

"Are you sure?"

"Mister President . . . to save your presidency, to continue to serve this nation for the next four years . . . you need to make the call. Otherwise . . . well, you're clearing the way for a West Coast governor to kick you out of the White House in four weeks. The same governor, I'll remind you, that three hundred leading economists said last month would destroy our nation's economy if he were elected."

Parker's words resonate with him. There's been progress here and around the world, but there's still so much more to be done.

And he knows he's the man to do it.

Parker is right.

He hesitates, picks up the phone, talks to the on-duty communications officer, who has the talents and technical ability to reach anyone with a phone, anywhere in the world:

"Please get me the First Lady."

# CHAPTER 4

*BUCK UP,* THE First Lady thinks, and with the lights in her office still off, she strides over and picks up the receiver.

"Yes?"

From the crackle and snap of static, she instantly recognizes the call is coming from Air Force One, and the communications officer flying up there somewhere says, "Please hold for the President."

Grace leans against the edge of her desk.

Waits.

She's amazed at how calm she is.

"Grace?" comes the voice that used to excite her, intrigue her, and now, for the last years, often disappoints her.

"Yes," she says, not wanting to say anything more.

More cracks and pops of static. Let him go first, let him set the tone.

"Grace, I don't know what to say, I mean, I'm so sorry about—"

"Shut up, Harry," she says. "Save it for your girl, whoever she is ... And who is she?"

"She's uh, well, we can talk about it when I get back—"

She interrupts him. "Talk? What shall we talk about? Is she the first? Is she? Or is she one in a long line of eager young ladies looking to service the President of the United States?"

"Yes," he snaps back. "She's the first. And the only one. And she's not just—"

"Oh, spare me, Harry, how she's much more than just a mistress or a woman you've cheated with," she says. "Don't tell me that this secret, sordid business of yours was so special, so romantic. Are you proud of yourself? Are you? You've managed to humiliate me, make a mockery of our marriage, and you've also given voters something else to think about when they vote in four weeks. When they get into that voting booth, what are they going to see? The honorable Harrison Tucker, President of the United States, or a cheating husband?"

"Grace, please, I hope we can—"

She talks right over him. "Hope?" she asks, voice rising. "Here's what you should hope, fool. You better hope that the American voters are stupider than you think, that they'll ignore the blatant . . . idiocy of sinking your chances a month away from Election Day. That they won't sign on with that yogurt-and-granola-loving governor and kick your sorry butt out of the Oval Office. And to drag me down with this . . . drama of yours. Harry, I won't have it. I've put up with enough from you over the years, from Columbus to DC, and you know the sacrifices I've made . . . what I've given up."

Her voice chokes, finally, and she bites her lower lip to prevent a sob from coming out. And she doesn't dare tell him what else is on her mind, that all the good work she's done as First Lady in the past four years—to rescue the most helpless and vulnerable in this nation, fighting for them even when he and his bastard chief of staff wouldn't—will now be ignored for the gossip-filled stories to come.

The tears are now rolling right along. Harrison has hurt her, but she doubts he knows just how deeply.

Through the static on the phone—coming from Air Force One's extensive telephone encryption system—her husband's voice comes through, soothing and apologetic.

"Grace, please . . . I made a mistake. A serious mistake. No excuse, it's all on me . . . but please . . . can we discuss this, work through this—"

Now his voice isn't that of a loving and contrite husband. It's the voice of a practiced politician, trying to make a deal.

It's too much.

She interrupts him one last time. "When are you getting to Andrews?"

"In . . . less than two hours."

"And you want to talk it over after you land?"

"Grace, please. Can we do that?"

The First Lady takes a deep breath. "I don't want to talk to you now, or then, or ever."

And she slams the phone down.

# CHAPTER 5

ABOARD AIR FORCE ONE, President Harrison Tucker gently places the phone back in its cradle. Parker Hoyt lowers his phone as well, having listened in to the strained and angry conversation between the President and one very hurt First Lady.

Parker looks closely at his friend and President, the man he has helped push, drag, and propel from the State House in Columbus to the White House in the District of Columbia. Except for a few years working for an international arms and intelligence corporation—to bank some serious change and make important defense connections here and abroad—Parker has always been at Harrison Tucker's side. The President is a smart man, a tough man in a very tough job, and Parker's role is to give him the additional resources and toughness to get the job done. The President is in a light-gray suit and white shirt, no necktie, and even with the troubles of this morning, he's a handsome man, with a ready smile, dark black hair with the obligatory white highlights at the temples, and except for a crooked nose— broken as a high school quarterback—he almost looks like a younger brother of George Clooney.

He's smart, sympathetic, and he has the "gift." Only a few presidents in Parker's lifetime have had the gift. Lyndon Johnson had it, as well as Reagan, and God, did Bill Clinton have it...the ability to work a room, to be the focus of attention, to smile, schmooze, and above all, to get things done.

But only if he stays smart and focused.

Which, Parker thinks, is a challenge this morning.

Harrison looks wearily at him. "What the hell do you think she means by that? That she doesn't want to talk to me now or ever. That sounds so...final."

He gives his President a reassuring smile. "It'll all work out. Trust me. Look at what happened the last time a First Lady caught her hubby cheating...there were a few rough months but he came back stronger, won reelection by a landslide, even gained seats in Congress. You've got a lot going in your favor, including that you weren't fooling around with an intern."

Harrison says, "But we don't have months."

Parker gives his President a reassuring touch on his wrist. "You've just got to trust me."

The President shakes his head. Parker goes on. "That's my job," he says. "To protect you. To protect your vision and this administration. And I won't let that bitch—excuse my French—do anything to hurt you."

If Harrison is offended by the obscenity, he doesn't show it.

The President speaks quietly. "Ever see a high-wire act? You know, where the guy walks across the wire with a pole, balancing himself so he doesn't fall?"

Parker doesn't know where the President is going with this but decides to play along. "Sure, who hasn't?"

Silence. They are in the most exclusive flying cocoon in the world, but right now Parker wants to get to work to save this man sitting across from him.

Harrison goes on. "You can see that guy up there, going along, slow and steady, making progress. Like this administration: slow, steady steps. Nothing flashy or fancy." He smiles, the white-toothed smile that has wooed so many millions of voters. "That's been us the past four years, hasn't it?"

"Yes, sir, it certainly has. And the voters will reward you come November."

The quiet tone of the President's voice doesn't change. "But all it takes is one slip, one misjudgment, one mistake. Then the wire starts to wobble. One foot and then the other slips. And off you go. All that progress...gone...as you fall to the ground."

*Jesus Christ,* Parker thinks, *let's get our man back on track.* "True, sir, but you forgot one thing."

"What's that?"

Another reassuring touch. "There's a safety net at the bottom. To rescue the high-wire guy. So he can bounce back up and go right back to the high wire."

The President says not a word.

Parker says, "Mister President...I'm your safety net. And I'm going to save you. That I promise."

The President's eyes are moist; he nods and then pretends to take interest in the forested landscape passing below them.

Parker checks his watch again. After they land, he'll start making the necessary phone calls, to cast a very wide net—safety or otherwise—to keep things under control.

Air Force One is a magnificent flying machine, with enough communications equipment to enable the President to command a war while forty-five thousand feet in the air, but in these troubled times, Parker doesn't trust the integrity of these communications systems.

Plans are starting to come to mind, plans he will keep away from his friend and boss, and especiallyWikiLeaks and the Russian intelligence agencies.

He will do what has to be done no matter what, no matter the risks.

To protect the President.

And to hell with the First Lady and anyone else who gets in his way.

# CHAPTER 6

GRACE FULLER TUCKER emerges from her office and stops, stunned, as her entire staff stands before her and starts applauding. Her face flushes with joy and embarrassment—joy at the support and love her children are showing her, and embarrassment because they had no doubt listened to her loud voice going through these old and thin walls as she yelled at the President.

She holds up a hand, blinking back tears, and just murmurs, "Thank you, thank you."

They eventually stop applauding, and some of them brush tears away from their eyes. Grace takes a long, deep breath, wonders what she could say that would make any difference at all to her staff. Despite herself, she glances up at the three television screens, still all reporting what's being called the Ambush in Atlanta.

To hell with that.

Grace turns back to her staff, folds her hands. "I . . . it's going to be a rough time for all of us in the hours and days ahead. All the good work you've done with me—in helping children in need, children hurt and abandoned by their families or society—

unfortunately, all of that good work is now going to be over-shadowed. For those of us in the East Wing, there is going to be only one story for the foreseeable future. For that . . . I am so very sorry."

Grace needs to go on, and she quickly looks at the carpeted floor to regain her composure. "But . . . as hard as it might be . . . ignore that story. Focus on the good that you've done with me . . . focus on the children whose lives have been improved or saved by you . . . and at some point . . . someday . . . this . . . nonsense, this scandal, will be forgotten."

Another burst of applause, and she smiles and joins their applause, then catches the attention of her chief of staff, Donna Allen, and gestures her back into Donna's office. Grace doesn't bother closing the door behind her because she only needs her chief of staff for a minute.

Grace asks, "My schedule for the rest of the day. Remind me, please."

Donna is a slim, pretty woman with glasses and short black hair who seems able to operate efficiently on only four hours of sleep. She goes to her desk, picks up a sheet of paper. "Ma'am . . . let's see. You have a luncheon with the Senate wives from the Party, a group interview with prominent political bloggers at two p.m., an early evening reception at five p.m. with the ambassador's wife from Japan. Then . . . er, dinner with . . . um, the President and an eight p.m. attendance at the Kennedy Center, for that—"

Grace nods. "Cancel it all."

Donna looks up, shocked. "Ma'am?"

"You heard me, Donna," she says, turning around and going out into the East Wing offices. "Cancel it all. I'm leaving."

Donna follows her out. "But . . . but . . . where are you going?"

She sees her Secret Service lead agent, Pamela Smithson, a tiny blonde who looks like she weighs ninety pounds soaking wet but who supposedly is an expert in hand-to-hand combat and close-quarters shooting. Pamela is speaking into her blouse cuff, and Grace knows what she's saying: "CANARY is on the move."

*Boy, am I ever,* Grace thinks.

At first she had hated the Secret Service code name, but now she embraces it. Canaries have a long and noble history, especially when it comes to warning miners of trouble coming, and she likes to think that's been one of her roles — warning American society that they can't keep ignoring the children trapped in the deep, dark holes of poverty.

She wants to say something once more to her staff, all of whom are looking at her now with love and concern.

What to say?

Grace Fuller Tucker, First Lady of the United States, turns and leaves her East Wing offices for the last time.

# CHAPTER 7

PRESIDENT HARRISON TUCKER didn't think it was possible, but in fact his mood is improving as Air Force One slowly taxis to its special spot at Andrews Air Force Base. He knows the pilots of Air Force One pride themselves on always arriving on time, but he also knows their secret: on time means coming to a halt at the wheel chocks, and they will either reduce or increase their taxiing speed to ensure they make the goal.

Secrets.

God, if only his one secret had been kept, at least for another month.

Parker Hoyt has been at his side for the last few hours, insisting that they play hand after hand of cribbage, and even though Harrison lost every hand to his wily chief of staff, he has enjoyed those few hours of distraction. It has done him well.

But now the cards and cribbage board have been put away. He glances out the window. Thank God this is a military base, and the public and press can be contained.

"What now?" he asks.

"You should try the First Lady one more time," Parker says.

"It's a long shot, but maybe we could get her to stand with you for a moment, some sort of photo op on the South Lawn when Marine One comes in for a landing…"

Harrison says, "Oh, come on, Parker, there's no way she's going to do that."

"Don't be so sure," his chief of staff says. "Without you, who is she? Another housewife with big dreams and ambitions. If she wants to continue her do-gooding ways, she needs to be with you. Sooner or later, she'll come to that conclusion, she'll smile for the cameras, and she'll bear it."

Harrison ponders what Parker has just said. He sounds…correct. Harsh, but correct. "What else?"

Parker says, "We need to meet with your senior campaign staff, and reps from both the House and the Senate. Not the congressmen or senators…Jesus, we don't need those blowhards making a statement out on the South Lawn after they leave. We'll want staff members from the Hill that we can quietly slide in and brief."

"And say what?"

"That we're facing a bumpy week or two, but we'll be fine. They bring that message back to the Hill, and that will reassure most of the crew up here. They may be angry at you for what you've done, but they're also scared to death to see the governor of California get sworn in next January."

"Who'll be making the briefing?"

Parker says, "It has to be you. Anybody else, the staffers will smell blood in the water and they'll race back up Pennsylvania Avenue on their young and chubby legs and tell their senator or representative to start backing away. First and foremost, they're politicians, wanting only to save their skin, and if they see any sign of disarray or weakness from this White House, they'll abandon you, sir. You need to show them remorse, but most of all, you need to show them strength."

Harrison still hates hearing what's coming from his chief of staff, but he knows he's right. "Sounds reasonable."

"Good," Parker replies. "But first things first, sir. Make the call."

He picks up his phone. "Get me the First Lady, please."

When he puts the phone down, he says, "What about the press back there?"

Parker offers a thin smile. "Let Jeremy"—the President's press secretary—"earn his pay for once. He'll keep them in place until you're safely on Marine One."

"But what will he say to them about what…what happened in Atlanta?"

"Don't worry, I'll take care of Jeremy, and he'll take care of the press. You just take care of the First Lady, try to calm her down. That's your goal for the day…oh, and one more thing."

"What's that?"

Parker says, "You get off the steps here at the base, you do the usual meet-and-greet with the military at the bottom. The only camera will be a pool camera, to see if you fall on your ass as you leave the aircraft. Don't trot down the stairs like you're in a hurry, and don't blow by the Air Force folks at the tarmac. Take your time. You're a guy who's messed up but who's confident he can come back."

Harrison nods. "I see what you mean."

"Same thing at the White House. If you can persuade the First Lady to show up, perfect. That means the turnaround will take place quicker than I hoped. But if she's still in a pissy mood and won't show up, no problem. You step off Marine One, wave, and saunter back into the White House like nothing's wrong, like you're totally in control."

"Fair enough," Harrison says, and he remembers something from that morning with Tammy. "But I need you to do one more thing for me."

Parker says, "My to-do list is pretty long, but go ahead."

Harrison says, "Congressman Vickers. Last night's speech was a near disaster, with a lot of my supporters being turned away. I want him out."

"But that might—"

"I don't care," Harrison says. "He's out by the end of the day, all right?"

"We're up by six percent in Georgia."

"Five point six percent," Harrison says, remembering what his Tammy told him. "And it would probably be up another half point if it wasn't for him. He's gone."

Parker nods, and Harrison sees there's relief in his eyes. His chief of staff is seeing the President of the United States is back at work.

A soft rap on the door, and Harrison says, "Yes, come in."

In comes the head of his protective detail, Jackson Thiel, and the large man looks troubled.

Harrison is suddenly afraid.

"Yes, Jackson, what is it?"

"Sir...the communications officer...he contacted me after you requested to talk to the First Lady."

"All right," Harrison says. "But why are you here?"

"Sir..."

"Yes?"

Jackson hesitates for the briefest and most frightening of seconds, and in a quiet and stone-cold voice, says:

"Sir...the First Lady...she can't be located."

# CHAPTER 8

IT'S COOL AND dimly lit where I work, the better to see the surveillance monitors and the televisions broadcasting the latest news, gossip, and screaming headlines. I look up, scanning the screens, and for the benefit of my fellow Secret Service agents this morning, I try to keep a sense of professional decorum and manage not to laugh. The man I've sworn to die defending has just gotten caught putting his presidential pen into an unauthorized inkwell. He isn't the first, and won't be the last, and I don't particularly care. The Secret Service is a protection agency. We're not America's Morality Police. There's the low murmur of voices, the tapping of keyboards, and radio chatter from police scanners covering Metro DC and all of the local police departments, so we always know what's going on with our somewhat friendly law enforcement neighbors.

My immediate deputy—Assistant Special Agent in Charge Scott Thompson—stands next to me and says, "What do you think, Sally?"

"Right now I want you to put the word out, especially to the Uniformed Division," I say. "We're going to get increased attention from the news media and the usual publicity hounds. I don't want any fence jumpers, wanting to give the President romantic advice or a Bible, got it? Double up the patrols on the sidewalks...anybody approaches the fences, looks like they're going to go over, we're to stop them on the public side. Got it?"

"Got it, boss," Scott says, and goes back to his desk. Scott is an ex-Army Ranger, bulky and tough, and respectful of me and everyone else in the chain of command, which makes him a keeper.

I shift my gaze from the network screens—AMBUSH IN AT-LANTA seems to be the winning headline this morning—and glance at the electronic status board. We and other members of the Presidential Protective Division are fortunate with this administration in that there are no spoiled kids running around, trying to ditch their agents at bars or dance clubs, or slightly nutty mothers-in-law claiming that Peeping Toms are gazing at them undressing in their guest quarters. There's just the President and First Lady, which makes my job a hell of a lot less complicated than my predecessor's.

According to the status board, CANAL is on Marine One, seconds away from landing on the South Lawn, and CANARY is—

"Hey, Scotty," I call out, just as he's picking up the phone. "Mind telling me why CANARY is at a horse farm in Virginia? Her Plan of the Day this morning didn't indicate that."

He says, "Last-minute change of plans, boss. After the news this morning...well, who can blame her? Not me, that's for sure."

"Yeah, I get that," I say, as I head back to my desk. I don't like last-minute changes. You don't have the time to prep the visiting area, check out the neighborhood, track down those nuts on the class three list who have made threats against the First Family in the past. The only upside is that with something as sudden as this horse farm visit, you can surprise any bad guys out there hovering around.

And the downside, of course, is that any bad guys out there—especially the patient and tough ones—can react quickly to an opportunity and kill your protectee.

Not a good way to get promoted.

I call over to my assistant. "Hey, Scotty. When you're done there, contact CANARY's detail."

"Sure, boss. What do you want?"

A little whisper of concern seems to be on my shoulder. "Make sure everything's fine."

"If it weren't fine, you'd be the first to know."

"Scotty," I say. "Make the damn call."

And I try to get back to work.

# CHAPTER 9

MY DESK IS shoved in a corner of the White House basement office called Room W-17, which is the command center for the Secret Service at 1600 Pennsylvania Avenue. Since I've been assigned here, one of the few jokes I've told about the place to friends and family is that my staff and I are closer than anyone else to the Oval Office, only seven feet away.

That usually brings ooohs and aaahs of appreciation, until I tell them the punch line: I and the others working in Room W-17—also known as Horsepower—are seven feet *below* the Oval Office.

Not exactly within spitting distance.

My desk has a wooden nameplate my eleven-year-old daughter, Amelia, made for me two years ago with wood and a burning tool that says, in clumsy letters, SALLY GRISSOM, AWESOME AGENT. The only agent who ever laughed at the nameplate is now with Homeland Security, inspecting cargo containers in Anchorage. What the nameplate should say is SALLY GRISSOM, SPECIAL AGENT IN CHARGE, PRESIDENTIAL PROTECTIVE DIVISION, but as much as Amelia enjoys making me gifts, I think if I asked her to make me a new one with my correct title, she just might cry.

A closed-circuit feed from one of the scores of surveillance cameras shows Marine One landing on the South Lawn. *Hoo boy,* I think, I bet the President wishes he was still up in the air, circling around, high up from his angry wife and the very hungry news media.

Then I get back to work.

No doubt the rest of the nation is going to be shocked by what's been uncovered about the President, but not me. Unlike 99 percent of the rest of the Secret Service detail, I'm a DC girl, through and through, and know all about the rumors and scandals that always bubble below the surface here among the pretty old buildings. Politics is politics, and human nature will always be human nature, so why pretend to be stunned?

Mom worked at the Department of Education, while Dad worked for the Capitol Police, and they're both now in Florida, enjoying sunshine, practicing Tai Chi, and fighting with each other. I have two sisters, one who works for the Government Accountability Office (GAO), and the other for the NSA, and let me tell you, family functions are lots of laughs, with one sister going on and on about budgets and spreadsheets and the other not able to say anything about what she does.

On my crowded desk are two framed photographs: one of Amelia, with her sweet smile and long blond hair—unlike the frizzy brown mop I wrestle with each morning—and another of the both of us, grinning with red, sweaty faces as we finished last year's Marine Corps 10K, both of us wearing Secret Service T-shirts: "You elect 'em, we'll guard 'em."

There's also an empty space that once held a photo of my soon-to-be—God-willing—ex-husband, Ben, one of the faceless, nameless bureaucrats in the Department of the Interior who helps keep our national parks and other treasures running.

That photo's been gone for almost a year, and since he and his rat bastard—excuse me, *overzealous*—attorney have come to their senses, our divorce should be final in less than two weeks.

My desk is small, crowded, and located just where I like it. I have another office across the street in the Eisenhower Executive Office Building, where I host the occasional dignitary and, more rarely, fire an agent who's screwed up, but I don't like being in the big office with all the nice furniture and bookcases and couches and coffee tables. I like it here, right up close with the Man and my people, who spend every waking second of their lives preparing to die to protect him and his poor, put-upon wife.

Then again, I'll probably use that big office later to debrief Jackson Thiel after his shift ends today and find out how long this affair has been going on—and why he hadn't told me. Definitely not good, but something for later. I grab a file folder from a thick pile and again wish I spent half the time wasted on paperwork out in a gym or on the range keeping my weapon qualifications current. The phone rings.

"Agent Grissom," I answer, which surprises some of my coworkers. According to protocol, I should answer the phone, "Special Agent in Charge Grissom, Presidential Protective Division," which is too much of a mouthful. Suppose someone is in the East Room, tossing off a smuggled hand grenade in the time it takes me to announce myself?

But there are surprises, and then there's this one: on the line is Mrs. Laura Young, the President's secretary. I can't recall the last time she phoned me.

"Agent Grissom," she says, "the President would like to see you, right away."

"Ah..."

Then one of my agents makes a handwritten notation on the backup status board, reflecting the electronic board. One of the changes I had implemented months ago, in case the power went out. "CANAL is in the Oval Office."

I say, "I'll be there," and I hang up the phone.

I don't like it.

Scotty sees me and says, "Everything all right, boss?"

I stand up and start walking.

Unless there's a major emergency or crisis, the President never calls the head of the Presidential Protective Division like this.

Never.

"Boss?" Scotty asks again.

I keep on walking to the office door.

Fast.

# CHAPTER 10

ABOUT THE ONLY entertainment source that has gotten the White House right in my opinion is *The West Wing*. Oh, not because of the crackling dialogue or the staff members arguing while walking backward or a President depicted as one who relaxes in the afternoon by strolling on top of the Reflecting Pool, but because *The West Wing* showed just how crowded and busy the place is.

There's always lots of people scurrying around, everyone save a special few wearing an access pass around their neck, color-coded to keep the serfs (excuse me, the *workers* and *volunteers*) isolated from the West Wing. I nod to those staff members I know fairly well, and one of my agents, Carla Luiz, opens the door to the Oval Office.

Little-known secret: the doors to the Oval Office have special doorknobs, meaning that if some crazed tourist from Idaho breaks free from a tour and manages to race his way here, he'll waste precious seconds trying to figure out how to open the door before he gets Tasered to his knees.

The office door closes behind me and there's the President,

standing up from one of the two couches. Sitting next to him is his chief of staff, Parker Hoyt. They're both well dressed and groomed, of course, but they look like cousins who've just learned their family farm is under six feet of floodwater, with a swarm of locusts due in once the waters recede.

"Mister President," I say, and then, "Mister Hoyt."

"Sally," the President says, gesturing to the couch opposite him, past a low-slung coffee table. "Please, have a seat."

I glance around and see we're alone.

I instantly don't like it. Usually there's an aide or three hovering in the background, to fulfill any request from getting a cup of coffee to getting the president of France on the phone, but no, we're alone. The famed desk of the President is to my left as I sit down, flanked by the American flags and his own standard. Thick bulletproof windows look out to the Rose Garden, and I see the back of another agent out there, keeping watch.

I flash back to my sixteen weeks of training at the Secret Service's James J. Rowley Training Center over in Laurel, Maryland, where my class and I were put through hours of different scenarios involving gunshots and explosions and violent assaults, but I don't think any of these scenarios are going to prepare me for what's going to happen next.

The President says, "Agent Grissom . . . er, Sally, we have a situation."

"Sir," I reply, content to let him tell me what's going on without lots of questions.

The President looks to Parker, as if for reassurance, then takes a deep breath and says, "We need your assistance."

"Of course," I say, and I wait, wondering what the hell is going on.

Hoyt gives me a self-satisfied look of knowing something he shouldn't know and says, "Impressive record you have there, Agent Grissom."

I don't feel like saying anything, so I don't. I just nod.

He says, "Especially the incident two years ago involving the Iranian ambassador. Why don't you tell the President about that event?"

*Hoo-boy,* I think. "I'm sorry, sir, I'm restricted in responding to your request due to its classified nature."

Hoyt says, "I'm sure the President has the ability to waive any restrictions you might be under."

CANAL says, "By all means, Agent Grissom. Do tell me."

I could make a stand, but what would it gain me? "Sir, at the time I was tasked to provide diplomatic security for a very unofficial summit meeting in Maryland with the Iranian ambassador to the United Nations, the Israeli ambassador to the United States, and the Secretary of State. An attempt was made on the Iranian ambassador's life. It was successfully thwarted."

The President says, "How come I've never heard of this?"

"It happened during your predecessor's term in office," Hoyt explains. "But Agent Grissom is downplaying her role in the event. The summit was held in the private room of an exclusive restaurant in Chevy Chase. A man pretending to be a waiter had gained access. Agent Grissom detected his presence, attempted to disarm him, a gun battle broke out, and Agent Grissom not only killed the would-be assassin but also covered the Iranian ambassador's body with her own."

"Is that true?" the President asks.

"True enough," I say.

"How did you detect the waiter?"

I give a slight shrug. "This particular restaurant is so exclusive it doesn't even have a website. But I saw the waiter's fingernails had dirt under them. He didn't fit."

CANAL grins. "I bet the Iranian ambassador was one happy man."

"Truth be told, sir," I reply, "he did his best to push me off as quick as possible once the gunfire stopped. He didn't want to be touched by a strange woman."

Hoyt says, "You see, Mister President, Agent Grissom is not only brave and resourceful, but also knows how to keep a secret. Which is why you're here, Agent Grissom. We need your skills, and your ability to keep a secret."

"What secret, sir?" I say to the President.

He grimaces and says, "The First Lady...appears to be missing."

I look at them, wondering if this is some sort of elaborate hoax or joke, maybe something to mark my birthday or hiring anniversary, but there's no humor on their faces.

I manage to speak. "Sir...she's at a horse farm, in Campton, Virginia. With her detail."

Parker speaks up. "We know that's where she's been." He glances to the President and says, "But for the past hour, we... the President has been unable to contact her. She won't pick up her cell phone, and her security detail...they say they can't locate her."

A chunk of ice seems to be working its way right up my throat. "That's impossible. They...I should have been contacted if something like that had occurred." I start to get up and say, "Mister President, Mister Hoyt, if you'll excuse me—"

"Sally, please," the President says, voice all dark and somber. "Sit down. Just for a moment."

I'm still standing up. I don't belong here. I need to run back downstairs to W-17, start contacting CANARY's detail, find out—

Parker says, "We need to keep this quiet. For now."

"What?"

He goes on. "This is a . . . delicate time. And the First Lady . . . she's not well."

I start moving away from the couch, and the President says, in a sharp tone I've never heard before, "Agent Grissom, sit down! Give us another minute. Please."

I slowly sit on the couch, my back stiff, not allowing myself to lean back against the cushions. "Mister President, with all due respect, this can't be right. If something has happened to Mrs. Tucker, I'd be the first to know. Her detail would have put out the call . . . we would have instantly responded."

Parker leans forward, his hands clasped together. "An hour ago the President tried to contact the First Lady, prior to Air Force One's landing. He was unable to do so. The communications officer aboard Air Force One was able to reach her detail with the assistance of Agent Jackson Thiel. That's when we learned about her . . . situation."

Another flash of memory, of grammar school, wondering why the boys out on the soccer field won't let me play, why I am being shut out, ignored. "I . . . the office here should have been instantly informed."

The President says, "I told them not to."

The ice that's clogging my throat has spread to my stomach, and my hands and feet are cold as well.

Training scenarios back at the sixteen-week Secret Service Academy?

Oh, yeah, this one has never come up.

"Mister President . . . this can't be true. You can't . . . I mean . . ."

Parker leans forward even more. "Again, this is a delicate situation. We're a month away from the election. The American people need to go to the voting booth with one thing in their mind, and one thing only: which elected official will do right by this country. Not the distraction of an ill First Lady, a missing woman. It wouldn't be fair to her or the nation to make this public."

I say, "What exactly are you saying, Mister Hoyt?"

Mister Hoyt doesn't reply, but our mutual boss does.

The President stares right at me. "We want you to find the First Lady."

# CHAPTER 11

I SAY STRAIGHTAWAY and without hesitation, "Impossible. If she's missing, you need to contact the FBI, Homeland Security, DC Metro Police, the Virginia State Police, and I'd even bring in—"

The President holds up a hand. "That's exactly what we don't want. The news coverage, the various agencies jockeying for position and headlines, a massive search and hunt…that won't be helpful. That's why we want you, and a few agents you can trust, to find her."

"Sir, with all due respect," I say, taking in all of the history that has occurred in this very Oval Office, wondering what twist of fate has put me right in the center of probably the biggest story to come out of here in fifty years, "I can't do that. We're a protective agency. Not investigative."

Parker says, "Bullshit. You *are* an investigative agency. You have access to intelligence information from Homeland Security. You go out in the field and investigate threats made against the President. You work with law enforcement agencies from cops in one-streetlight towns all the way up to New York City."

I feel like slapping that smug face, hard. "As part of our protective duties, Mister Hoyt. Not to find a missing person."

He says, "A person isn't missing. The First Lady of the United States is missing."

"But—"

The President says, "Agent Grissom, I'm ordering you to locate the First Lady, and to do it quietly, confidentially, and quickly. Otherwise, in all of the news stories that come out if we do anything else, and eventually locate the First Lady, there will be other stories as well. Those tales will also focus on how you and your highly skilled and highly trained agents...lost my wife. Do you want to go up to Capitol Hill and try to explain to a special congressional committee how that happened? On your watch? Do you?"

I say, "I'd rather do that than...what you're asking me."

Parker settles back on the couch. "How's Amelia?"

I'm stunned again, for the second time in less than ten minutes. "My daughter? She's...fine. Why are you asking?"

He grins, showing very firm and sharp teeth. "Divorce is always hard on kids. No matter how much work a single mom does, no matter the therapy sessions and counseling, there will always be scars, will always be permanent damage. The best a mom like you can do is to mitigate the damage."

It's like there are only two people in this famed room, him and me. "I don't see what you're driving at...Mister Hoyt."

His smile gets a bit wider. "Your husband...Ben, isn't it? Works for the Interior Department, has a little problem with the bottle, and with college interns...I can see why you're in the midst of divorcing him. His lawyer is Albert Greer, am I right?"

I now know where this is going, and I feel trapped, like I'm in the back of a Diamond Cab in a sleet storm, the driver having lost control, and we're spinning out as we slide into ongoing traffic in Dupont Circle.

"You're correct, Mister Hoyt."

"Sure I'm right. I don't know Albert Greer, but I know his firm. Lockney, Trace, Fulton and Smith. Big DC firm, does a lot of work, both public and private. Back when I was VP of operations at Global Strategic Solutions, we tossed a lot of business their way. I even let Mister Lockney beat me a few times at golf over at Burning Tree. So he and his firm owe me a number of favors."

I look to the President, to see what he thinks of all of this, but he's staring over my shoulders, looking at a painting of a sailing ship over on the opposite curved wall.

"You're a piece of shit," I say, surprising even myself.

"No, not a piece," he replies calmly. "Just the biggest chunk in all of DC... so let's make this clear, so there's no misunderstanding. You do what your President wants you to do, and we'll give you everything you need... all the backup and information necessary, so long as it's kept quiet and under the radar."

A pause for effect, no doubt. He goes on, his tone sharper. "But if you leave here without saying yes, then you're going to find out that your tentative divorce settlement is going off the rails. There'll be lots more motions... hearings... expensive delays... and you can expect a final divorce when your pretty little girl is about ready to enter college... if she still has it together to go on beyond high school and if you have any money left for tuition bills."

I'm breathing and staying conscious, but just barely. I stare at the chief of staff, and he doesn't flinch or flicker, giving it right back to me. I say, "I see how you've gotten so far."

"All those nasty rumors about me?" he says. "They're true. We're wasting time. What's your answer?"

A small part of me wants the President to intervene, to make it all right, to make the bad man go away, but the President isn't going to help me today.

I get up.

"Two answers," I say. "The first one is yes."

I walk away from the couch with the two men sitting there, one of whom I had once admired.

"And the second answer is go to hell."

I exit the Oval Office and then remember something else important.

Because of its design, it's impossible to slam the door in anger.

# CHAPTER 12

IN THE OFF the Record bar at the luxurious Hay-Adams Hotel in downtown Washington, practically across the street from the White House, Marsha Gray laughs at the dumb joke her mid-morning date has just told her, and she reaches under the table to give his upper thigh a tender squeeze.

"Really?" she asks, softening her voice. "That's really why the chicken crossed the road? All these years and I never knew that."

Her date's face flushes. He's a sweet young fellow, maybe a few years older than she is, and he's wearing a nice Savile Row gray suit with matching red necktie and pocket square. He's from one of the "stan" countries that popped up after the collapse of the Soviet Union, and he has a first and last name made up mostly of consonants—but she calls him Carl, and he thinks that's adorable.

"Are you sure?" he asks, his voice betraying only the slightest of accents. His skin is light brown, and his eyes and carefully groomed hair are both ebony. "I always thought...well, that's one of the oldest jokes in the world."

She gives his thigh another slight squeeze. "Oh, Carl, it is...but just the way you say it...well, it made me laugh."

His eyes crinkle as he smiles in return, and she slowly withdraws her hand and says, "What time is that reception of yours?"

Carl looks at his TAG Heuer watch. "In...two hours. It's a lunch meeting."

She smiles, leans forward so she is nearly popping out of her low-cut, little black cocktail dress. "Then let's go up to your room."

He smiles back. "I...I don't think there will be enough time."

"Oh, Carl..." she says, her voice dripping with disappointment. The Off the Record bar—one of the most famous watering holes in the District—is a busy place this late morning, which is perfect. Marsha leans over and kisses his ear, runs her tongue gently around the lobe, and whispers, "That thing you've always wanted to do...I'll let you do it to me now. Honest."

She leans back and already he's fumbling at his napkin with one hand, signing the check with the other, and she picks up her little black leather purse and he's smiling like some teen boy, finally getting his driver's license. In his sweet, low voice, he says, "You...you're a green-eyed *djinni*, you are. The way you make me do what you want."

Marsha waits for him to come around the small table, then stands up and crooks her arm. He slides his arm into hers, and they walk out of the bar, into the grand and posh lobby of the Hay-Adams Hotel, which is made of columns, high ceilings, polished wood, and quietly efficient staff.

Three bulky men in ill-fitting suits are sitting in comfortable chairs, eyeing the two of them as they walk by, and Marsha just keeps the smile on her face. The elevator is quick, silent, and in the few seconds they are in there, she turns her head and buries her face into his neck, gently nibbling and licking. He tastes of vanilla. She continues to taste him, ensuring her face isn't seen on the elevator's surveillance cameras.

Down the hallway and poor Carl's hand is practically trembling as he tries to use the keycard once, twice, and then on the third attempt, he gets the door open. Marsha sees the front of his trousers is bulging out.

Inside, he waves her in, and again she takes just the slightest breath at the expense and expanse of the suite that Carl has been living in these past two weeks. There's old-style furniture, a sitting area, a gorgeous and well-designed bedroom, and windows actually overlooking the White House.

She turns and kisses him ravenously, holding him tight, rubbing a black-stocking-covered thigh against his crotch, and he moans with lust and anticipation, and she breaks away, breathing heavily. "Carl...just a moment...all right?"

"Yes...my *djinni*...anything you want."

Marsha goes across the room, thinking that even a one-night stay in the smallest room in this hotel costs more than a month's pay when she was in the Corps, and she draws the curtains closed so the White House is no longer visible, in the process hiding the room's interior from any Secret Service spotters on the White House's roof. She opens up her small purse, fumbles inside for something, and then walks back to Carl, smiling widely, reaching back to unzip her dress.

Carl is way ahead of her, his coat and tie off, his shirt unbuttoned to reveal one dark and hairy chest, and he's working at his belt with his shaking hands as Marsha comes forward and kisses him, gives him one last hug, and then kills him.

# CHAPTER 13

THE PRESIDENT OF the United States sits in silence with his chief of staff for a minute after the very angry and very determined head of his Presidential Protective Division has left the Oval Office. He gets up from the couch and walks over to his wooden desk, Resolute, a gift to the nation from Queen Victoria. Harrison sits down behind the small and ornate desk, the same one used by JFK and Bill Clinton, reflecting that they too had women problems—just like him, just like now.

The Oval Office... how many times has he spoken to the nation from this room? How many times has he had his photo taken with visitors and dignitaries in this historic place? How many meetings held here with cabinet members or news reporters?

Now, he has just concluded a meeting about secretly looking for his missing wife on the same day his relationship with Tammy Doyle was brutally made public. Twenty-four hours earlier he would never have thought that was possible.

Parker comes over, sits next to his desk in a handsome striped cushioned chair. Harrison turns to him and says, "Do you think she'll do it? We're asking a lot from her."

Parker smiles. "You know what they say, once you have 'em by the balls, their hearts and minds will follow."

For the first time since he left Atlanta, Harrison manages a laugh. "She's a woman, you fool."

His chief of staff smiles back at him from the chair. "Like you're an expert on women. Look, she'll do her job. You went after her based on her career. That didn't make her budge. But I went after her personally, with her and her daughter. That was the trick."

Harrison looks at his phone, knows at some point today he will have to reach out to Tammy Doyle. Along with the growing fear of what's happened to Grace, there's the shame of how he abandoned Tammy back in Atlanta, with that baying pack of reporters chasing after her. The woman he loved, tossed away, left to face those media wolves by herself. He can't remember the last time he's felt so ashamed.

"Where do you think Grace is?" he asks.

"Not far," Parker says. "My guess is that she dumped her Secret Service detail at that horse farm, borrowed a pickup truck, and maybe scooted out to a motel somewhere for a good cry, or maybe a few drinks."

"How long before we find her?"

"No worries, Mister President," Parker says. "She's one of the most recognizable women on the planet. How far do you think she can go? I wouldn't doubt it if we get this thing wrapped up by the end of the day. This Agent Grissom...I've read her background. She'll get the job done."

"Tell me about her," he says.

"She's been in the White House as long as you, was named

head of the Presidential Protective Division last year," Parker says. "She started out with the DC Metro Police, went to the Virginia State Police, and then joined the Secret Service. And that Iranian deal...she managed to save a man who hates her because she's a woman working for the Great Satan. Plus, she's kept it a secret all these years."

Harrison says, "I don't like what you did, threatening her... with her divorce proceedings. And her daughter. That's not right."

Parker says, "It got the job done."

"I still don't like it."

"Then forget it, and don't ask about it again."

Parker Hoyt is trying to gauge what's going on behind the steel-gray eyes of his President, and decides this is as good as any time to press him.

"Mister President, I think Agent Grissom will do her best to locate the First Lady...but she might come up against roadblocks that will...be against her nature to try to get through. I think we need another resource, a backup, if you will."

"What do you have in mind?"

"Best you don't know."

The President hesitates for a moment. "Just as long as you find her."

"And protect your presidency?" Parker asks.

He nods. "Yes. Find her and protect the presidency."

"I've got it covered," Parker says, standing up. "If you'll excuse me, sir, I've got to get to my office."

"And...the news media. We need to get something out to them."

"I've got that covered, sir. I'll be back in ten minutes."

Parker gets up and walks out of the Oval Office, through the door leading to Mrs. Young's office, past a Hispanic Secret Service agent, and then makes a sharp right into his own office. Money, prestige, power...all coins of the realm here in DC, but what really counts is access to the President. Parker is one of the very few people in this house who can see the President at any time, without an appointment, and he's the only one in this building who has what he has, on the corner of his desk: a private phone that doesn't go through the White House switchboard and that took a lot of arm-twisting and name-calling to get installed over a weekend four years back.

He closes the door, looks to the phone. There are two numbers he could call to help him in this matter, but which one? How to choose? Both are equally dangerous.

What to do.

It reminds him of that classic short story, "The Lady, or the Tiger."

Which door to open?

What number to call?

His office phone rings and rings, and he ignores it.

No time for regular business.

He makes a decision, opts to leave the other number for later.

Hoyt quickly dials a series of digits and it rings once and is picked up by an associate of his, from when he was working for Global Strategic Solutions.

"Yes?" a man's voice answers.

"I need to see...Gray. Straightaway."

"Where?"

Parker tells him.

"Hold on..."

Parker waits.

"Thirty minutes."

"Good."

He hangs up the private phone, thinks about what the President told him.

Find the First Lady.

Not save her, rescue her, or help her.

He just said, "Find her."

And that's just what he intends to do.

# CHAPTER 14

HIS EYES WIDEN as she steps back, the tiny one-shot hypodermic still concealed in Marsha Gray's right hand, her fingernail polish quite red and stark. He trembles, tries to breathe, and she wonders if she could say one last word to him before his spirit travels to whatever afterlife he believes in just as Carl collapses to the floor.

Marsha maneuvers around so she can zip the dress back up, and then goes back to her leather bag, puts the empty hypodermic back in. A slick little drug that will fade away in Carl's bloodstream within minutes, and when—or if—he's autopsied, the only thing a medical examiner will come up with is death by natural causes, perhaps a myocardial infarction, but whatever the official medical outcome, Carl will still be dead.

Mission accomplished.

Near the office space with the pretty upholstered chairs and a mahogany desk are two identical black leather briefcases.

Tempting.

From her little purse she pulls out a pair of light-blue latex gloves, snaps them on, and then opens up each briefcase. She's surprised they're both unlocked.

Each briefcase is full to the top with bundled one-hundred-dollar bills.

She whistles.

"Dear girl, temptation is surely knocking at your door," she whispers.

She gives one more appreciative glance to the money, closes the lids.

Poor Carl back there is—or was—the son of a prominent politician and oil executive (being one and the same in that particular nation ending in "stan") and was due to meet with some prominent American oil officials and representatives from his nation later this afternoon.

She is sure his unexpected death will cause a lot of turmoil, distrust, and maybe even a grudge killing or two, but that isn't her concern.

She is focused only on getting out of the Hay-Adams safely.

She picks up her small leather purse and goes into an adjoining bathroom about the size of her first apartment back in Cheyenne.

Forty-four minutes later, Marsha Gray is sipping a Diet Coke at a Subway six blocks east of the Hay-Adams. The same drink that she spent $1.99 for here at the fast-food place would probably have cost ten times as much back at the Hay-Adams, but having successfully slipped out, she's in no hurry to get back, especially with the shit storm of police, FBI, and EMTs that are descending there at this moment.

While in Carl's enormous bathroom, she had quickly and efficiently gone to work. The green-tinted contact lenses were flushed down the toilet. Her black nylons stripped off, replaced by sheer thigh-highs. A few tugs of her specially designed cock-tail dress eliminated the deep cleavage and lowered the hem about six inches. Two quick tugs on the high heels of her shoes turned them into flats. The auburn-colored wig was taken off and placed at a key point under her now-modest dress, along with the heels, making her look like she was a few months in the family way. A pair of black-rimmed glasses with clear lenses went from her small purse to her face. And with that out of the way, she had slipped out of Carl's room, taken the elevator back down to the lobby, and walked out past Carl's three bodyguards, none of them even glancing in her direction.

Now she sips on her Diet Coke, checks the time, wonders how long she'll have to wait before getting another job.

Her iPhone starts ringing. She examines the screen and smiles.

Not long at all.

# CHAPTER 15

BEFORE I KNOW IT, I'm back in the darkened and—despite the police scanners chattering along—reasonably quiet confines of Room W-17. My heart is pounding hard enough to make me think that I've just finished another road race. That thought draws me to the photo on my desk, and my sweet Amelia, and what Parker Hoyt has threatened. I check the status board and the screens and even the television feeds, each of them repeating the same footage again and again, of the Man upstairs and his mistress. Or lover. Or girlfriend.

I sit down, look at the photos of my girl once more, and my fingers briefly trace the wooden sign she's made for me.

I take a deep breath. So many years of hard work, late nights, and travel to get to this point, the pinnacle of one's career within the Secret Service. And the first woman to ever head the Presidential Protective Division.

And just as much hard work and dedication to achieve the other part of me, mother to one young lady named Amelia Grissom Miller, who's got her whole life and future ahead of her.

My fingers drop away.

I don't move.

Parker Hoyt is right.

I'm wasting time.

"Scotty!" I call out.

"Boss," he replies, hunched over a keyboard, punching in some report or update with his strong fingers, attacking each letter on the keyboard like it's an enemy that deserves to be struck hard. "I tried CANARY's detail and couldn't reach them. I tell you, our radio system has to be upgraded before—"

"Never mind that for now," I say. "Sign out a sterile Suburban. You and I are going for a ride."

He picks up a phone. "You got it. Where are we going?"

I grab my work bag, black wool overcoat, and bright-red scarf, and say, "Disaster...or in this case, a horse farm in Virginia. Come along."

A fully loaded and fully undercover black Chevy Suburban from Secret Service headquarters on H Street is delivered to the White House, and I let Scotty take the driver's seat as we slowly move around the long, curving driveway of the south side of the White House. He punches in the address of the Virginia horse farm to the Suburban's GPS, and after I buckle up, he says, "What's up? Unannounced inspection tour of the First Lady's detail?"

I settle in, my bag on the floor between my feet. "You could say that."

We're waved out of the security gatehouse and are on 15th Street, Northwest, heading south to Constitution Avenue, past the Treasury Library and other faux-Roman-looking government structures along the four-lane road. It's a crisp autumn day but the sidewalks are packed with people, either tourists looking agape at all the historical buildings, or locals—the lobbyists, bureaucrats, and a few elected officials—talking on their cell phones, moving rapidly through the meandering crowds, all believing that they, and only they, are the vital ones in government.

And scattered among that smaller group is an even smaller handful, my fellow agents, dressed to blend in, acting like tourists or bureaucrats, save for one thing: their ever-moving eyes, the eyes of a hunter, looking for those who would harm the Man.

"Boss?"

"Yeah, Scotty," I say, breaking my eyes away from the crowded sidewalks. We are now past the buildings, and to my right is the greenery of the Ellipse (I brought Amelia here last December for the lighting of the National Christmas Tree, dressed for the cold, me holding her shoulders, mine wrapped in my early Christmas gift from her), and before us, the Washington Monument is now coming into view.

"What's really going on?" he says. "This isn't an inspection tour, is it? I can tell. You're too tensed up."

The government types out there like to talk about turf battles, but Scotty's been in the real-deal turf battles, fought with M4s and AK-47s, car bombs and air strikes. He's lived this long with all of his body parts intact because of his strength, smarts, and especially because of his ability to sniff out things that don't make sense.

"No, it isn't," I say.

"What's up, then?"

Traffic slows down and I grab hold of my seat belt, tighten my grip, and say, "The First Lady can't be located."

Scotty, bless him, is a pro. "Status board says she's at that horse farm, in Campton. And her detail hasn't reported anything wrong."

"That's because they've been ordered to keep their mouths shut."

"By who?"

"The First Lady's husband, that's who," I say. "And he and his chief of staff have ordered me to go find her...and do it quietly, and quickly, without waves or headlines."

"But..."

"There's a scandal on the TV right now, Scotty, a month before the election. News breaking about a missing First Lady...it'd sink the Man in a heartbeat. There's too much at stake here. This White House isn't going to let that happen...and let that California majority become the next President. You hear what that governor said about the Chinese buildup in the Pacific? That we shouldn't worry about their bases because climate change will eventually sink all of their islands, and we should be able to cut the DoD budget by half because of that."

We slow down in the thick traffic as we get closer to Constitution Avenue.

"Well, shit," Scotty says.

"That's right."

I think for a moment, and say with a bit of reflection, "You know why I joined the Secret Service?"

"Not for the pay or benefits."

I manage a laugh. "Yeah, you're right. It's just that I grew up here...and then I was in law enforcement, protecting a chunk of turf. But I wanted to guard something bigger. The dreams and hopes that first built these pretty buildings here. Sounds silly, doesn't it? But I got to go to work every day knowing I was protecting something bigger than myself."

I wait, trying to figure out why this is all coming out now. "And today, I was just reminded that for some, I'm still nothing more than just a cop, cleaning crap up."

Traffic gets heavier and time is dragging on, and I cross my arms and say, "Remember what I said earlier, about keeping everything quiet?"

We seem to be about twenty feet away from the intersection. We've been out of the White House grounds for nearly ten minutes and have hardly moved at all.

"Yeah, I do, boss," he says.

"Change of plans," I say. "Light 'er up."

His right hand moves and flicks a few switches, and the Suburban's siren starts screaming, red-and-blue lights start flashing in the grille and at the top of the windshield, and slowly, sluggishly, the traffic starts to move, and in just a few minutes, we're on Constitution Avenue, heading west to take the Theodore Roosevelt Memorial Bridge into Virginia, passing over the Potomac River.

With the siren sounding, there's no real chance to talk to my assistant, which is fine, because at the moment I can't think of anything more to say to him.

The traffic really thins out for us, and I settle back into my seat as we cross the Potomac River and race into Virginia—and head into whatever disaster awaits us.

# CHAPTER 16

AFTER SPENDING SOME time with the President, crafting a statement mostly full of mush—the key phrases being the President confessing to a relationship that "was not appropriate," which he hopes will satisfy the press for at least a day, along with a nearly sincere apology to his "dear wife" and "the American people"—Parker Hoyt leaves the grounds of the White House and takes a walk by himself to the south, to Pershing Park, overlooked by the crowd of ignorant tourists, most of whom would probably have trouble naming the President's predecessor. He takes a bench near the fountain and the large pool that is used as a skating rink in the winter. There's a slight breeze, and most of the passersby are bundled up from the apparent cold, though Parker doesn't feel it. Growing up in Cleveland on the bitter shores of Lake Erie, you quickly learn what cold really feels like.

A short, dark-skinned woman with fine black hair, brown eyes, and wearing a Navy pea coat and jeans comes over and sits down on the bench next to him. Parker eyes the tourists one more time. If one out of a hundred could tell him who Pershing was or what he accomplished, he'd be surprised.

Parker says to the woman next to him, "The Marine Corps says your confirmed kill was forty-two."

"Sixty-three," the woman answers in a strong voice. Marsha Gray, former USMC, now a contract worker for Global Strategic Solutions, and right on time.

"Why the difference?"

Her hands are in her coat pocket. "The Corps has pretty strict rules when it comes to confirming sniper kills. You need secondary confirmation. Most guys, that's not a problem, because you have a spotter working for you—he can confirm a hit. But I worked alone. That means it took after-action intelligence reports or drone footage to confirm what I did."

"Odd thing to work alone."

"I worked in odd places," she says. "My family background gives me the skin color to blend in. I wear a chador or something similar, most men leave me alone. Under the chador, though, I had a nice special-model Remington X600 sniper rifle. I could break it down so I could sling it over my shoulder—nobody could spot it. I'd find the high ground, reassemble the gear, find and terminate the target, and by the time the blood stopped flowing, I was walking along the street like a nice, quiet covered woman, submissive to the nearest smelly bearded man and God."

"Good for you."

Marsha says, "What's the job?"

Parker says, "What do you think of our President?"

She shrugs. "No better, no worse, I guess. Though his little man sure has gotten him into trouble. Why do you ask?"

Parker thinks about how to phrase it, and decides just to let it go. "President Tucker...he gets stuff done. Not earth-shattering, or headline-making, but he gets stuff done. For the first time in a long time, we've got a President who isn't involved in a vicious fight with the other party or even with the news media. It took decades for us to get into the mess we're in, and it's going to take decades to climb out, but at least this guy is turning things around. He's made a good start."

Marsha doesn't look impressed. He goes on. "I grew up in Cleveland. Joke city of the Great Lakes. My dad, and his dad, and my great-grandfather, they had opportunities in the mills and foundries. Places to go. Good jobs that allowed them to buy a house, leave something for the kids, maybe get a vacation cabin for the summer. Families like that, they weren't entrepreneurs they weren't thinking of new Internet apps, stuff like that. So they were abandoned, forgotten. This President...he's remembered them. And he's remembered my family. That's why I work for him, and that's why I'm dedicated to his safety and success. His opponent...he thinks if we all grew kale, held hands together and sang Kumbaya, then we'd be ushered into a new world of light and happiness. I can't allow him to win. It would be an epic disaster."

Marsha says, "Nice sales pitch. What's the job?"

He says, "You grew up poor in Wyoming, didn't you? Orphaned daughter of a Basque sheep farmer, up there in the mountains. Your parents died in a truck accident during a blizzard. You joined the Corps to get out of there, make a living. It must have been pretty rough out there in Wyoming before you left."

She says, "You had a big lake. We had mountains. You had it better."

Parker says, "The First Lady is gone. The Secret Service doesn't know where she is."

"Good for her," Marsha says. "You see the knockers on that other gal? I'd be missing from my husband too, if I found out he'd been stepping out with her."

"There's more to it than just that," Parker says. "Something screwy is going on with her sudden absence. She might be missing, might have left on her own. I'm not going to allow her to sabotage the President's second term, so we're keeping the search for her secret. I'll give you information about the Secret Service's investigation, and I want you to shadow them . . . and if the situation requires, terminate."

Marsha crosses her legs. "How will I know when the situation requires it?"

"I'll be in constant contact. You'll know."

A group of chattering schoolchildren go by, two female schoolteachers desperately trying to corral them away from the pond. Parker says, "You okay with that?"

Marsha says, "Just to be clear . . . just her or do what's necessary?"

"Pretend you're out in the field, no way to contact anybody else. Do what has to be done."

Another slight shrug. "Not a problem."

"You sure?"

"I've never liked her anyway," Marsha says. "Not a problem."

"Good," Parker says. "I need you to start right away."

"Fine," she says.

"Great," he says. He rattles off a series of digits. "That's my direct line at the White House. Give me a call in thirty minutes and I'll give you what I know, and we'll proceed from there."

"Deal," she says.

Marsha gets up, and Parker says, "Ask you one more question?"

"You're not on the clock yet, so yeah, ask away."

"Who's Pershing? You know, the guy this park was named after."

For the first time since he had met this killer, she smiles.

"What is this, a joke? General John Joseph 'Black Jack' Pershing. Head of the American Expeditionary Force during the First World War. Chased Pancho Villa through Mexico earlier but never caught him. You need anything else?"

"No," Parker says. "Go along, and don't be late calling."

Marsha says, "I won't," and she walks away, and like snipers everywhere, she quickly blends in with the crowds and trees and disappears.

Parker takes that as a very good sign.

# CHAPTER 17

AT THE WESTBROOK Horse Farm just outside of the rural Virginia town of Campton, a forty-minute drive from the White House, Scotty parks our Suburban next to two other black, identical-looking Suburbans situated in a dirt lot surrounded by a chest-high white wooden fence.

I get out and Scotty tries to catch up with me as I stride over to the First Lady's three-person security detail, standing in a group like little animals huddling together for protection, and I lose my professional composure and attitude and let them have it for about three wasted minutes, yelling and jabbing my right arm at them like I was about to step over and punch each of them in the throat.

The detail, two women and a young man, take it without flinching, and then I stop, take a deep breath, and say, "That wasn't necessary. My apologies. I've wasted time. Pamela, give me a briefing."

Pamela Smithson steps forward. She's blond and barely made the weight and height requirements for female Secret Service agents, but she's an expert in hand-to-hand combat, and at some agent's birthday party last year, I saw her take some clown from Homeland Security who had been harassing her and toss him into a swimming pool.

"CANARY wanted to come out here for a couple of hours of horseback riding," she explains. "She finds it relaxing, and her doctor recommends it for her as part of her recovery."

Around us are millions of dollars' worth of barns, outbuildings, fencing, and lots of horses. This area is set aside from the main area of stables. I can see a number of children at play with ponies and horses in a corral about thirty meters away.

"What's going on over there?" I ask.

Pamela says, "Part of the stables here are owned by a charity—Green Grass for Kids—that brings inner-city kids and others with special needs to the farm, gets them some fresh air, let's them see what horses are all about. It's one of CANARY's favorite charities."

"Okay, run me through what happened."

Pamela looks back at the other two agents—Tanya Glenn, a heavyset African-American woman, and Brian Zahn, a slim guy who doesn't look like he's old enough to shave—and she says, "Once the news got out about Atlanta, the First Lady dumped her schedule for the day. She wanted to come out here for a relaxing ride."

"So there was no prep, no sweep, nothing made ready."

Tanya speaks up. "We didn't have the time ... and after being on her detail as long as we've been, you know that when CANARY makes a decision, that's it. She wanted to go riding. She went riding. She says this is one of the only two places in the world where she can relax."

"What time was this?"

Pamela glances at her watch. "Near three hours ago."

I say, "All three of you have horseback riding experience. So why weren't you with her?"

The wind shifts and I hear kids squealing with laughter and joy from many meters away. Tanya says, "We always go with her, hanging back or riding ahead. But not today...she wanted to be alone, and she said she'd be back in sixty minutes."

"Why wasn't I notified when she didn't return?"

Pamela looks both defiant and upset. "Orders."

"From whom?"

"The President."

"Tell me more," I say.

"Just when she was overdue, and wasn't answering her phone, that's when I was contacted by the communications officer on Air Force One. I talked with Jackson Thiel, the head of the President's detail. He told me to hang on for a second. I did just that. Then the President came on the line and told me to stand down, that he would take care of it."

"And he told you not to call me?"

Pamela looks miserable now. "He told me...that I should keep quiet and not tell anyone. Anyone at all."

I bite my lower lip and don't say anything for a moment, knowing with sadness that Pamela's career and those of the rest of the detail have crashed and burned. No matter. Depending on how this is going to play out, my career is probably going to scream right into the ground next to them.

"Where do you think she might be?" I ask.

Tanya speaks up again, and I note that Brian, the only male and the newest one on the detail, is keeping quiet. She says, "Sally, there's miles of trails out there...you go down one and it branches off, and then it branches off again, and goes on...she could be anyplace. My guess is...she switched her phone off, or dumped it, and is just sitting under a tree, being miserable."

"Does she have her panic button with her?"

Pamela says, "Absolutely."

Every protectee has a hidden panic button—the President's is an Air Force One challenge coin he carries in his pocket at all times, the First Lady's is on a small brooch she wears on a gold chain around her neck—and when it's pressed, it sends off a strong beacon alarm and a GPS signal that gives out the exact coordinates down to one foot.

"But it hasn't been activated."

"No," Tanya says. "It hasn't."

I glance once more at this miserable-looking trio of agents, who've done something even worse than having their protectee injured or killed: they've lost their protectee.

To Pamela, I say, "When you have a moment, call the supervisors for your replacement shifts. Make up a plausible story, but tell them that all three of you are staying on duty. We need to keep this as close-in as possible."

Pamela nods and I say, "All right, do you have a map of the area?"

Pamela goes over to the hood of the near Suburban, where a map is spread out, and she points to a marked area where the parking lot is located. She jabs a finger and says, "Since that last call with the President, we've gone out as runners down the near trails, seeing if we can spot anything, one of us always staying behind in case she shows up."

"Okay," I say.

Pamela goes on, "This farm is huge, hundreds of acres, but the outer perimeter is secure, with hired security personnel working the fence line and some surveillance cameras. I haven't talked to the management about securing the recordings there because of our orders, but it's up to you when you want to get them, Sally."

I start to answer, but I'm interrupted when Brian, the male agent, shouts out, "There she is!"

I whirl around, relief running so quickly through me that I think I'm going to faint.

The First Lady's black Morgan horse is trotting back to the parking lot from the main trail leading out.

And I kick the near front tire and curse very loudly and emphatically.

The horse is riderless.

# CHAPTER 18

HER FLIGHT IS five minutes away from landing, and Tammy Doyle sits stock-still in a wide seat in first class. This wasn't her assigned seat, but soon after the Atlanta to Dulles flight had taken off, the lead flight attendant had motioned her forward and had grabbed Tammy's carry-on luggage from the overhead bin.

She could have been Tammy's mom, with her brisk attitude and dyed blond hair, and after she had settled Tammy in a row by herself, she'd leaned over and whispered, "It's always the man's fault, but they always come after us."

Her ears had felt warm all the way through the flight, thinking of the other passengers back there, all connected to the world via airborne Wi-Fi, and she felt sure that most of them knew her secret: the President's lover. Mistress. Slut.

Back in Atlanta, Harrison had told her of his plans, to gently break the news to Grace about their relationship after Election Day, then to separate officially, and then quietly introduce Tammy to the White House and the world during his second term.

But now?

What will Harrison do?

The sudden thump of the plane landing jolts her, and another thought quickly gets her attention:

What is *she* going to do now?

It takes just a few minutes to taxi the aircraft to the gate, and her friend, the senior flight attendant, again takes control. She helps Tammy with her carry-on and blocks the aisle to give her a chance to get ahead of the exiting passengers, then squeezes her shoulder.

"I'll pray for you," she whispers, and Tammy just nods, unable to speak, and then quickly goes up the Jetway, her travel bag rolling along, her large black leather purse on her shoulder.

As she enters the concourse, she slips on a pair of sunglasses and a navy-blue beret, and starts walking. Here in this gated area she doesn't see any news media, which is a relief. With the hard-ass TSA out there keeping watch, there's no way they would allow them in without a boarding pass.

Which means they're waiting for her at the main terminal. Her heart starts to pound, knowing she's going to get ambushed for the second time during this long and horrible day.

With a number of other passengers, she gets on the AeroTrain that takes them to the main terminal. She sees a large Hispanic family—grandma, mom and dad, half-dozen kids—and she moves closer to them, smiling and nodding at the harried mom.

The train jerks and quickly gets them moving, and almost as quickly, they come to the end of the journey, and—

Those same damn bright lights from television cameras.

Damn it!

The Hispanic family jostles through and she slips in between them and starts walking briskly. There are shouts, questions, and other passengers are streaming off, and thank God it's a busy day in the main terminal, for she quickly moves in and out of the crowds. Lots more questions and she ignores them all, moving along, and at one point, an insistent photographer pushes through and tries to cut in front of her, and she swings her left arm with her heavy purse and knocks him back.

*Fools,* she thinks. *I grew up in the projects in South Boston, interned every summer on Beacon Hill, and fought and clawed my way to K Street. You think I'm really going to stop and give you a statement?*

She maneuvers again, gets outside and to the taxi stand, and she gives the businessman at the head of the line two twenty-dollar bills to take his place. In a few seconds, she's in the rear of a black Washington Flyer taxicab, seat belt fastened, now en route to her home in Arlington.

Her chest is aching, and she realizes why as she sits back.

She's nearly forgotten to breathe.

The cab is thankfully driven by a man who introduces himself, says hello, and keeps his mouth shut as they exit the airport. Tammy squeezes her hands together, remembering all of Harry's promises, including about someday flying on Air Force One during his second term, once he separated from the First Lady.

"It's something to look forward to, I promise," Harry had said. "You never touch your luggage. Any kind of meal you want. The gentlest, quietest flight in the world. Your own cabin with me up forward, with hundreds of movies to choose from, or live television, or anything else you want for entertainment. Damn, there are so many attendants on Air Force One I swear to God there's one tasked just to pick up your napkin if you drop it. It's an experience you'll never forget, one you're going to have, and soon. I promise!"

Now?

Now a dark, deep part of her wonders if all those promises had been empty words, not pledges. Ever since the start of their . . . relationship (she felt like calling it an affair cheapened it), he had followed through by protecting her, always keeping his promises about their get-togethers, and treating her . . . well, like a woman liked to be treated. With respect, affection, and love.

Then, back in Atlanta a few hours ago, he had abandoned her, letting the Secret Service hustle him away without seeing if she was all right in the midst of the ambushing reporters.

And—

On the opposite highway she now sees something horribly wrong at a road construction site, something not right, as a black pickup truck speeds and bounces over the dirt median, and she shouts at the driver as the truck grows large in her vision, slamming into the side of the cab, plunging her into pain and darkness.

# CHAPTER 19

MY CELL PHONE starts ringing just as the First Lady's horse trots closer, and I yell, "Somebody grab that damn horse and check it out!"

Brian Zahn is the closest agent, and he manages to get up to the horse, grab its bridle and reins without spooking it. "What am I looking for?"

Another ring from my phone. "Damn it, any blood, or signs of injury, or her freakin' foot torn off and still in the stirrup!"

I answer before the next ring. "Grissom."

"Hey, Sally," comes the concerned male voice. "It's Gil."

I nod with satisfaction. Gil Foster, a trusted colleague of mine who works with the Secret Service's Technical Security Division, and a man I had called earlier while we were just a few minutes away from the horse farm, siren off.

"Gil," I say. "Tell me you have something."

I make out a shaky sigh. "I can tell you that the First Lady's cell phone was on and operating as of three hours ago, and based on the cell phone tower triangulation and the internal GPS transmitter, the phone was at the Westbrook Horse Farm, fifty meters to the east of the main stable."

"Great," I say. "That's where I am right now. Anything else?"

"At eleven sixteen a.m., it went dark."

"How did it go dark? Did the battery die?"

Gil says, "Even if the battery were to die, the GPS would continue to signal. It's powered by a radioactive source, good for a year."

"Then what happened?"

Gil says, "Something happened to the phone. It was damaged or destroyed."

"Wait, I thought those suckers were pretty much indestructible."

"They are," he says. "But if someone really wants to do something...like take a blowtorch to it or put it through an industrial-strength shredder, or break it open and dunk it in the water, then—"

A thought comes to me. "Gil, okay, thanks, you've been great."

"Sally," he says quickly. "I've got to know...when you called me, you said this was an unannounced drill, right? A security drill to see if the First Lady can be found via her cell phone."

"That's right," I say. "Just a training drill."

"But...well"—and he utters a nervous laugh—"the way you're talking, well, it seems like it's the real deal. Not a drill."

"Gil?"

"Yes, Sally?"

"Anybody asks, from your shift supervisor to a congressional committee someday, to the best of your knowledge, this was a goddamn drill."

I switch off. "Pamela!"

She's over by the horse, along with Brian and Tanya, the other agent. She looks up, and I say, "Show me that map again."

Pamela joins me back at the SUV, and I say, "Nearest body of water to the trails. Right now."

She doesn't hesitate, traces a blue line on the map. "Here. Taccanock River. Cuts right through the property. Not much of a river...more like a wide stream."

"Her horse...what's his name?"

"Arapahoe."

"The trail Arapahoe came down—"

She says, "Yeah, the trail heads up there, then runs parallel to the stream."

"We're going there, right now," I say. "Her dead phone...one of the ways to disable it is to break it open and dunk it in water."

"Like she fell off the horse."

"We go. Now."

I take control and make the arrangements, and to Scotty I say, "Stay here. Get Arapahoe back to the stable...but you're our command post. And keep any press away, or curious kids, or anybody else."

Scotty's eyes narrow. He doesn't like the assignment, but he's a good agent and will do what he's told. I hustle the detail into the near SUV, and Brian says, "We're driving out on the trail?"

"We are."

"The owners...they won't like it."

I climb into the rear. "They'll get over it."

And I notice something else before closing the SUV's door.

All three of these agents from the First Lady's detail have reddened eyes.

I know why.

They've been weeping over the fact that they've lost their protectee, the First Lady of the United States.

*     *     *

The trail is barely wide enough for the SUV to pass through without branches or well-trimmed brush scraping the windows or fenders. At points, other wide trails leave from the main one, and I say, "There are no signs. How do the riders know which trail to take?"

From the front Pamela says, "If you ride here, you know. It's a given, like if you have to ask how much something costs, you can't afford it . . . hey, Tanya, not so fast!"

True, because even with seat belts and harnesses fastened, we're bouncing up and down, and something from earlier puzzles me, and I say, "Hey. What's that you said before, about CANARY riding for medical reasons? What medical reasons?"

The SUV engine growls as we continue along the trail. Pamela shifts in her seat, looks back at me. "It's . . . well, a secret, I guess. Back when the President was governor of Ohio, the First Lady, she had breast cancer. For whatever reason they kept it quiet back then . . . and still do."

"How is she now?"

"Fine," Brian speaks up next to me. "More than five years have passed . . . but horseback riding, it relaxes her, helps with her blood pressure . . . and other things."

"What other things?"

Another moment of silence. The other agent in the detail, Tanya, works the steering wheel and keeps her eyes forward. "Because of the treatments she received, the ones that saved her life . . . she had early induced menopause."

"Oh," I say.

"That's right," Tanya says with disapproval. "Her husband delayed and delayed having kids until it was too late."

# CHAPTER 20

THE SUV BREAKS free from the woods and now we're in a field, the dirt-and-gravel path for the horse trail clearly visible as it shifts to the right. The drive goes on for another minute, and then Tanya hits the brakes and we slide to a halt.

Up ahead is the body of water that Pamela Smithson calls a stream.

The water races by at a high rate of speed, sending up waves and plumes of spray as it hurtles past exposed rocks and boulders. What she calls a stream is wide, deep, and menacing.

We all get out and walk to the water's edge. There are woods across on the other side and a hint of the Blue Ridge Mountains in the distance.

"Hell of a stream you got there, Pamela," I say.

"The rains we had last week...the runoff...who knew..."

I bite my tongue, thinking, *You and your detail should have known,* and then I get back to work. "All right. Brian and Tanya...go upstream, see if you can find a place to ford, get across, and start walking downstream. Pamela and I will work this side...and let's make it quick. If she fell off, she's probably injured, and we don't have much time before it gets dark and cold."

Brian and Tanya do as they're told, and I move downstream with Pamela, the detail leader, and I think to myself, *This isn't right; we should have a full-scale search going on here, this isn't right...*

And I remember.

Orders.

I say, "You three...you seem pretty dedicated to CANARY."

"Absolutely. She's different," Pamela says. "Doesn't want to accumulate power, doesn't want to save the world, doesn't care how much anybody weighs...but children—that's always been her focus, ever since Inauguration Day."

"That's why she comes here?"

"And other places too," Pamela says. "The press only sees a portion of what she does. From the start, she didn't want a big detail. Jackie Kennedy...she made do with three, and Mrs. Tucker, that's exactly what she wanted. Three, to keep it quiet and relatively unobtrusive. And lots of times, when the President is traveling, she goes out to area shelters or soup kitchens, or foster homes, and volunteers or makes donations, or just...listens. She's a great listener."

A shout. I look over, and Brian and Tanya are on the other side of the rushing water—they wave, then keep on searching. Their pants are soaked up above their knees.

"What else?" I ask.

"She takes care of her detail, I can tell you that," Pamela says, eyes to the ground and to the stream, just like me. "Any holiday-related trips—like Thanksgiving or Christmas—always happen a week later so we can spend that time with our families. And the letters she gets...lots of letters, asking for help, asking for cash.

And she answers every one of them, most of the time enclosing a check or money order. Ever see that in the news?"

"No," I say.

"And look where that gets her," Pamela says. "She's out helping kids and moms, face-to-face, and her husband is screwing some bimbo."

I say, "That particular bimbo is an executive at one of the biggest lobbyist firms on K Street. She didn't get that job because of her cup size. So let's not blame her right away, okay?"

Pamela doesn't reply. I don't care. We continue, scanning, looking at the field, at the stream, at the banks of the stream, a constant to and fro.

I say, "Besides being tossed by the horse, do you think she's run off? Or hiding? Or anything else?"

"No," Pamela says. Then she looks to me and says, "Some scarf."

"Thanks," I say. "My daughter made it."

"She's good."

"I know."

Her talking is now distracting me and I want to tell her to shut up, but I see something fluttering in the water, like a leaf, a white leaf, like—

I hold up my right arm. "Stop."

Pamela stops and I stare, wanting to make out what's caught my eye.

White. Jammed up against the rocks. About three feet into the stream.

"What is it?" she asks.

"Don't know," I say.

Across the stream the other two members of the detail are still working. Good. If this turns out to be nothing, why delay them?

I step forward and look closer.

Seems to be a bit of trash, or a piece of paper.

Well?

"I'm going in," I say.

"Don't fall."

"Gee, thanks."

I slip off my shoes and wince as I get into the strong, cold water. The fast-moving current tugs and pulls at me, and I'm barely up to my soaked knees. I take one step, then another step, and on the third step I meet up with one slippery rock and nearly fall in. Only by some serious windmilling of my arms and tilting back and forth do I get to stay up.

Close now, only a few more inches.

There.

A sheet of white paper, that's all, battered and torn by the quick water, jammed up against an exposed rock.

I gently peel it free, reverse course, and head back to the bank. Pamela extends a hand and helps me up.

"What is it?"

I don't say anything because I don't know anything.

I'm starting to shiver from the cold, and I kneel down on the muddy dirt and grass, do my best to gently unpeel the soggy piece of paper. The thick red wool scarf lovingly knitted by my Amelia flips over and hits the mud, and with a quick reflex, I toss it back over my shoulder.

"Holy crap," Pamela says.

I recognize the stationery.

At the top is a stylized drawing of the White House, and below that is the imprinted phrase FROM THE OFFICE OF THE FIRST LADY.

And just below that, in a clear and crisp cursive handwriting, is this:

*My dear ones, after the events of today, I just can't take it anymore. It's clear that . . .*

The rest of the message is a mess of blue ink, where the water has washed away the writing.

Kneeling down next to me, Pamela murmurs, "Sweet Jesus, a suicide note?"

"Don't jump to conclusions," I say sharply. "Focus on what we have, which is bad enough."

I look to the rushing waters.

"A missing First Lady."

# CHAPTER 21

A CONCERNED MALE voice, saying, "Missy? Missy? Are you all right, missy?"

Tammy Doyle opens her eyes, winces. The right side of her head is throbbing. The passenger-side door is open. Her cabdriver unbuckles her seat belt, gently helps her out, as she steps onto the dirt and—

Chaos. Complete and utter chaos.

The taxicab she was in is halfway off the highway, facing the wrong way. The trunk is smashed in and nearly torn off. Broken taillight glass and bits of metal are scattered across the asphalt, on top of skid marks. There are also tire tracks in the dirt median where the pickup truck had raced across. Traffic is slowing down on both sides of the highway, three lanes westbound and three eastbound.

She jumps when the cabdriver touches her shoulder, offers her an open bottle of Poland Spring water. Tammy takes a deep swig, and the driver is smiling. "Lucky me, lucky us, eh? Back home, I was in the ENDF and—"

Tammy shakily says, "What's the ENDF?"

"Ah, yes, the Ethiopian National Defense Force...drove... what you call...armored vehicle." He laughs, motions with his hands. "For two years, I fought in the desert against the rebels— you know when you see armored vehicle appear suddenly out of a sandstorm...learn to swerve...I see this madman coming at us...I swerve!"

There's bleeding from his left temple, and Tammy says, "Hey, you're hurt."

"Ah, nothing," he says, taking out a handkerchief and holding it to his head, "But my cab...my poor cab..."

Sirens are off in the distance, and the slow-moving traffic starts to make room for the approaching police cruisers and emergency vehicles. Her driver leans into the open door of the cab, removes his cell phone, and starts talking rapidly, and a dim part of Tammy recalls that Ethiopians speak Amharic, a Semitic language, and he gets off the phone and says, "My cousin Jamal...he will be here shortly...he will take you home..."

Tammy leans against the cab, takes another swallow of water, and realizes her legs are quivering hard.

Home seems very far away.

The Virginia State Police troopers who arrive take a brief statement from Tammy—they seem much more interested in her driver—and as another cab rolls to a stop and the first driver races over to talk to his cousin, she says to the near trooper, "Where's the truck?"

"The one that hit you?" he says, looking down at his clipboard, filling out a form. "No idea. Seems to have swung back on the highway...bet the driver was either drunk or texting, lost control for a moment. He'll be caught, I promise you that...you sure you don't want to go to the hospital?"

"No, I just want to go home."

The large trooper says, "I can see why. This was lucky for all of you."

*Lucky.* That's a word that doesn't make sense to her.

The drive home is quick, and Tammy is sure she's still in shock at how close she came to being seriously injured...or even killed...if her Ethiopian cabdriver hadn't moved so quickly. Good Lord.

And something he had said...it's nagging her. She doesn't know why.

Tammy looks at the expensive homes and developments in this part of Arlington and once again feels quiet pride that she's made it this far, and she wants to go home, dump her laundry by the washing machine, relax, and think about what tomorrow will be like at her K Street lobbying firm, Pearson, Pearson, and Price, but Tammy knows she hasn't gotten this far by being weak or scared or—

Her new cabdriver, Jamal, slows down, turns his head back. "Miss?"

She looks up, about to ask what's wrong, and then she doesn't have to say a word.

There's a mob of press out in front of the gate leading into her condo complex, five satellite trucks with their dishes up, photographers, reporters with hand mikes and—

A burly man with a tan vest holding a large camera spots the slowing cab, points, and then the scramble starts, the mad rush, and Jamal slows down and—

"Move!" she shouts, fumbling in her purse for the key card that will open the sliding gate.

Jamal slows down, jerks forward as camera flashes light up the cab's interior. She turns her head away from the mob and the shouts start, blurring into just one constant mess of words, yells, questions, taunts, and demands.

The cab goes forward, stops again, and Tammy gets a hand into her purse, finds a twenty-dollar bill, and she shoves the bill over Jamal's shoulder. It falls next to him on the seat, and she says, "Another twenty...just get me through the gate!"

A sharp turn to the left and there's a black wrought-iron gate with a key-card reader in a center median. A bronze sign with raised lettering says ARLINGTON ACRES in the center of the gate along with NO TRESPASSING VIOLATORS WILL BE PROSECUTED.

"Pull up, pull up," she says, as she lowers the window. Microphones are shoved in her direction, like spears or daggers, and she flashes her key card at the reader.

The gate doesn't move.

She moves closer, tries one more time.

Success.

The gate slides to the left and she sits back, still keeping her head away from the flashes, the microphones, the yells, and shouts, and then Jamal mutters something and the Washington Flyer cab slowly moves through.

"My God," she whispers.

The gate reverses itself, and she sits back in the seat in relief.

Okay. Another minute or two and she'll be safe at home, and—

"What?" She leans forward, looking ahead, and she can't believe what she sees.

This is a private, gated community, with only residents or invited guests allowed inside, and holy God, there's another knot of news media in front of her complex.

Her home!

Her cabdriver sees the smaller crowd and turns to her. "No worries, missy. I'll take care of you. Stay with me, all right?"

Before Tammy can answer, he stops the cab, jumps out, reaches for her carry-on bag, and sprints around to her door. She releases the seat belt and Jamal opens her door, and turning, with her bag held up to his chest like a battering ram, he pushes his way through the mess of reporters. She follows right behind him, like a ship following an icebreaker, opening the way, and she ignores all the shouts.

Then she's in the foyer of her condo, breathing hard, front door closed, ignoring the ringing bell and the pounding on the door. Jamal smiles. She's not sure of the fare and just hands him a wad of bills, and he nods, scribbles a receipt on the back of a business card, and then, shyly, asks her, "Excuse me, have I seen you before?"

Tammy says, "No."

When he leaves she turns and starts up the carpeted stairs. Her unit is on the second floor, and after going up three steps, she's had it. She lets go of her carry-on bag and it tumbles to the tile floor. To hell with it. It's too heavy and she'll get it later. She needs a bath, a glass of wine, some Ibuprofen, and as she unlocks the front door and walks in, something else is seriously wrong.

Smoke.

Is something burning?

Is her condo on fire?

Tammy goes through the entryway, now realizes she's smelling burnt tobacco, and someone is here, someone has broken in, and this person is smoking!

In her home!

She walks into her living room, and something heavy seems to hammer against her back.

An older woman is sitting in one of her comfortable chairs, a lit cigarette in one hand, her fingernails painted bright red, wearing a short black skirt, an ivory blouse, and a black jacket with pearls around her neck. Her face is perfectly made-up and she has a prominent nose, with short, bright-red hair.

"Well?"

Tammy stands still, breathing hard. This woman is Amanda Price, one of the partners in her lobbying firm, and her boss.

"How . . . how did you get in?"

Amanda smiles with her sharp, white teeth. "Don't ever underestimate my negotiating skills, Tammy. Your property manager . . . he's an easy mark."

Tammy tries to think of what to say, and Amanda taps the ash from her cigarette into one of her prized teacups, part of a set that once belonged to a distant aunt when she had been on the embassy staff in Beijing in the early 1980s.

"So you're screwing the President," Amanda says. "Care to tell me what that's all about?"

# CHAPTER 22

SNEAKING THROUGH A forest once more in her life, Marsha Gray moves quietly and efficiently through the woods—which are part of this prestigious and oh-so-precious horse farm in Virginia—a rucksack over her back, dispatched by Parker Hoyt, heading to where she's sure the Secret Service unit looking for the First Lady has been going.

She had spotted a black Chevrolet Suburban going out of a parking area and into the woods, and she had trotted along past the trees and low brush, hearing the growl of the engine, wondering why in hell it was always Suburbans, Suburbans, and more Suburbans.

Didn't Ford have any vehicles usable for the Secret Service?

Now she sees the parked Suburban by the river and moves along, keeping herself concealed, noting there are only four of them out here.

Four agents?

Looking for the missing First Lady?

Marsha had seen the news that morning about the President and the lobbyist he had been banging. Maybe POTUS really dislikes FLOTUS.

Why else would there be such a weak response?

Two women agents stop by the fast-moving river. One wades in, and the other stands back.

No boots, no real outdoor gear. Like they were sent here in a hurry, no prep, no planning.

What's going on?

She takes the rucksack off her shoulder, gets to work, un-zipping it and quickly assembling the experimental Remington sniper rifle she has used so well over the years in dark and dirty places overseas. She thinks it will be nice to use her weapon at least once in a land that has running water and flushing toilets, the true and only sign of civilization. Once the sling is in its place along with the telescopic sight, she finds a good hiding area within some low brush and takes a look.

*No, not the time to shoot,* a scolding voice inside of her speaks.

Just information gathering.

And what is she gathering?

All she knows is that the First Lady has gone missing some-where on these horse grounds, and something has brought these agents to the river.

But what?

The agent in the water seems to be senior, and she's wearing a black wool coat and a thick red scarf around her neck. She's got a mop of frizzy brown hair and one determined look, and she picks up something... white?

Yeah, white.

Movement on the other side of the riverbank. Two other agents, a young man — barely a man — and an African-American woman. They stop as they observe the movement in front of them.

Marsha moves her scope over to the near riverbank, checking

out the other agent, another woman, this one skinny and blond. This agent is focused on her boss in the water, oblivious to anything else that's going on. Poor situational awareness. If she had the intent and the orders, with four quick squeezes of the trigger, and three quick movements of the rifle's bolt action, she could cut down these four agents in less than a minute.

Marsha takes a deep breath.

Boy, wouldn't that be fun.

The agent in the water climbs out, the young blond agent helping her, and it looks like the older agent has retrieved a soggy piece of paper.

Marsha shifts the scope, but she's too far away and the scope isn't powerful enough to make out what was found.

The two agents huddle together and examine the paper. The older woman's red scarf falls to the ground and she tosses it back over her shoulder.

Damn poor clothing choice, Marsha thinks. If that agent had to run or chase down someone, or toss a protectee in the back of a moving Suburban, that scarf would get in the way.

Marsha checks out the two agents on the other side of the river. They're looking, examining, and the young man halts.

My word, such an easy job, to take all four of them out.

So easy.

She checks the near two agents again, thinks of the dark secret that all good snipers contain, deep inside that special part of someone's soul that's rarely examined and never talked about in polite company.

And that dark secret is . . .

It's so much fun.

Because consider it, she thinks again, eyeing the two agents on the other side of the fast-moving water, where else in the world could you have the power of life and death not in your hand, but in your finger?

That's all!

One slow motion of her finger and that young male agent, now wading into the water, would be dead. All of his dreams, hopes, aspirations, and plans for the next half-century or so snuffed out.

By her.

By Marsha Gray, poor daughter of an even poorer Basque sheepherder in Wyoming and his silent, dutiful wife, both dead and forgotten, and now their poor, overlooked child is out here, with the power to kill someone with just the tiniest tug of her finger.

Somewhere inside of her are the jumbled memories of her past missions in Afghanistan, Iraq, Iran, Nigeria, and other places...and she knows that publicly and in books and documentaries, her fellow snipers have talked about feelings, emotions, of just getting the job done despite the guilt...which is pretty much crap, Marsha thinks.

Now the young man is knee-deep in the water, shouting and holding something up.

The truth is, for her at least, that she loves it. Loves the viewing, the hunting, the anticipation, and most of all, the killing.

She loves it more than life itself.

Marsha shifts the sniper scope once more to the young man. He's holding up...what?

A piece of jewelry.

That's it.

A gold necklace with some sort of brooch dangling from one end.

Belonging to the First Lady?

Perhaps.

Marsha settles in, sighs.

Times like these, she wishes she had spent just a bit more time learning something other than the best way to kill someone.

Like lip reading, so she'd know why these four Secret Service agents are so excited.

# CHAPTER 23

TAMMY DOYLE DROPS her purse on the near couch. "You're smoking."

"Very observant," her boss says, gently tapping another length of ash into her aunt's priceless teacup.

"You shouldn't be smoking in here, Amanda."

Amanda Price shrugs. "I didn't see a sign. I needed a smoke. There you go." She leans forward and says, "You've got a hell of a bruise on your cheek. What happened?"

A wave of exhaustion and the need to bawl comes over her, and Tammy struggles to push it back. Besides still being freaked out over what just happened, she's sweaty, her clothes are a mess, and she just wants to be left alone.

"Car accident," she says. "My taxi...a pickup truck hit the trunk...could have killed us if it was just a few feet in the other direction."

Amanda shakes her head. "Interstate Sixty-six...what a horror show that can be. Are you okay?"

"Just...shook up." She touches the tender side of her face. "Why are you here, Amanda?"

Amanda takes a deep drag from her cigarette. "How long has it been going on?"

"Put the cigarette out."

"Tammy, you—"

"The cigarette goes out or I keep my mouth shut." The side of her face is really throbbing and she wants to take a couple of painkillers now, but Tammy's not in the mood for showing any weakness in front of Amanda.

A few seconds pass as her tougher-than-titanium boss locks eyes with her, and Tammy stares right back. Then Amanda widens her sharp smile, stubs out the cigarette in the teacup, and puts the cup down on a coffee table. "Sharp lady," she says. "I've always liked your style."

"You want to talk style, or you want to tell me why you're here?"

Amanda says, "You and the President. Tell me what's going on."

"None of your business," Tammy says.

"None of my business? Hah." Amanda crosses and recrosses her long legs. "Tammy, m'dear, anything and everything you do, on the clock and off the clock, reflects on Pearson, Pearson, and Price. Clear? If you were pulled over for drunk driving, well, that's a manageable problem. But you've been caught banging the leader of the free world. We need to talk, or you're going to be unemployed and no lobbying firm in the western world will hire you. Unless we have . . . a satisfactory conversation."

Tammy waits and the hard look from her boss returns, and Tammy knows she won't win this staring contest.

"We've been together about eight months, since a fund-raiser in Denver," she says, feeling like she's surrendering to the older woman. Her boss nods in satisfaction, knowing she's won this one.

"You in love with him?"

Something thuds in her chest. "God, yes."

"Is he in love with you?"

"Yes."

"He make promises?"

"I—"

"Tammy, what the hell did the President say to you?"

"He…" Damn it, tears are starting to pool in her tired eyes. "Yes, he promised me that after the election, after the inauguration, he would separate from his wife, and that eventually…he'd introduce me to the American people…and bring me publicly into his life. That we would get married during his second term."

Amanda chuckles, a dry, scary sound. "Leaving the First Lady and marrying you later? That damn ship has sailed and is now circling the Cape of Good Hope, on its way to the Pacific. Nope, those plans have been blown out of the water."

More silence, except Tammy can now make out the low buzz of the news media talking among themselves, out on the street. Amanda says, "Expect rough times ahead. He'll probably dump you publicly, to save his bacon."

She says the words without thinking. "No, he won't."

Amanda looks like she is going to laugh again, but doesn't. "Perhaps…I could be wrong. It's been known to happen."

Tammy says, "I've answered your questions. Now it's my turn. Do I still have a job?"

Amanda's inked-in eyebrows rise. "Of course. You're one of our best, Tammy, and your notoriety is going to get our phones ringing with new business. But please don't do anything more to embarrass the firm. Got that? The work you've done with Gideon Aerospace and Romulus Oil has fast-tracked you to a partnership. Even if you're a Harvard girl and a Red Sox fan, which I've never held against you."

Tammy manages a smile. "There are three pastimes in Boston: sports, politics, and revenge."

Amanda gets up. "A good trio to learn. All right. Be at the firm at your usual hour tomorrow. Stroll in like you don't have a care in the world. And for God's sake, don't even think of talking to the press. Or your neighbors. Or anyone else, for that matter. You could talk to your best friend tonight, under a cloak of secrecy and Häagen-Dazs chocolate ice cream...and she'll turn around and sell your story to the *National Enquirer* in a heartbeat. Do you understand?"

"Yes, I do," she says, glad to think that her boss is leaving her home.

"Good," Amanda says, walking to the door. "Now I need to start working our potential client list, including that rube from Oklahoma, Lucian Crockett."

Tammy waits a second and calls out to her, "Just so you know, I'm getting a cleaning company in here as soon as I can, and I'm going to bill it to the firm."

That brings an amused nod of the head from Amanda. "You do that. And just so you know...and this isn't for distribution either—the First Lady appears to be missing. At least that's the rumor I've heard."

Tammy can't smell the old tobacco smoke anymore. "Missing?"

"Yes, as in she's disappeared. Not for public information, but I hear that she was so pissed at the President that she ducked out from her Secret Service detail and is on the lam." Another dry chuckle from her boss. "If I was her, I'd be on a one-way trip to Reno, to get divorced and laid by some twenty-year-old stud, just...because."

She leaves and the door shuts behind her, and Tammy rubs her tired face.

Holy God.

What now?

Tammy lowers her hands, picks up her purse from the floor, takes out her iPhone.

Usually it's her favorite object, enabling her to communicate with anyone on the planet, but now...it looks and feels like an unexploded hand grenade.

She almost puts it back into her purse...but she has to know something.

Tammy turns on her phone, slides through a couple of screens, and—

Holy shit.

One hundred and twelve missed calls.

A hundred and twelve!

She skims through them, seeing familiar networks and the names of familiar reporters, *skim skim skim,* and no, there's no familiar number, not the one she's looking for.

Tammy jumps when her phone starts ringing.

The caller ID function on her phone says 202-456-1414.

The White House main switchboard.

She gingerly answers it. "Hello?"

"Miss Doyle? This is the White House. Please hold for the President."

# CHAPTER 24

AFTER BRIAN ZAHN finds the First Lady's untriggered panic button, I make a phone call to Parker Hoyt. He starts arguing with me, until I say, "Mister Hoyt? This particular pile of shit is mine until the President takes it away. I'm not asking permission. I'm just telling you what I'm doing. Have a nice afternoon."

I then make one more phone call, to an old friend who's now working for the enemy. Luckily I have his private number, and when I tell him what I need, I still have to repeat myself three times before he reluctantly agrees.

"All right, Sally, you've got it," he says, "but if I have to, I'll throw you under the bus so fast that only your pistol and shoes will be recognizable."

"Randy," I say, speaking to a very handsome and very capable ex-Secret Service agent whom I briefly dated prior to marrying my soon-to-be ex-husband, and with whom I spent many a lonely hour, standing watch in hotel basements or empty rooms. "Trust me, that will be one very fair and happy exchange."

After I hang up, we're all together, all four of us sopping wet from just above our knees to our soggy shoes. I've taken the wet piece of stationery and slid it into a plastic envelope for later examination by our forensics section, just to make sure it's CANARY's handwriting. In another plastic envelope is the panic button pretending to be a piece of jewelry. I walk around in a big circle with my arms folded before me and see the three agents are staring at me. I shrug. "Now we wait."

"How long?" Brian asks.

"As long as we have to," I say, and then I check the setting on the Motorola XTS 5000 radio attached to my belt—along with a set of handcuffs, pepper spray, my SIG Sauer P229 pistol, and ASP expandable baton—and then I toggle the microphone at my wrist and say, "Scotty, Sally calling."

This is an encrypted channel, and I don't like fooling around with code names that can be forgotten under pressure. "This is Scotty, go."

I say, "We're going to have visitors coming shortly. Send them along."

"Got it," he says. "What about the stable's owners? They've already come around once, wondering where...someone is, and why I'm out here."

"Tell them...damn, I don't know," I say. "Tell them something. Sally, out."

When I lower my wrist, my phone rings, and I check the incoming number and whisper an obscenity. "Todd, this is Sally. What's up?"

Todd Pence, my neighbor and a Navy vet, says, "Sally, I'm sorry, but I gotta leave in a few minutes."

I turn away from the other three agents. "What's going on? Is Amelia okay?"

"Oh, she's great," he says. "But my older sister Phoebe...she lives alone and is older than me and is on the Social Security, and her damn water tank is leaking. She tried calling a plumber but the rates they charge—"

"Todd, please..." I take a few more steps. "Put Amelia on, will you?"

Some seconds pass and a sweet voice comes on and says, "Mom? You busy?"

Good Lord, what a question. "Um, yeah. Look. Mister Pence says he has to leave ahead of schedule. Are you okay with that?"

I can sense her eye-rolling through the tone in her voice. "Oh, Mom, I'll be fine. Honest."

"Okay. You sure?"

"Of course I'm sure," she snaps back. "But...when do you think you'll be home?"

"As soon as I can, hon, as soon as I can," I say. "But make sure the doors and windows are locked and that you carry the phone around with you, okay?"

"Yes, Mom," she answers, putting about a ton of attitude into each syllable.

"Good girl," I say. "Put Mister Pence back on."

My neighbor and child-care provider—last year Amelia got angry with the term *babysitter,* and I promised never to use it again—comes back on the phone and we have a brief conversation. I put the phone away just as the sound of the helicopters reaches us.

Two UH-60 Black Hawk helicopters come into view, low, over the near trees, the branches whipping around from the wash coming from the spinning blades. They land downstream at a wide, grassy spot, and as the engines slow down, I run to the near one. A gold banner encircles the low part of the fuselage, where black block letters read HOMELAND SECURITY.

The side door slides open, and a man jumps down, wearing

a dark-gray jumpsuit and black combat boots. Around his slim waist is a black leather utility belt, holding a handheld radio and a pistol holster that's also strapped to his muscular upper thigh. He pulls off a pair of sunglasses to reveal a face that is flush and rugged, and his sandy brown hair flutters from the moving air. A name tag says ANDERSON, and we exchange a brief handshake as we move away from the engine noise.

"Randy," I say.

"Sally," he says. "All right, let's get to it."

I take a very deep and troubled breath. "I need . . . a search mission. Up and down this river for a white female, midforties."

His gray-blue eyes bore right into me. "A search or a recovery?"

"A training mission, remember? That's what this is. An unannounced training mission."

His gaze doesn't flinch. "I might need a higher authority than you, Sally. I'm sure you understand."

I say, "How does Parker Hoyt sound?"

Two more helicopters approach and land on the other side of the river. Randy lifts his voice. "Sounds pretty heavy."

"Yeah, like lead."

We stare at each other for a moment, and he says, "I'll leave Mister Hoyt alone for the moment."

"That's wise."

A nod. "All right, just remember, back in Santiago . . . you warned me off that woman at the bar, at the Ritz-Carlton. You were pretty damn insistent, and I put up a fight, but later . . . the bitch turned out to be working for Cuban intelligence. Ruined the lives and careers of three other agents. But we're now even."

"Agreed," I say. "We're even."

He takes the handheld radio, turns and mutters some orders I can't make out. Then he turns back to me, replaces the radio, and says, "But I need to know. It's always bothered me. How did you know she was working for the DGI?"

"Ask you a question first?"

"Sure," he says. "Make it snappy."

"How do you like working for the dark side, the clumsy side, Homeland Security?"

He doesn't seem insulted and even smiles a bit. "Secret Service is part of Homeland Security," he says. "We're all part of the same team. The hours are better and so is the pay. You should think about coming over, you being a single mom."

I say, "Not today. Not ever."

"All right, you made that clear," he says. "Santiago. Answer me now."

I take three steps forward, gently touch his hard chin. "I didn't know. Honest."

"What?"

I say, "I had no idea she was with Cuban intelligence, or Chilean intelligence, or Bulgarian intelligence for that matter. She was hot-looking and I was jealous, and I wanted you for my-self…which happened later in Bogotá, if I recall. But I needed to separate you from her at the bar. You were practically glued to that curvy torso of hers."

His eyes widen just a bit, either in humor or horror, I can't tell, and his hand reaches out and skips my face, touches the scarf. "You…how's your Amelia?"

"Right now my Amelia is an eleven-year-old girl who's home alone for the first time, that's how she's doing. If I'm lucky when I get home tonight, at least my bedroom and the bathroom will be in survivable shape."

"You okay with her alone?"

"I'll manage," I say. "She knows to keep everything buttoned up, not to answer the door, and to call nine-one-one and me at the same time if something scares her."

"Sounds good," he said. "Sorry about your divorce from Ben."

"Don't be," I say, and then, "Come on, Homeland Security, get to work. You know what they say about the Secret Service: you can either play ball with us, or we'll shove a baseball bat up your ass."

A crisp nod follows; he steps back and grabs his waist radio one more time, and says, "You and me. No one else knows, or ever will know. This is officially an unannounced Homeland Security training drill. But, Sally . . . who are you really looking for?"

"A bird," I say.

"A bird?"

"Yeah," I say. "A goddamn canary."

He opens his mouth and starts asking more questions, but luckily for me, four black Humvees from Homeland Security growl their way in, their combined noise drowning out whatever my old friend is trying to say.

And it's about the only luck I get that day, or the next.

# CHAPTER 25

THE AFTERNOON MEET-AND-GREET with his top campaign staff is due to be over in five minutes, but Harrison Tucker is done. He stands up and says to his half-dozen top officials, "Very good, that'll do for now. Thanks for coming in and...my deepest apologies again for putting all of you in this very awkward position."

The head of the delegation, a heavyset man in a brown suit who's the senior senator from Ohio, takes the lead and says, "We won't let you down, Mister President. The margin might be tighter, but we sure as hell ain't gonna let that nutcase from California get in here next January."

The delegation smiles and murmurs as Harrison, assisted by one of his aides, ushers them out of the Oval Office, but the oldest person in the group, the former majority leader from the Ohio State House, lingers behind.

"Mister President," Miriam Tanner says. "Please...just a word."

He hesitates, but he owes a lot to Miriam, and with a hand he gestures his aide to leave, so it's just the two of them, standing by the open door. Miriam is eighty-one years old, face worn and wrinkled, wearing a simple floral dress—probably from Walmart or Target, he thinks—but she's been in the business for more than six decades, and her instinct for politics is one of the best he's ever known.

Miriam says in a low but strong voice, "What the hell do you think you were doing, stepping out like that?"

The tone of her voice nearly knocks him back. "Miriam, I—"

"Shit, Harry, if you wanted to get laid, there are plenty of high-priced, security-cleared young ladies in this town who'll take care of you, quietly and discreetly," she says sharply. "What were you thinking? Damn it, son, you've had a grand first term, with promises of an even better second term, and you threw it all away for a bit of tail?"

"Miriam . . . it wasn't . . . isn't like that."

"Then there's Grace," Miriam says, pursing her lips in displeasure. "She may be an ice queen, a stubborn bitch, and come from a family that thinks they crap pearls, here and back home, but by God, she has her heart in the right place. She's helped thousands of poor kids as this country's First Lady, and what's her reward? Being nationally humiliated. What the hell did you see in that chubby lobbyist?"

Desperate to get her out of the Oval Office, Harrison says, "Miriam, please . . . I'm in love with her."

His old political ally shakes her head. "Harry, you should know this by now. Presidents can't be human. They can't get drunk, or cry, and they certainly can't fall in love."

With one more disgusted shake of her head, she's gone.

The on-duty Secret Service agent tugs the door shut, and the President of the United States walks back into the empty Oval Office, having succeeded in at least gaining a few minutes to himself. That is a treasure, to have those precious seconds, for his day is always planned down to the exact minute.

But . . . still no news from Parker.

He goes to his desk phone, picks it up to connect with the lead operator at the White House switchboard, and simply says, "Please get me Tammy Doyle."

"Yes, sir."

After he hangs up, Harrison impatiently paces the office—careful never to step on the Presidential Seal in the center of the rug, which is considered bad luck, and he doesn't want any more bad luck today—and the dark part of him wonders, who does he want to hear from first? Parker Hoyt, telling him where Grace has been found? Or the anonymous telephone operator somewhere on the grounds, telling him she's located the woman he really loves?

What kind of man is he, he thinks, what kind of husband is he, that he would worry about both his wife and his mistress at the same time?

Good question, he thinks.

And no answer.

He reaches into his left pants pocket, takes out a thick challenge coin, stamped with an outline of Air Force One over the White House, and on the reverse, the logo of the 89th Airlift Wing, and its Latin motto, *Experto Crede*. If he were to push the center of the coin and hold it down for three seconds, this room would be flooded with Secret Service agents.

His wife wears a similar object around her neck.

It hasn't been activated. He puts his challenge coin back into his pocket, seeing that as a good sign. If she were in trouble—

The phone rings. He goes to his ornately carved desk, picks up the phone. "Mister President," says the clear voice of the switchboard operator, who again sounds neutral and professional on this "Ambush in Atlanta" day of days, "I have your party on the line."

"Thank you, thank you very much," and there's a *click*, as the line is secure, belonging to him and his caller, and he says, "Tammy? Are you there?"

"Oh, Harry," comes her sweet and tired voice, and he sits down with relief in his leather office chair. At least one wait is over.

But there's something off in the tone of her voice. "Tammy, are you all right?"

And then the love of his life starts sobbing.

# CHAPTER 26

THE PRESIDENT OF the United States says, "Tammy...
please...what happened?"

The sobbing goes on for long seconds, and that sound stabs at
him, for it's the first time in their relationship that he's ever heard
her cry. He may be the most powerful man in the world at this
very second, but he feels so damn helpless.

Over the phone he hears her take a deep breath. "Oh,
Harry...I'm sorry. The flight home was all right but then I got in
a car accident and—"

"A car accident? What happened? Are you all right?"

Her voice sounds stronger. "Yes, I'm fine...a bit achy, but the
cab I took from the airport was hit. We were on the highway just
east of Dulles when a pickup truck crossed the median and hit
the trunk of the cab. Spun us around and thank God the cabbie
was a sharp guy, otherwise...oh, Harry. What a rotten day. And
the media were camped out at my condo when I got here."

He swivels the tiniest bit in his chair in front of his ornate
wooden desk. "What did you say to them?"

"Harry? What?"

He instantly realizes his mistake. He isn't acting as her lover, her friend, her man. He is responding as a politician, trying to minimize a mistake. Not trying to take care of a woman he loves. Shit.

"I . . . I just wanted to see if you said anything to them. Or if they said anything to you. It must have been rough."

"No, Harry, I didn't say a word . . . I mean . . . what could I say?"

He rubs at his eyes. This isn't going well, damn it.

"That's good. I'm . . . sorry, I know you won't say anything."

Tammy says, "Harry . . . what am I going to do? What are we going to do?"

"You . . . take care of yourself, first and foremost," he says, thinking rapidly. "Call in sick tomorrow if you have to. Or work from home. And we're going to fix this."

"We?"

"Parker Hoyt . . . he's working on it right now."

"By doing what?"

"He's . . . doing a lot of things. And he's working on . . . doing what's right."

God, he thinks. Another close miss with Tammy. He was about to tell her that Parker Hoyt is looking out for him and his re-election, which of course, would lead to the question, well, what about me?

What about Tammy, indeed. He can't tell her what his advisers told him not more than ten minutes ago: dump her, and dump her publicly.

"Is there . . . anything I can do for you?" he asks, rubbing at his eyes.

A bitter laugh. "Arrest the reporters outside my condo?"

He manages to laugh back. "If I could, I would . . ."

A pause, and she says, quietly, "When can I see you, Harry?"

"Not for a while," he says. "You know how it is."

Her voice is sharp. "For at least four weeks, right?"

"Tammy..."

He rubs at his eyes again, and she says, "How are things with Grace?"

A jolt of surprise. In the months they've been together, she's hardly ever asked about the First Lady.

"Angry. Upset. You can imagine."

"I can," she says, voice soft, full of understanding. "Where is she now? In her office, practicing throwing lamps?"

He turns in his chair, peering out at the three greenish-tinged glass windows, floor to ceiling, which are green because they are bulletproof.

"She's...in the East Wing," he says, speaking quickly. "Trying to gather her thoughts together."

"But is she going to speak to the press? Is she still going to keep her public schedule?"

He can't do this anymore. From the very beginning, he's always been straight with her, never making promises he can't keep, always being upfront as to when he can see her and when he can't.

But now?

"She's...ah...look, Tammy, I have to go. All right? Hang in there...we'll get through this together. Honest."

And he hangs up the phone, disconnecting the secure call, swivels his chair once more.

What a rotten conversation.

And what was that all about, her asking about Grace?

Then he realizes something else.

For the very first time, he's lied to the woman he loves.

Tammy is stunned as the President brusquely cuts her off.

Of course he's under pressure, and of course the news of their . . . relationship is on his mind, especially with the election so close.

But never had he been so short with her and never had he . . .

Lied?

She recalls what Amanda Price told her, just a few minutes ago.

The First Lady can't be found.

But her Harry—the President of the United States—just told her something else, that Grace Fuller Tucker was in the East Wing, definitely not missing.

And when Tammy tried to press him on that

He hung up on her.

Her phone rings and she's startled, and she checks in the caller ID.

CBS NEW YORK.

She switches off the phone.

Curls up in her chair.

Waits.

For what, she doesn't know.

But the hard core inside of her, that took her from a dumpy three-story tenement building in South Boston to Beacon Hill and Boston College and then Harvard and then to the center of the world—the District of Columbia—knows she won't wait forever.

His phone rings, and Harrison Tucker waits a moment before picking it up.

Tammy's news about her car accident has caused a memory from his political past to surface, from back when he was running for re-election as a state senator. It had turned into an unexpectedly close race, until his opponent—a retired univer-

115

sity professor—had gotten into a serious crash one rainy night outside of Toledo.

And he remembers Parker Hoyt smiling at him, when he told him the news the next day: "Accidents do happen...especially at the right time."

Harrison had laughed it off then, thinking Parker was just joking.

But now?

Parker...could he? Would he?

His phone rings and rings.

# CHAPTER 27

MARSHA GRAY MOVES back about three meters, wanting to remain concealed from the burly and fast-moving Homeland Security fellas, who are fanning out along the riverbed and the tree line, looking for the First Lady. The lead Secret Service agent had a bit of a serious discussion with a hunky guy in a gray jumpsuit who seemed to be in charge of the helicopter crews and those arriving in the Humvees.

From her coat she takes out an earpiece and slips it in, and her fingers maneuver over the iPhone at her side. She puts the iPhone down on a nearby rock so she can whisper into it without being overheard, then slides a few fingers over the screen

The phone rings only once. "Hoyt."

"You know who this is," she says.

"What do you have?"

She whispers, "What I have looks like a reunion of a Homeland Security training class."

Hoyt swears. "How many?"

"Scores," she whispers again, "with more arriving every minute. They're setting up a search, both sides of the river, sweeping downstream and upstream. We also have three Black Hawk heli-copters overhead, and about a half-dozen Humvees. All that's missing now is a keg."

Another foul obscenity. "Where's Agent Grissom?"

"About twenty meters away, running the show. I can see her from here."

"Have they…found anything else yet? Besides that piece of paper and the piece of jewelry?"

"Nope," she says. "And it's going to get dark soon. What do you want?"

A pause. "Grissom is key. She's the one. Follow her, no matter where she goes."

"All right," Marsha says. "What kind of cover story have you got? Eventually somebody's gonna wonder why Homeland Security and Secret Service are going up and down the river."

"The story is that they're assisting the Virginia State Police and the Virginia Conservation Police in looking for a lost canoeist."

"Good cover story," Marsha says. "Do either of those agencies know that yet?"

"They will."

She shifts again, keeping an eye on Grissom, the lead agent. For some reason—even at this distance—the woman is bugging her. She reminds Marsha of the various female Marine officers she had met in her career, the bulk of them being bossy, kiss-ass broads who'd do anything and betray anybody to advance their career. The way Grissom is pacing around, talking, ordering, and looking…well, she's fitting the pattern.

Marsha focuses the crosshairs of her sniper's scope on the base of Grissom's neck. "Hoyt?"

"Make it snappy," he says. "I'm expecting a bunch of congres-sional staffers who need cheering up."

"I could do it now," she says. "One shot, one kill. Drop Grissom and really throw things into confusion. What do you think?"

"Hell, no!" Parker snaps back, his voice loud and sharp in the sole earpiece. "For now, just observe. All right? And if there's any hint that the First Lady has been found, you contact me, right away."

"You don't have to yell," Marsha says. "Ever."

He hangs up without another word.

Marsha tracks the agent again, the bossy broad with the black wool coat and lumpy red scarf, strolling up and down, talking sometimes to that handsome Homeland Security guy, and other times to the three Secret Service agents.

More engines. She looks to the left, where there are Humvees and the original Suburban parked. Trucks arrive with trailers, the trailers carrying large, portable powered light systems.

Looks like it's going to be a long night. Marsha doesn't mind. She has passed long nights in places where starving dogs roamed after dark, with open sewers sliding through broken neighborhoods, the horizon lit up by the explosions of IEDs.

Spending the night here would be a nice change of pace.

But now Marsha sees that Grissom looks to be leaving. She gets into a Suburban with another agent and the taillights flicker on, and seeing that, she starts breaking down her rifle, opening up her rucksack.

On the move.

Part of the job.

Still…part of her was always thinking about that classic dorm-room poster, showing two vultures sitting on a tree branch, one saying to the other, "Patience my ass. I wanna kill something."

Words to live by.

Her gear packed, she's ready to move into the darkness.

But one more thing.

Her earpiece is still in, and with a few swipes of her fingers on her iPhone, a recording from earlier pops up:

Her: *"Just to be clear…just her or do what's necessary?"*

Him: *"Pretend you're out in the field, no way to contact anybody else. Do what has to be done."*

Marsha removes the earpiece, puts the iPhone away, thinking she hasn't gotten this far and made so much money by ever trusting men.

Parker Hoyt has a few minutes to spare before the first of the congressional staffers arrives, and he stares at his special phone on his desk. This is going longer and darker than he had anticipated. The First Lady…all right, he figured she'd be one angry wife, that was to be expected.

But this?

Disappeared?

And what he has learned from Agent Grissom…some sort of note and the woman's panic button, untriggered.

Not good.

So what now?

He wants this settled, nailed down, completed…so he can focus on what's really important—getting that talented man in the office next door re-elected.

Parker picks up the phone, dials the second number, the one he hadn't wanted to touch earlier.

But that was then.

No more time.

The phone rings.

Rings.

Rings.

It's answered, and from the ambient noise, Parker knows the person on the other end is outside.

"Yes?" comes the quick, impatient reply.

"It's Hoyt," he says.

"Can't talk."

"I know you're busy . . . but . . ."

"Make it quick."

Parker says, "I need to know exactly what Grissom is doing, what she's thinking, what she's planning, second by second."

"She's planning right now to go home to her kid."

"But—"

The voice says, "I know our deal. I know what you've promised. But don't ever call me again. I'll be the one making the contact."

The phone is disconnected.

Parker hangs up on his end, leans back in his chair. It's now dark, the lights of DC visible.

That call . . . just checking on his insurance policy.

Someone connected out there, working for him.

Highly illegal, highly unethical, and in the end—considering how much he's been paid—highly effective.

And that's all he cares about.

# CHAPTER 28

PAMELA SMITHSON QUICKLY and efficiently gets me back home, to an apartment complex in Springfield, Virginia, which is closer than going back to the White House, where my personal vehicle is located. I use my cell phone to arrange a Secret Service driver to pick me up overnight if need be.

Pamela pulls into the parking lot and leaves the engine running. I say, "You call me the second you find anything."

"You know it," she says.

"If it weren't for my daughter, I'd still be at the river."

"We know that, and Sally, no offense, I want to get back there as soon as possible..."

I put my hand on the door handle. "Okay. Pamela, where is she?"

Pamela looks rattled, which is what I'm going for. Good.

"Sally, I—"

"Back at the farm, just before we started the search, Tanya said something about the farm being one of the two places where she feels most comfortable."

No reply.

"So where's the second place?"

"I . . . I don't know. None of us know."

I go on. "I also asked you that besides being tossed by the horse, did you think she had run off. Or was hiding. You just said no and instantly changed the subject."

Still no reply.

"Who is he?" I ask.

She turns and looks over at the parking lot. "Pamela! Who is he?"

Pamela's face is still turned away from me. "I don't know."

"How long has she been with him?"

"I . . . not sure. A few months at least. I've heard her talking to him. Three or four times. They communicate only by phone, best I can tell."

"Hers?"

Pamela says, "No, a burner phone."

"How in hell did the First Lady of the United States get a burner phone?"

She turns to me, and under the lights from the parking lot, I see her eyes filling up. "How do you think? She makes a request to a staffer, the staffer makes a request to a low-level staffer, and passes it on to an intern. The intern pays cash for a debit card, buys the phone anonymously, sets up a fake Gmail account to activate it, and then it's handed back up to the First Lady. Nearly impossible to trace."

"Who is he?"

"I don't know."

"Pamela . . ."

She wipes at one eye, then the other. "It's . . . a man. That's all I know. I've overheard her talking to him a few times over the past months . . . and once . . . I heard her say, 'I love you so much.'"

I take a breath, feel like punching her in the face. "Pamela, your career went down in flames this morning when you and the others lost your protectee. Now...in the next fifteen seconds, however you answer me will determine whether you're allowed to quietly resign or whether you're going to appear in court as a defendant."

She just nods. I say, "Do you have any idea, lead, or hint of who this man is and where he can be found?"

"No."

"The other shifts?"

She shakes her head. "I've...sounded them out over the past couple of months. Nothing serious, just testing to see if they've noticed anything. Not a thing."

"All right, then," I say.

I start to open the door, and Pamela says, "I need to tell you one more thing."

I think of my eleven-year-old girl, up in our apartment alone. We had moved here nearly a year ago, when I found out my husband and her father had been taking interns to our condo during his lunch break, and I refused to live in that place for one second more than I had to. This place is pricey, in poor shape, and in a lousy neighborhood, but I had no other choice.

"Make it quick."

"Back in May, we were having a going-away party for one of the night shift agents on her detail," Pamela says. "We had rented a room over a bar in Georgetown, but the First Lady...when she found out about the party, she knew that her three on-duty agents would miss it. So with no announcement, nothing made public, she showed up. A surprise. Took time out of her own schedule so her three on-duty agents wouldn't miss the party, and she laughed, danced, and knocked back a couple of glasses of wine with the crew. That's who she is...the best protectee I've ever worked for, and Sally, if I had the slimmest lead on who this guy might be, I'd be out there now. You've got to believe me."

I open the door. "I do believe you. Just hope you can convince a judge or a congressional committee if the time ever comes."

From a parked Honda Odyssey minivan on the street, Marsha Gray watches the lead agent depart a Suburban in an apartment complex parking lot. She has night-vision gear at her side but decides not to use it. She loves minivans because they're so anonymous and blend in so well, and having a night scope up to her face definitely won't make her blend in.

The Suburban has been here for about ten minutes, so she's sure there's been some chitchat going on inside between the two agents, but what? Marsha wishes she wasn't by herself, working alone, because she'd have that Suburban bugged and wired so she would know for sure what they were talking about.

Grissom walks across the parking lot, and Marsha sees shadows emerge from between two parked cars.

Things are about to get interesting.

I'm walking to the apartment complex and something flickers ahead of me, and I quickly realize that I'm seeing shadows from two people behind me.

I turn and there's two youngsters walking quickly in my direction. They have on baseball hats, and the hoods of their jackets are pulled up over them, making it hard to tell what they look like, which is probably the plan.

They keep on walking toward me, fast and deliberate.

I say, "Help you fellas?"

The one on the right says, "Hey, yeah, my bud here, I think he hurt his left knee. You know where the closest walk-in clinic be?"

"No, I don't," I say. "But he's not limping."

"Appearances can be deceiving, sweetie," the other one says. "Maybe I'm just faking it, who knows. Maybe we just needed a reason to come talk to you and then take your money."

I take a step back, swivel a bit, reach under my coat, remove my collapsible baton, pop it open, and swing it hard across the knees of the guy on the left. He yelps, and the pain drops him on the pavement, arms splayed out. His standing buddy is frozen.

I say, "Now he's not faking it."

I walk backward a bit, until I'm sure the threat is gone. Then I turn and go to the front door, punch in the access code, make my way through the smelly foyer, and trot upstairs to the third floor. At my apartment I unlock the door, which I had strengthened and the cheap lock upgraded when we moved in. I call out, "Honey, I'm here!" which is my everyday code word so Amelia knows it's mom coming in and not some creep.

Inside, there's a small living room, a kitchen to the right, and a hallway leading to a bathroom and two bedrooms, one for me and one for Amelia.

The place smells of burnt food.

In the kitchen, Amelia turns, smiling at me. She's wearing a white apron smeared to mid-thigh with tomato sauce. A pot of pasta is close to boiling over on the stove, there are open cans on the counter, and the sink is piled high with dirty dishes. The small wooden table is set with clean ones, and she says, "Mom! I made us dinner!"

I drop my purse and bag in a near chair, and I just nod, taking off the scarf she made for me and then my black wool coat. I should hang them up in the closet, but I'm so very tired, and I toss them on the couch instead.

"Honey...you didn't have to. We could have gotten takeout from Chang's."

There's sizzling noises as the pasta pot fully boils over. Amelia squeals and goes back to the burner, turns it down, and she says, "Mom...we had takeout from Chang's last week. Twice. I wanted to make dinner tonight. Besides..."

"What?"

She picks up a ladle, stirs tomato sauce in another pot. The sauce splatters on her apron and the floor.

"Besides, Mom, I'm not dumb. I know we need to save money."

What to say to something like that?

I can't.

"I'll be right back," I say, and walk down the hallway, slip into my bedroom. I switch on a light and take off my jacket, use a key to open a top drawer, and deposit my baton, radio, SIG Sauer, handcuffs, and pepper spray into the padded interior.

The last thing I put in is my service book that contains my Secret Service badge.

Imprinted in bold letters on the dark leather are these words:

DUTY AND HONOR.

I close the drawer.

The words are mocking me.

# CHAPTER 29

THE SPAGHETTI IS chewy and could have been boiled for another two minutes, and the pasta sauce has tiny flakes of burnt material floating throughout—from where it stuck to the bottom of the pan—and there's homemade garlic bread (toasted bread with melted butter and garlic powder shaken over it) that's stone-cold, but as I eat, I give my daughter a big smile and say, "Honey, it's delicious. Thanks so much. You did a great job and I appreciate it."

She gives me an ear-to-ear smile that lightens my spirit and makes me feel the best I've felt since this rotten day began so many long hours ago. As we eat Amelia goes on about her school day, about two friends named Stacy and Amy who are now fighting over a boy, a math test that went well, and how upset our neighbor Todd Pence was when he had to leave early.

Amelia says, twirling a piece of spaghetti on her fork, "Do you think I'm still gonna need to have Todd come by?"

I think of the two kids I had dispatched earlier. "For just a while, hon, until we can move into a better place."

Her sweet face brightens up. "Are we moving back in with Daddy? In our old home?"

My sweet, airy feeling is gone, brought back to earth by the ongoing disaster that's my divorce from her father. "Amelia... please. We've talked about this, haven't we? We both love you, very much. But...things aren't right between the two of us. It has nothing to do with you. You will always be our special girl, our daughter. But...we...I'm not getting back together with your dad."

Amelia lowers her head, doesn't speak for a while, even while we're washing the dishes. There's an unexpected knock on the door.

Amelia turns, dishcloth in hand. "Mom?"

"Hold on," I say, and I go back to the bedroom, retrieve my SIG Sauer, and head to the door, which has a thick security chain across the top.

I call out, "Who's there?"

Another knock.

Well?

My hand lowers to the doorknob, pistol hidden behind my hip.

Marsha Gray watches people go in and out of the apartment building, still impressed at how quickly Grissom dispatched the two punks who had approached her.

Tough broad.

Need to remember that.

She yawns.

How long before she could leave?

Until the lights up there are all out.

Still...she wishes she had more info, more intelligence about what Grissom is doing. Marsha hates relying on a man for her livelihood, especially Parker Hoyt. He's given her calls about Grissom's movements, but she refuses to completely trust him.

Something has to be done, and soon, about getting better information.

I undo the door and step to one side and—

A familiar, smiling, cautious face is looking at me.

"Hi, Sally, can I come in?"

Amelia runs from the kitchen. "Daddy!"

I close the door, undo the chain, and let him in. Ben Miller, my straying husband, walks in, his smile wider, his black hair trimmed well, wearing gray slacks and a black turtleneck. A brief flicker of my old love and affection slides through me, and I instantly kill it, remembering all the lies, the betrayals. He gives Amelia a big hug, and there's a jolt of jealousy in seeing how joyfully she returns the hug to her father.

I slide my pistol in my rear waistband. "Ben...what a surprise."

He kisses the top of Amelia's head. "Love giving my little girl a surprise."

"Why...how...why are you here, Ben?"

He closes the door behind him, as Amelia turns around and he puts his arm around her. Amelia's smile is as sweet as anything I've seen in a while. Ben kisses her again and says, "I called here earlier. Amelia said Todd, the babysitter—"

"Dad, he's not a babysitter!"

"Sorry, kiddo," he says, squeezing her shoulder. "Amelia said Todd the neighbor had to leave and she wasn't sure when you were coming home, so I offered to come over and keep her safe."

*This isn't what we've agreed to with the visitation schedule* is what

I want to say, but I buck up and go into the kitchen. "Great. Come along, Ben, you can help us finish the dishes."

Marsha waits and waits and then the lights in the apartment unit start going out. Good. Across the street is a 24/7 Walgreens with a well-lit parking lot. She'll slide in there and catch some catnaps during the night, and be ready in case Grissom leaves.

She remembers again how quickly that Secret Service agent moved. She hates to admit it, but when Grissom was facing those two creeps, Marsha was really tempted to go out and help her.

It was the urge to do something good.

Marsha turns on the ignition.

Better watch out and make sure it didn't happen again.

# CHAPTER 30

AFTER THE DISHES are wiped dry and put away, I'm yawning because of the long day, but I won't go to bed yet. Ben and I keep a cordial and polite conversation for the benefit of our girl, and there's chocolate ice cream for dessert. We then go out into the small living room, and I not-so-gently aim Ben to a battered reclining chair, while Amelia and I sit on the couch.

Amelia puts on a television show about not-so-real housewives somewhere, all made-up, Botoxed, and dieted to within an ounce of their lives, and it seems most of their time is spent yelling at each other and eating at expensive restaurants.

My daughter is calling up photos of national parks on her iPad in preparation for some school project, and Ben comes over and kneels down next to her, pointing out the history of each park that Amelia brings up. I try to stay awake as I watch members of my own sex disgrace themselves on national television, but then I'm shocked into sudden awareness at the exchange next to me.

Amelia oohs and points to a photo on her tablet. "Oh, Yellowstone. And that geyser, Old Faithful. Does it really spout out like that on schedule?"

Ben rubs her shoulder. "It sure does, honey. I was there last year and saw it twice, right on time."

Amelia says, "No way, Dad," and her dad says, "Sure…maybe I'll take you out there next summer."

"Really?" Amelia turns to me and says, "Mom, did you hear that?"

I force a smile. "I sure did, sweetie, and look at the time. Let's get you into bed."

For once she doesn't whine or argue, but she shuts down her iPad and says, "Can Daddy spend the night? Can he?"

Ben says quietly, "Yes, can he?"

I take Amelia's hand, gently pull her up from the couch, and lead her out of the room without saying a word.

After she's washed up and settled down in her small bedroom, I go out and Ben is standing there, looking uneasy, pretending to pay serious attention to a talk show now on Bravo. I stand in front of him and say, "Mind telling me what this is all about?"

He looks up at me, not ignoring me, which is at least a step forward, although a step overdue by a number of years. "I called her up to see how she was doing. She told me Todd had to leave because of some family emergency. And that you were running late. She sounded scared, Sally, so I told her I'd come right over. You know this isn't the best of neighborhoods."

I cross my arms. "And whose fault is that?"

Ben holds up a hand. "Please…can we not fight? Please? For Amelia's sake?"

"For Amelia's sake?" I step closer and lower my voice. "You should have thought of Amelia a long, long time ago, before your drinking got out of control and you started humping interns half your age."

His voice is bleak. "I'm in a program. I've stopped the drinking and...I've been faithful these past months. Sally, how many times do I have to apologize?"

"I'll let you know," I snap back. "And here's another thing for Amelia's sake. You're confusing the hell out of her. We've agreed to a visitation schedule, and you coming tonight...okay, she was scared, but I was here before you showed up. It's tough enough for our daughter without her thinking there's a chance we're getting back together."

His eyes seem to moisten, and I step back and say, "But fair's fair. You take the couch, get out before she gets up for school."

He nods. "Thanks, Sally."

"Don't be so happy," I say. "If I get called out during the night, you're going to have to stay and get her to school by yourself."

"Not a problem," Ben says.

I leave the living room. "And either turn that damn thing down or turn it off."

In my bedroom I hear sudden silence from the living room as Ben switches off the television, like he's some holy pilgrim somewhere, following his superior's orders, hoping for redemption.

Sorry, Ben, I think, curled up in my bed. No redemption tonight.

And after a while, I figure, no sleep as well.

Not after the day I've had.

So many thoughts are racing around in my mind that it's hard to keep track of them, and instead of counting sheep, I'm counting all of the problems I'm facing—each problem looking like a rabid wolverine rather than a cuddly sheep—and then the bedroom door creaks open.

I whisper, "Amelia?"

"No," comes the embarrassed reply. "It's Ben."

He comes in, closes the door, and says, "Sally, I'm sorry. I can't sleep. That couch...it's got some metal bar in it that digs into my back."

"Then go home already."

"Can't...can't I just come in here? With you? I promise, I won't disturb you."

His shape is outlined by the glow from the bedside clock and other electronics. I don't want to even glance at the time.

"You could still go home."

"Sally, please...must you always be angry at me? Always?"

I think of him and I think of my commander in chief, and I wonder where the First Lady might be, and maybe there should be some consolation that even the highest and mightiest of us all can have marital problems, but I'm not seeing it. The First Lady saw her betrayal live on television earlier today. I saw mine about a year ago, when a presidential visit was canceled at the last minute, meaning I got home early to see my drunken husband in bed with an intern from the Department of the Interior, with another one waiting for him in the kitchen, smoking a joint.

"All right," I say. "You can join me."

There's movement and a soft rustle of clothes being removed, and the bed shifts as he stretches out next to me. We both remain silent until Ben says, "Not a day goes by that I don't regret what I did, Sally. Honest. I'm ashamed, I'm humiliated, and I'm so sad for what I've put you through, and Amelia. Especially Amelia, I never meant for it to—"

"Ben?" I ask in the darkened bedroom.

"Yes?"

"Go to sleep," I say, "and if you touch me or try to come over to this side, I'll break your fingers."

# CHAPTER 31

MY INTERNAL CLOCK usually gets me up at 6:00 a.m., and it's rare that it fails me, but this is one of those damnable mornings. I wake up in an empty bed, *Good,* I think, and glance over at the clock—6:45 a.m., *definitely* not good—and I jump out of bed and toss on a robe and yell out, "Amelia!" as I go down the hallway.

Then I smell coffee and bacon, and I get to the kitchen, and Ben's there, grinning, standing by the stove, and Amelia is setting plates and says cheerfully, "Look, Mom, Daddy and I made you breakfast!"

*Holy crap,* I think. I check the time again and say, "Ben . . . for Christ's sake, she's got to be down at the corner in ten minutes to catch the bus."

Ben's face colors. "I thought the bus picked her up at seven fifteen."

*Before I caught you, you fool, and when I swore I would never set foot in that place ever again,* is what I think.

I say, "Ben, that was at . . . the old place." I turn to Amelia and say, "Your bag all packed? You got money for lunch?"

"Mom—" she starts, and I say, "Hurry up and eat as much as you can."

And I turn and race back to the bedroom.

Nine minutes later I'm outside with Amelia, dressed, with just a comb through my hair and wearing about 80 percent of what I was wearing yesterday. I've made a call to get a pickup from one of the Secret Service staff at H Street. I also make two other phone calls, one to Scotty and one to Pamela Smithson, and both calls confirm what I had suspected: no progress in the search for Grace Fuller Tucker.

"All right," I tell them both. "Keep at it. I'm going to work matters on this end."

When I'm done I see the bright yellow school bus grumbling its way to us in the thick morning traffic. Amelia stands there, looking small, her brightly colored knapsack almost as large as she is. Ben had given her a quick kiss and awkward hug a few minutes earlier before quickly strolling away, shoulders hunched over.

"Hey, hon," I say, "what's up?"

"You don't have to be so mean."

"Amelia . . ."

Her head snaps right to my direction. "Daddy came over last night because I was scared! And he helped clean the dishes. And make breakfast. And you weren't nice to him at all . . ."

"But Amelia . . ."

"He came out of your bedroom this morning," she says. "That means he still loves you, Mommy. Don't you see? If you stop being so mean to him, we can move back to our real home, and you don't have to get a divorce and it can all go back to the way things were."

Her bus comes to a stop, and I note a black Suburban up the way that's my ride this morning.

"It's . . . more complicated than that, honey. And we're not getting back together. I'm sorry."

The door to the bus swings open, and she's now bawling. "If you were nice to him, he'd take us back! He'd take us back, I know he would! We can all be together again!"

"Honey . . ."

She jumps off the sidewalk, goes up the steps into the school bus, her knapsack bouncing on her little back, and she turns and in a high-pitched voice that always cuts me, no matter how much of a tough mom I think I am, she calls out, "If you weren't so mean, we'd still be a family! Why do you have to be so mean?"

The door whispers shut. Amelia goes to a seat. The times I've waited with her at the bus stop, she's always turned and waved out the window at me.

Not this morning.

The bus lurches forward into the traffic, and the Suburban stops. I open the door and climb in, and I say to the young driver, "Not a word to me or I'll toss you out and drive myself."

Even with his sharp dress and clean-cut looks, he appears scared.

Good.

"Yes, ma'am," he says.

I fasten my seat belt. "Those were two words. Don't let it happen again."

And then we're off.

# CHAPTER 32

PARKER HOYT HAS been at his desk for three hours already this morning, working the phones, soothing scared senators and representatives, bucking up important donors, all the while waiting and waiting to see if the First Lady is going to be found today. The news is still grim from Atlanta, but there's a hopeful tone in some of the commentary, about the President coming forth yesterday and admitting his mistakes. And the bulk of the coverage and opinion pieces share the same thread: the President's campaign has received a serious blow, but there's still time to recover, especially if the First Lady comes forward and offers some forgiveness.

But there are also questions . . . where is the First Lady?

Parker rubs at the back of his neck. Publicly, she's in seclusion. Privately . . . about a half-dozen people know her real status, and in DC, that number will start growing in the next few hours until he finds that bitch, either dead or alive.

At this point, Parker doesn't particularly care.

His phone rings, and his secretary says, "Special Agent Grissom to see you," and he says, "Send her in right away."

The door opens and Agent Grissom comes in, and she looks awful. Eyes bleary, hair a mess, skin blotchy, and it looks like she's wearing the same plain outfit from yesterday. A nasty part of Parker quickly wonders how in the world she managed to find a husband and to have a child...and also thinks, well, she found a husband, but she sure didn't find a way to keep him.

"Sit down," he says, but she's already descending into a chair when he says, "Why are you here?"

Grissom says, "I have a capable crew out searching the river. And I've got other work to do in town."

"Anything new to report?"

"Not a thing," she says. "The horse came back riderless. Nobody at the stables saw anything unusual. There's only one road in and out of the farm. Surveillance tapes were reviewed and she didn't sneak out."

"And the note and the panic button?"

"Still in our possession, and I got a call a while ago from our forensics outfit," she says. "It was legit. Does the President know?"

"He does," Parker says. "The Homeland Security unit still out there?"

"They are."

"The cover story about a lost canoeist still holding?"

"It is, so far...but I don't know for how long."

Parker brushes away a speck of dust on his otherwise clean desk. "How did you get that unit out there on such short notice?"

"Appealed to their better nature," Grissom said, voice snappy, and Parker decides not to press the point.

He says, "What did you say earlier, about other work to do? What the hell does that mean?"

Grissom says, "It means the President's wife is still missing.

There are search teams in the area where she was last seen. Having me out there supervising won't accomplish a damn thing. Talking to people back here can help."

"What people?"

"The President's lead protective agent, for one."

"And who else?"

Grissom says, "I need to talk to the President. Privately."

Parker shakes his head. "Impossible."

"Then make it possible, and this morning," Grissom says. "Right now, there are no leads. None. Zero. And I need to ask some questions, poke around to see what comes up."

"She might be dead," Parker says. "That note...I thought it looked like a suicide note."

"Perhaps, but I'm leaving all options open."

"You think she might be faking a suicide?"

Grissom says, "Like I said, I'm leaving all options open. And I need to see the President, as soon as possible."

"Agent Grissom..."

"Make it happen, Mister Hoyt," Grissom says. "The best way for a successful resolution, and a quick one, is to run this down like any other criminal investigation. Which means I get to talk to people. And that's going to include me talking to the husband of a missing woman. When a wife goes missing, the husband needs to be interviewed. Like any other case."

Parker says, "This isn't any other case, you know that."

Grissom stands up. "You can keep on thinking that, Mister Hoyt, but I can't afford to do so. Otherwise she'll never be found."

After she's gone, Parker picks up his phone, reluctantly calls one of the two numbers he's been using since this mess started.

Again, the phone is answered by his contact; again, from the ambient noise, he can tell the person is outside.

There's no hesitation on the other end of the phone. "Don't ever call me again, all right? I'll call if I have any information, and right now, I don't."

Parker says, "I just want to verify that there are no new developments."

No answer, as the person on his private payroll hangs up.

Parker stares at the phone and then glances at a printed piece of paper carefully placed to the side of his desk. He picks up his White House phone and reaches the President's secretary.

He lets out a big sigh as she answers the phone. He says, "Mrs. Young, I need fifteen minutes of the President's time this morning...so tell the Better Business Bureau delegation they're going to have to make do with the Secretary of Commerce."

# CHAPTER 33

IN A CRAMPED, windowless interview office adjacent to Room W-17, I finally meet with Jackson Thiel, the head of the President's detail, the agent most often at President Tucker's side. There's no decorations, no plants, no framed photographs in the office, just a telephone and a metal desk and two chairs that seem to be leftovers from the Carter administration.

I sit down, and Jackson sits across from me, impeccably dressed as always, face impassive but slightly troubled, and I decide to get right to it.

"When did it start?"

Jackson doesn't hesitate. "When did what start?"

I make sure he hears my audible sigh. "Okay, if that's how you want to play it, I'll let you be. In a day or two, the usual congressional knuckleheads are going to demand a special prosecutor to find out what laws were broken while CANAL was stepping out on his wife. Then the Secret Service and Homeland Security are going to decide whether to defend you rogue agents, or toss you all under the nearest Metro bus. When that happens, you're going to be on your own, Agent Thiel. In other words, if some agents who'd take a bullet for CANAL have their lives and careers destroyed, so be it."

Jackson makes to speak, and I roll right over him, no patience at all. "Your work in sidestepping proper procedures and enabling the President to bed his mistress was completely rogue and unauthorized. You work for me, and the moment I found out was yesterday morning. Do you think I'm going to let that slide? Or that the director will?"

"But I—"

My rolling over him continues, and maybe I'm not being fair, but I don't care. "You know your history. You know what happened to the agents caught up in the Clinton–Lewinsky mess? They had to hire private lawyers. They lost their homes, their savings, their college funds. And their careers crumbled like dust. You know a good lawyer, then?"

I gather my notepad and bag, stand up, and Jackson's face softens. "Eight months ago."

I sit down. "Where and how?"

"It was a post-fundraising get-together in Denver," Jackson says, voice quiet. "Miss Doyle was part of the group. There were about two dozen there, a meet-and-greet, photo taken with CANAL, that sort of thing."

"Go on."

"Then CANAL asked if we could delay getting back to the hotel for a while," Jackson says. "He and Miss Doyle went into a private room off the banquet hall for about a half hour."

"Was this the first time they ever met?"

"To my knowledge, yes."

"Did she entice him in any way?"

"Entice?"

I lose my patience again. "Crap, Jack, you know what I mean.

Did she have a low-cut dress on and drop some cottage cheese down her cleavage in front of the President? Did she laugh a lot and touch his shoulder, touch his hair? Did she turn and flip up the back of her dress to show him she was wearing a thong? Anything like that?"

Jackson shakes his head. "No, nothing like that. Miss Doyle... she's a class act."

That's a comment too far. "Excuse me for being rude, but she's banging a married man, and not just any married man."

Jackson is stubborn. "She...makes him happy. That's all I know. And a happy President...well, it's a good thing."

"Was she a stalker? Hanging around the Man's campaign events? Trying to sneak into Camp David? Send him books of love poetry?"

"Not at all. Like I said, she's a class act. A fine woman."

I bite my tongue and say, "How often did they get together?"

"Two, three times a month."

I can't believe it. "You've got to be kidding me."

Jackson shakes his head. "Nope."

"How in the hell did...how did you think you were going to get away with it? How did you think *he* was going to get away with it?"

He says, "You know how it is. CANAL goes to a campaign event, or some political meeting, and at some point the press secretary, he says, the lid's on, no more news for the night, the President's gone to bed. And the hotels he stays at...secure, staff discreet, we rent the floor the President's on and the floor above and the floor below. After-hours...easy enough to go out a back entrance, or a service area, or any other place for a...meeting."

"So you helped arrange these...meetings."

"We did."

"Not really in your job description, is it?"

He shrugs. "Just following orders."

I say, "This Tammy Doyle . . . you think she has violence in her heart? Wants to hurt the President? Or the First Lady?"

"Absolutely not."

I wait for a moment. "Anything else?"

He waits for a moment as well. "I'm hearing . . . rumors. About the First Lady. That she might be . . . well, someplace where she can't be reached."

I get up. "That's all, Jack."

"You asked about Tammy Doyle and the First Lady. There's something going on, isn't there?"

"Jack, your career has already been bombed into destruction. What, you have an appetite to make the rubble bounce?"

He stares up at me. "But if you're doing something about the First Lady being . . . unavailable . . . it's not our job. It's the FBI, DC police, whole lots of other agencies."

I say, "You know the drill. Just following orders."

# CHAPTER 34

AFTER THREE HOURS of purging her emails and phone messages, Tammy Doyle finally sits back in her office chair and takes a breath. She managed to slip into the K Street building holding Pearson, Pearson, and Price by going into an adjacent structure and walking through a maintenance hallway.

In her office, there's been looks, a few smiles, but mostly she's been left alone, which is fine. The firm's receptionists are screening any incoming calls, the media can camp out on the sidewalk for as long as they want, and she's in a little cocoon of safety here in her office.

Tammy's feeling better, even though her face is still tender from yesterday's car accident and that side of her body is achy. The bruise on her cheek has been covered up with some foundation, and no one's noticed a thing. She's ignored the news this morning, and right now, all she wants is a third cup of coffee, and then there's a knock at her door.

"Come on in," she calls out, and Ralph Moren, her group's admin aide, steps in and says, "Tammy, there's a woman here to see you."

Tammy says, "I doubt it. I don't have any scheduled appointments."

Ralph nods, his face bright red above his equally red bow tie. "I know that but this woman...she's from the Secret Service. And she says she needs to see you, straightaway."

Tammy waits for a moment, says, "All right, Ralph. Show her in...and get me a cup of coffee, the way I like it. And see if she wants one as well."

Ralph slips out, and about ten seconds later, the Secret Service agent comes in. Tammy stands up, extends a hand, gives her a close look. Tammy has gotten to know about a half-dozen Secret Service agents after meeting...Harry, and she's not one of the protective team that travels with him. She's older, tall, and very tired-looking, with frizzy brown hair and swollen eyes. She has on a black wool coat that goes down to her knees, along with a red scarf that looks handmade. After the initial awkward private meetings with Harry, she'd gotten along well with his Secret Service detail, with smiles and little shared jokes here and there.

This woman doesn't seem to be in a joking mood.

She reaches into her leather bag, pulls out a small wallet, which she displays, showing a star-shaped badge and a photograph of the woman. "Miss Doyle, I'm Sally Grissom, special agent in charge, Presidential Protective Division for the Secret Service. Thanks for seeing me."

The Secret Service agent sits down, and Tammy does as well, and then the door opens up again and Ralph comes in with a large white coffee mug branded with the firm's blue logo, and she says, "Are you sure we can't get you anything, Agent...Grissom?"

"No," she says, and Tammy denotes hard steel behind that one syllable. Ralph leaves, and Tammy says, "Do I need a lawyer?"

"Do you think you do?" Grissom shoots back.

"I'm not sure . . . why are you here?"

Grissom says, "You're a smart woman, you've worked here for three years, you know the ways of the world in DC. And I'm sure you know that the agents who . . . allowed you within the President's company were violating Secret Service regulations."

"But they were . . . well, the President knew."

"The President isn't their boss," she says, voice hard and sharp. "I am. And I'm here to do an interview, to ensure you weren't a threat then, and are not a threat now."

Tammy at least a swills, smiles, and takes a healthy sip of her coffee. Outside is the constant hum of traffic on K Street, with her windowed office overlooking the key avenue in this town, where deals are struck and money changes hands, all in the name of greasing the so-called wheels of power up on Capitol Hill and at the White House.

"Please," she says. "I'm not a threat. Honest."

Grissom says, "When did it start?"

"Ah . . . you mean, when did I start seeing the President?"

"Exactly."

"About . . . eight months ago. At a function in Denver."

"Had you been following him prior to that?"

"Following? Like . . . stalking? No, I'm not a stalker."

"Your meeting in Denver, then, it was just an accident."

"Yes."

"How did it happen?"

Tammy doesn't like being put in the spotlight like this. It feels like a job interview that's going off the rails.

"It . . . happened."

Grissom says, "Sorry, that's not going to be good enough. I want details, or I can take you into custody right now."

"You're bluffing," Tammy says.

"Try me," Grissom says quietly.

Tammy pauses. "It was in Denver. My firm represents companies that have...pipeline interests in Colorado. There was a reception. We chatted for just a few seconds...and later, people were leaving, and Harry...I mean, the President, caught my eye. He motioned me to follow him...and we went into this little conference room. And...we talked. That's all. Just talked. About Denver. The campaign. Weather. And...you know what? He seemed lonely. The poor man...just lonely."

"And?"

Tammy says, "A Secret Service agent knocked on the door, told him his motorcade was about to leave. We embraced... kissed...and...he asked me if I was going to be at an event in Saint Paul the next week."

She feels warm now, thinking about that first time. "I lied. I said I was. And that's when...we became intimate."

Grissom says, "During your times together...did you say anything about the First Lady?"

Something is changing in Tammy's office. It's no longer the safe cocoon she loves.

"I'm sorry, I don't understand your question."

"Grace Fuller Tucker. Did you and the President talk about her? Did you talk about her as a rival? An enemy?"

Tammy says, "Not on your life."

"Prove it."

Tammy feels trapped by the cold eyes and look of the Secret Service agent across from her. "I...we hardly ever talked about her. Honest. Our time together was so limited that we made it count...and that didn't mean talking about his wife."

"Did the President make promises to you? About your future together?"

Tammy hesitates. Maybe now is the time for a lawyer, but still...she can't stand the thought of being dragged through that mob downstairs with her arms cuffed behind her, still being the lead story on every television and cable news network on the planet.

"Yes...he said that after the election, he'd put out news leaks about his relationship with the First Lady, that they had grown apart. And after the inauguration...he'd separate from her. And eventually bring me into public view."

Grissom says, "Nice plan. Tell me, how much do you dislike the First Lady? Have you been following her? Sending her anonymous threats? Or are you jealous about her relationship with the President?"

"No, no, I have...look." She takes a deep breath. "This is rotten. I know it is. But the President...he was lonely. And...we connected. The two of us. I love him, and he loves me. We hardly ever talked about the First Lady...and you know what? I admire her. She's trying to help homeless kids, she's trying to make a difference...and I admire her for that. Honest to God."

"One last question," Grissom says, and Tammy is nearly faint with relief.

"Okay."

"Did the President make any mention of the First Lady having an affair of her own, with another man? Did he have any suspicions that she was cheating on him?"

Tammy couldn't reply for the surprise she felt. She recovered and said, "No. Not a word. Not a hint...nothing."

Grissom abruptly stands up. "Very well. Thank you for your cooperation, Miss Doyle...and good luck in the days ahead."

Before Grissom reaches the door, Tammy calls out, "Can I ask you a question?"

The Secret Service agent, leather case in one hand, rearranges the handmade red scarf with the other. "Sure. I can give you that."

"I've heard...rumors. About the First Lady. Whether she's... really in seclusion in the family quarters at the White House."

Grissom says, "Take care of yourself."

And then she's gone, her non-answer raising lots more questions for Tammy.

She takes out her cell phone, feels that urgent hunger to call Harry to see how he's doing.

But...

Tammy puts the phone away.

The last time she talked to him on this phone, Harry had lied to her.

She doesn't want to give him another opportunity.

# CHAPTER 35

I'M IN THE President's private study, on the second floor of the White House, and I suppose I should be impressed, but I'm not. I'm thinking about the naughty things that have happened in this room over the years—Harding, LBJ, Clinton—and I force myself to keep a slight smile on my face as I sit down across from the Man. Parker Hoyt is hovering at his side, near packed shelves of leather-bound books. There are also small oil paintings of famed past politicians decorating the walls, and President Tucker is sitting at a small wooden desk.

He starts, "Agent Grissom, I want to apologize for the… brusque tone I took with you yesterday. You can imagine the… stress we were all under."

"I understand, sir," I say, sitting still, hands in my lap. I catch the attention of his chief of staff and I say, "Mister Hoyt, will you excuse us?"

The President's campaign may be in slow-motion collapse, and the comics and commentators may be having a wonderful time with the "Ambush in Atlanta," but I have to give Parker Hoyt credit: he looks as tough and as sharp as when I saw him last.

"Absolutely not," he says. "I stay here. I want to hear what's going on."

I smile at him. "Very well." I shift my gaze. "Mister President, do you know where your wife is?"

The President is puzzled. "No. Of course not."

"Thank you."

Still in the chair, I say, "Mister Hoyt, that concludes my investigation. You told me yesterday to do whatever it takes to find the First Lady, and I can't do that by conducting interviews in your presence. So your choice is either to leave and let me perform this investigation in a manner I see fit, or stay here and the investigation is finished. I'm unable to find the First Lady."

The President says, "Parker, she makes sense. Please leave."

"Mister President—"

"Parker."

He says not a word and then quietly and quickly leaves, closing the heavy wooden door behind him. The President says, "With everything else that's going on, you've managed to make an enemy for life, Agent Grissom."

"He'll have to take a number," I say. "Thank you, sir. I'll make this as quick as possible. I know your time is extremely valuable."

He nods, and I think of the times I've interviewed men while I was working for Metro DC and the State Police in Virginia, men who were suspected of being drug mules, serial abusers, or rapists. The fact that I'm using my interview techniques with the President of the United States boggles my mind.

"Again, Mister President, do you know where your wife is?"

"No."

"With the news about your . . . relationship with Tammy Doyle, I have to ask this . . . your marriage, was it in serious trouble?"

He nods, eyes sad. "Ah..."

He stops talking.

"Mister President...what you say to me I'll keep confidential. Even if I'm subpoenaed at some point. Right now I want to find your wife, and I need your help."

He nods, swallows, and that's when I no longer have the most powerful man in the world sitting in front of me.

In front of me is a husband whose wife has gone missing.

"It...started a couple of years ago. We both had our schedules, our demands. Often we were on the road on separate trips... and then...I started making compromises. Grace didn't—or wouldn't—understand that. Politics is a practical business, and it's better to get half a loaf than none. But she kept on pushing me, pushing me...even working behind my back to reach out to congressional leaders. We had a few private blowups, and then...we settled, I guess. We settled into our own universes, our own lives..."

I hear his words and I also see something else—my marriage, the long stretches of time I spent working and on the road, and Ben doing the same, out visiting the national parks, each of us juggling our own career, our own demands, while trying to raise a daughter.

"I see, sir. Please continue."

He shrugs. "Our marriage...it was for appearances only. An empty shell. There was no more romance, no more passion. A peck on the lips or on the cheek, a week or so here...a couple of times we tried to mend things, spending long weekends at Camp David; then we'd go back to the old arguments, our old patterns. But you have to know one very important thing, Agent Grissom."

"And what's that, sir?"

"I still have affection for her. I always will. And I do love her still. I couldn't have gotten here without her support, without her sacrifices. I want you to know I bear her no ill will."

I try to gauge his mood, what's going on behind that sad yet handsome face, and I say, "When was the last time you spoke with the First Lady?"

"Yesterday morning, when we had just left Atlanta."

"That must have been a difficult conversation."

Another swallow. "It was."

"How did it end?"

"Excuse me?"

Something just flickered across his face. "Your conversation with the First Lady," I ask. "How did it end?"

He seems to be struggling with something, and I decide not to press him. Too much pressure from my end and he'll wrap things up, and maybe get another compliant Secret Service agent to conduct this fouled-up investigation. An attractive option for sure, but I'm in so deep now that I'm going to see it to the end.

The President says, "She was angry. Very angry. And she asked me when I was going to get to Andrews...and she said, she said, 'I don't want to talk to you now, or then, or ever.' She hung up on me, and then my follow-up calls went unanswered, and...well, you know the rest."

I certainly do, which included violating a good half-dozen laws, regulations, and procedures in the process. "Sir," I ask, "do you know of any other place where she might be? Someplace that she might go to as a refuge."

"Our residence on Lake Erie, in Vermilion. The Erie White House, you'll recall."

"I'll alert the Secret Service detail there, but I don't think she would have been able to leave the horse farm and get there without being noticed," I say. "But her detail has told me that besides

Camp David, she did have another place where she could be alone and relax. Does that strike a bell with you at all?"

The President shakes his head, and I sense his frustration. "No, no, I wish I could help you...honestly, I wish I could tell you something useful."

I take a deep breath, decide it's time for the Big Question. "Mister President...did you have any indication, or suspicion, or even a suggestion...that the First Lady might be having an affair as well?"

His eyes widen in shock, and I guess that's my answer. "No...nothing like that, I mean..." And his voice rises. "What in hell are you suggesting? Who told you that?"

"It doesn't matter now," I say. "What matters is that my source tells me that he or she overheard your wife talking to a man, expressing her love and affection."

"Can't you trace that call, find out who he is?"

"Your wife was using a burner cell phone, apparently secured by someone from the East Wing."

The President shakes his head and leans back in his study chair. "I...I can't believe it. When could she do it? How could she do it?"

I think if I bite my tongue any harder it will be severed in half—*That's what you did,* I want to say, *and that's what my husband Ben did. Why are you surprised?*—and thank God, I'm interrupted by my phone ringing.

I see that it's Scotty calling, and I say, "Sir, please excuse me, I need to take this call."

I get up from the chair and cross to the door, open it and step into the hallway. Luck is with me because this narrow stretch of fancy corridor with old paintings and furniture is empty.

"Grissom," I answer. "What's up, Scotty?"

A crackle and hiss of static, and the words, "—a body."

"Say again, Scotty? What is it?"

His voice bellows out. "We've found a body! Female…at the Quinnick Falls…about three miles south of the horse farm… you better—"

Another burst of static, and I lose the connection.

No matter.

I start running.

# CHAPTER 36

IT'S NEAR DUSK, and Marsha Gray is slogging through a swampy area, near Quinnick Falls, where she's been dispatched after getting a frantic phone call from Parker Hoyt. Supposedly the First Lady's body has been found, and Marsha certainly hopes so, because she's tired of hunting in the First World.

The muck and water are up to her knees as she slowly wades through brush and saplings heading toward the sounds of engines, loud voices, and the thumping hum of a helicopter overhead.

She gets closer, finds a dry spot near a maple tree, takes a breather. In the Third World, hunting could be as fun as trick-or-treating. Cops and security forces can be bribed to look the other way. Traffic laws were suggestions, not rules. And in most of her Third World hunting grounds, being a woman meant you were ignored, were part of the shiftless, covered background.

Which made hunting so much fun.

But here?

She drops her rucksack, opens it up, and removes a pair of binoculars with high-grade optics. She leans against the trunk of the maple, starts scanning what she sees. Damn thing is, here in the First World, if a local cop or a Virginia state trooper were to trip over her, she couldn't bribe them or persuade them to look the other way. Nope, she'd have to kill them, and that made the job just that much harder.

All right then.

The waterfalls look to be about thirty meters wide, with a drop of about two meters. Lots of exposed rocks, tangled limbs, and old tree trunks caught up in the water and debris. Homeland Security folks and a couple of Secret Service agents are on the far side of the river. A guy in a black wetsuit and with an orange rope fastened to a harness starts carefully working his way to an area just below the falls. Marsha focuses in and sees an arm flopping back and forth from the currents, the body obscured by the swirling foam and water.

"Bit chillier than the East Wing, eh?" she whispers, as she keeps watching.

Another guy in a wetsuit joins the agent, then slips and falls. Shouts and yells as he's pulled to shore, and then he steps out again.

"That's right," she whispers. "Be a hero. Drown for a dead woman."

The progress is slow and painful to watch. Marsha shifts her spot, scans the crew, and then another Suburban bounces along the shore, lights flashing, and yep, there she is, the Queen of All She Surveys, Secret Service Agent Grissom, black coat on and red scarf flapping around.

Grissom meets up with another Secret Service agent, and there's discussion, and the Queen borrows a pair of binoculars, scans the area. They then go to the water's edge. Behind them a white tent is being erected, and a generator kicks to life.

The two men in the wetsuits are at the location of the body. More ropes are deployed, securing the body in case the two heroes fall on the way back. Wouldn't be nice to have her let loose and bounce around for another mile or two in the rapids.

All right, then.

The two wetsuited men make their way free, the body slumped between them. Marsha swears. Not a good view at all. Just a slumped torso. They work their way through the water, past the rocks and debris. A line of men and women are waiting for them, men holding a wire Stokes litter. Wouldn't do to have the First Lady of the United States dragged into that examination tent like a sack of potatoes and—

Oh, shit.

Freeze.

Marsha stops, no longer breathing. She is focused on Grissom, the lead Secret Service agent, and the woman is staring right at her, motionless.

Don't move, she thinks. Don't breathe.

The worst thing that can ever befall a sniper has just happened to Marsha.

She's been spotted.

# CHAPTER 37

AFTER A BALLS-TO-THE-WALLS, screaming drive from the White House, I finally get to Quinnick Falls, a small park about three miles downstream from where I had found the First Lady's note. Although it drove me crazy with impatience, I kept off the radio and the phone through the hurried drive to Virginia, not wanting anyone out there with the ears and capability to learn why I was in such a hurry.

And to make this early evening even better, I get a phone call from my neighbor Todd Pence, with more apologies and excuses, saying another emergency from his sister means he can't look after Amelia tonight.

Damn, damn, damn.

My male Secret Service driver finds an empty spot near other Suburbans and Humvees, and before the vehicle comes to a complete stop and the engine is switched off, I fling the door open and start running to the mass of men and women gathered in a small picnic area, with wooden tables that are crowded now with ropes, grappling hooks, communications equipment, and other gear.

Scotty spots me and comes over, and I say, "What do we got?"

Scotty nods, looking tired, a set of binoculars hanging around his neck, and he points over to the rushing water, where a man in a wetsuit is starting to wade out, a bright orange rope attached to his waist. "About thirty minutes ago, a couple of kids fooling around by the edge of the falls saw a woman caught up in the rocks. Apparently drowned. Right about then a Homeland Security Humvee pulled in, as part of the search effort, and they waved it down."

"How do they know it's a woman?"

Scotty looks embarrassed. "Partial breast. Sally. The blouse is torn away and a breast is exposed...and, well, the body's a mess. It's been in those rocks for a while."

"Binoculars," I say.

He passes over his set without a word, and I check the turbulent waters. Something heavy, like a fifty-pound chunk of lead, seems to slide down my gullet. Through the binoculars I can see a bloated shape in the water, partially clothed, and an arm flopping around.

I give the binoculars back to Scotty. A power generator roars on, and behind us, a white tent is being set up. Somewhere in that mess of people is Randy Anderson, the Homeland Security officer I had shanghaied to conduct this unauthorized and probably illegal search.

"Where's her detail?"

"CANARY's detail? Over there, by that big wooden sign showing the history of the falls."

"Get them over here," I say.

Another wetsuited man is in the water, rope attached to his harness, and he slips and nearly falls. Scotty says, "Why?"

"Because when the body gets to shore, I want them and...

you, Scotty, I want the four of you to bring her into that tent, for examination."

Scotty nods. I say, "And another thing. Pass the word around. I see any camera flashes from anybody as she's being taken away, I'll shoot them dead, right on the spot. And I'm not kidding."

"I know," Scotty says, and he walks away.

I stand there, cold and hungry and just miserable, watching the scene unfold before me. This is not a new experience. In my years of law enforcement, I've seen lots of bodies recovered— from drownings like this one, from scores of traffic accidents, from burned-out apartments and trailers—but this recovery is just hammering at me. This one is going into the history books, the documentaries, the news programs, and only by the sheerest and slimmest bit of luck have we avoided having network television helicopters overhead.

The two men are there now, working in the cold, rushing waters, using ropes to secure the body, and then the body is free. The two men work very hard to keep their footing as they come back to shore.

Movement nearby. A metal Stokes litter is by the shore, and Scotty is there, and the three slumped and depressed members of CANARY's detail: Pamela Smithson, the lead, with Tanya Glenn next to her, and then Brian Zahn, the young male. He appears to be weeping, and no one notices him.

I turn back and—

Wait.

Hold on.

Something just happened.

Movement over there, on the opposite bank.

A little flash of light.

Gone.

But there was definitely movement.

But what was it?

I stare, and stare, and part of my childhood comes back, seeing that old show, *The Six Million Dollar Man,* and like when I was a little girl, I wish I had that bionic eye that could zoom in.

I now wish for a pair of binoculars, but they're with Scotty, and I'm not going to disturb him just as the slumped-over remains are brought in. Pamela is holding up a bright-yellow sheet, and when the out-of-view body has been placed into the Stokes litter, she lowers the sheet and gently tugs it into place.

The four of them lift up the Stokes litter and quietly—the only sound being that of the generator—the body is slowly brought into the white tent. No one commands anything, there are no orders, but every male and female agent removes his or her head covering as the body passes by.

The little procession gets into the tent. Near the opening to the tent I see Randy Anderson, and I walk to him, running through my mind how we're going to get the remains removed from here and brought to Bethesda Naval Hospital—no way we're going to end up at a civilian hospital—and then there's a shout and a scream.

Automatically I grab for my SIG Sauer, as Tanya Glenn bursts out of the tent, crying and screaming, and then laughing and yelling at the top of her lungs:

"It's not her! It's not her! It's not the First Lady!"

# CHAPTER 38

THERE'S CONFUSION AND a lot of movement and yelling going on over there by the tent and the people, and Marsha Gray is trying to figure out what's going on. When Grissom had moved away from the riverbank, Marsha had slipped to another viewing position—a wet patch of ground soaking her belly—and saw the Stokes litter being brought into the white tent. The folks over there lined up on each side as the body was carried in, with covers coming off their heads and salutes being made, as if the dead woman were part of the military.

Then about a minute ago the whole scene on the other side of the river just got tumbled up when a black woman ran out, and now she's laughing, crying, and lifting her arms up to the darkening sky.

Marsha whispers, "What the hell is this?"

She slowly moves the binoculars back and forth, trying to gauge what just happened. There's a sense of something being noticed, being released. The group over there had looked somber and tired, and Marsha sees that's all changed. They're relaxed, some laughing, others giving their buddies hugs and slaps on the back.

Okay then.

Two minutes ago, the First Lady's body was being recovered. It was dark and quiet over there, a funeral procession, and now it's different.

Smiles. Laughter. Happy people.

Grissom is now talking and gesturing with a Homeland Security guy, who's giving it right back to her.

Conclusion?

The First Lady is still missing.

That's not her body that was just brought in.

Damn

She slips out her iPhone, slides the earpiece in, starts sliding the phone's screen and working the numbers.

No answer.

Where the hell is Parker Hoyt?

The crowd over there is starting to disperse. Two Humvees have started up and have left the scene.

"Well, this sucks," she whispers.

What now?

What now is that something is going to change. Right now she's been a bird dog, following tips and orders from Parker Hoyt. Okay, that's the job. She's a big girl and can do what it takes.

She sees Grissom and the Homeland Security guy still talking, looking animated, whatever. If Marsha had been on the other side of the river, she could key in on what's being discussed, planned, where this so-called search would go next.

So Marsha knows what needs to be done, what she earlier had decided to do.

Time to slip away and get to Grissom's home, surveil the crap out of it, leave a little listening souvenir behind, and maybe—if things go well—do the same to Grissom's vehicle.

Still...

Let's make one more try to get ahold of her boss.

Once more, her fingers work away on the iPhone.

Still no answer.

Where the hell is Parker Hoyt?

# CHAPTER 39

ONCE I GET Tanya calmed the hell down, I say, "How do you know it's not her?"

Tanya wipes away tears from her eyes, but she's still smiling widely. "Her teeth! That poor woman...her face was beat up but you could see her teeth...and there's a lot of bridgework back there! It's not the First Lady! She's got perfect teeth."

I feel whipsawed, like a roller-coaster ride I'm on has suddenly jolted to a stop before the final steep descent.

"Are you sure?"

Pamela Smithson and Brian Zahn both come out of the tent, and based on the smiles on their faces, I know it's true. The poor drowned and battered woman in that tent is not Grace Fuller Tucker.

Pamela says, "Tanya's right...CANARY has perfect teeth. That woman in there...she's had a lot of work done in her mouth."

Well, what now? I turn away from everyone, grab my phone, make a call to Parker Hoyt. The phone rings and rings...and there's no answer.

What the hell? Based on his expression back at the White

House when I told him about the recovered body, I was sure he'd still be in his office, pacing back and forth, waiting for this call.

But no answer.

"Sally?"

I turn and it's Randy Anderson from Homeland Security, formerly of the Secret Service, and one tired hombre. His jumpsuit is splattered with mud and water, and he needs a shave.

He says, "Sally...that's it. We're packing up."

"But...you'll start again tomorrow, won't you?"

A firm shake of the head. "Not a chance," he says, and as he explains what's going on, I hate to admit it, but my old friend is right. Randy gestures to the Humvees, the tent, the men and women searching, and he says, "This...for a day I could pretend it was an unannounced drill, helping search for a mythical lost canoeist. The second day, Sally, I was putting my head on the chopping block...a one-day drill extending into two? Okay, I could make it work. A two-day drill was pushing it. I'm sorry. A three-day search is impossible."

Randy nods in the direction of the tent. "This is going to sound grim, but finding that poor dead woman is a blessing. It'll mean a round of nice publicity for the department, having an unannounced drill end with something special, and it'll get me a reprieve from management. Do you see what I mean?"

I hate his words, but I do know what he means. "Sure, Randy, I know."

Even in his exhausted state, he smiles. "Sorry, Sally. I really wanted to help you..."

"You did, no worries," I say.

"But CANARY..."

I nod, shove my cold hands into my coat pockets. "Randy, you have no idea what you're talking about."

"Sally..."

"Randy, this had nothing to do with the First Lady, and you know it. You...your Homeland Security unit was doing an unannounced drill along this river, and members of the First Lady's off-duty detail were assigned by me to provide assistance and to give them additional training in working with Homeland Security on short notice."

He rubs a hand across the bristles on his chin, slowly nods. "So that's how it's going to be."

"Randy, maybe it's my maternal nature, but I took care of you in Santiago, and I want to protect you again. So send everybody home...and thank you."

He says, "When this is over..."

I touch his unshaven cheek. "When this is over, come visit me in Leavenworth, all right?"

"I just might try to break you out."

"Don't be a foolish boy," I say. "Go."

And he walks to his people, and I take my phone, and call Parker Hoyt to let him know what's just happened.

But again there's no answer.

A few minutes later I huddle up with Scotty and the three members of CANARY's detail. The joy of learning the dead woman wasn't the First Lady is gone, and now they're slumped over, tired, worn down. Scotty doesn't say anything, and Tanya and Brian look to their detail leader, Pamela Smithson, who simply asks, "What now?"

I bite off what I want to say, which is *What now?* And is two days too late, and I say, "We take the night off. We're exhausted, and we'll start making mistakes."

*And you've already made enough mistakes,* I want to add, but I'm too tired to get into a shouting match at the moment.

"We'll start again tomorrow, eight a.m."

Tanya asks the reasonable question, "Where?" and I know we can't meet at my office, or the East Wing, or W-17...too many questions will roar our way tomorrow from other people who will be wondering why more than two days after the "Ambush in Atlanta," the First Lady has been neither seen nor heard. And I've got to lie once more to the other shift members of the First Lady's protection detail, which is going to take some imaginative and delicate untruths.

"The horse farm," I say. "We...the buildings there. They haven't been thoroughly searched. There's a chance CANARY might be there, lying low."

"Wouldn't the staff say something?" Brian asked.

"They're loyal to her, like you three," I say. "If she asked them to keep her presence there quiet, don't you think they'd do it?"

Nobody says a word, which tells me they're thinking it over.

"Go," I say, and they walk away, and Scotty comes to me and asks, "Boss, what about you?"

I feel like crawling in the tent with the dead woman and taking a nap on the wet grass. I say, "I've got to get home. And I need to update Parker."

"You need a ride?"

"I do."

Scotty says, "Got your back, boss."

"Thanks," I say, and I walk away and try Amelia.

No answer.

A little cold stab in my gut.

Okay.

I call Parker Hoyt, at his office and on his cell phone.

No answer at either number.

I hang up.

Vehicles are driving away, fewer people are around, and a Rockford County ambulance slowly approaches the white tent, here to take the dead woman away.

Where the hell is Parker Hoyt?

# CHAPTER 40

PARKER HOYT HANGS up his regular phone, interrupting a heartfelt call from the Senate majority leader, and grabs his special phone before it gets to a second ring.

Again, ambient noise telling him his caller is outside.

"Hoyt," he says.

"Not her," his caller says.

"What?"

"You heard me," the voice says. "The body's not hers. Back to work."

The phone is disconnected on the other end, and Parker replaces the handset and slumps into his chair. For the past hour he's been entertaining the notion of having a drowned FLOTUS. That would erase yesterday's news from Atlanta and give the President a sympathy vote that would outweigh any damage from the scandal. But now that hope is gone.

Damn.

Where the hell did that bitch get to? And how long can he keep a lid on this damn mess?

His regular office telephone rings, and his secretary, Mrs. Ann

Glynn, says, "Amanda Price is on the line, sir. From Pearson, Pearson, and Price."

"Thanks, Ann," he says. "Put her through."

A little *click* and the rough, smoky voice of Amanda comes through crisp and clear. "Parker, hon. How goes it?"

He says, "I've had better days. And if the Buddhists are to be believed, I've had better lives. What do you need, Amanda?"

"Your boy has been very naughty," she says in her familiar voice.

He shoots back, "And so has your girl."

She chuckles. "Let's get together and talk it over."

"Yes," he says with no reluctance. "Let's."

Thirty-three minutes and two Diamond taxicab rides later, Parker arrives in a tiny alleyway off M Street Northwest in Georgetown, west of the White House. This high-priced part of Georgetown is old brick-and-cobblestone streets, but the thick wooden door he approaches is bland. After punching a code into a keypad, the lock clicks open and he enters the Button Gwinnett Club.

The place is old, worn down, and the food and drink are comparable to the output of a kitchen at a soon-to-be-closed Holiday Inn in West Virginia. But with its initiation fee of $100,000, plus a penalty of ten times that much if the club's solitary rule is ever broken, the Button Gwinnett Club is exclusive. Parker goes through the motions as he goes down the wood-paneled hallway. With a small key, he unlocks a small numbered wooden locker in which he deposits his iPhone, watch, and wallet.

An old man, wearing a knee-length starched white apron, black trousers, and white shirt with black necktie, nods and says, "Sir...I believe your guest is in Room Three."

"Thank you," he says, and takes a turn past one door toward another marked with a brass numeral 3, and walks in.

Amanda Price is sitting at a small round table with a white tablecloth, sipping a martini, and he sits across from her. The room is private. All of the rooms in the Button Gwinnett are private, and with cell phones and all electronic devices forbidden in the dining areas, the club offers something that is rare in the District of Columbia: a place where the power brokers can sit and have open and fruitful discussions without any chance of being overheard or having their presence noted by the media, for that's the solitary rule of the Button Gwinnett Club.

Pure privacy.

The door silently opens, and a waiter delivers his drink—tumbler of Jameson Irish whiskey and an ice water chaser.

Amanda says, "Really, Parker, what was your boy thinking, going out like that? I thought he was smart enough to avoid what the little man tells him to do."

He takes a bracing sip. "Amanda, if you want to talk, talk. If you want to make jokes and snarky comments, I can go back to work and pick any random cable news channel to deliver what you're offering."

Amanda smiles with the face of one who knows a secret. "How's Grace handling this?"

"As well as can be expected."

"And where is she?"

"In seclusion. Look, Amanda—"

"How goes the search for her?"

The Jameson is threatening to crawl back up his gullet. "I don't know what you're talking about."

Amanda says, "Nice try, but don't treat me like an idiot. I know she bailed out on her detail yesterday, and I know there's a search going on for her. As low-key and quiet as possible, but there's a search going on."

Parker needs a moment to think so he takes another sip of Jameson. It tastes bland and warm.

He says, "What do you want?"

A sharp-toothed smile. "That's better. What I want is…to see what common ground we might share. In return for not passing on what I know to my friends in the media. It's always practical to make deposits in the favor bank, especially a deposit as big as this one."

The room is quiet, the doors and walls are thick, and the reclusive management of the Button Gwinnett Club promises hourly electronic sweeps of the premises to ensure there's no eavesdropping equipment, but Parker hesitates.

Amanda says, "Please. If this were to get out—highly unlikely—we'll both hang together, won't we?"

He says, "What kind of common ground?"

Her red-polished fingernail traces the top of her glass. "Let's just say that you and I could agree that having a First Lady that remains missing, or turns up deceased, would be a very good thing for certain parties."

"Go on."

"Hypothetically speaking…"

"Of course."

"There are certain insurance corporations and pharmaceutical firms that have been severely damaged and compromised by that woman's endless campaign to do good. They're not looking forward to another four years of being on the other end of her constant criticism."

Parker takes another sip of his Irish whiskey. "They may get their wish in four more weeks."

Amanda shakes her head. "No, then it would get worse. A retired First Lady, out from under the thumb of her cheating husband and the government agencies, would be free to really go to town on her activism. And that could last a lot longer than a four-year term. She'd be out of the White House, but some see her as the second coming of Jackie O. She'd still have a lot of influence."

The talk and the whiskey are making him slightly light-headed, a sensation Parker despises, for he feels its weakness. "Fascinating hypothetical you've got there, Amanda. And hypo-thetically again...what would encourage me to act...or not act...to assist you and your clients?"

Her smile is sweet and confident indeed. "If your boy can persuade the American people to send him back to the people's house for another four years, without that chattering albatross around his neck, you'll be thrilled at how cooperative my clients will be to work with Congress to get his agenda through. And if your boy loses, well, there's always room on our board of dir-ectors, and those of our clients, to reward those who have been helpful."

Another pause, then one last sip of his whiskey. "That's very intriguing. I'll see what I can do, to make sure that...chattering al-batross disappears from the President's neck. One way or another."

She nods in satisfaction.

He says, "And just to make sure we're clear, if you don't change those hypotheticals into stone-cold reality, I'll crush you—personally—and Pearson, Pearson, and Price."

Amanda says, "I wouldn't have it any other way."

He nods, takes a cleansing swallow of the ice-cold water. "I've never liked you, I've never trusted you, but I've always been able to do business with you, Amanda."

"Right back at you, Parker."

"But my boy . . . we've dealt with him. Let's talk about your girl."

"Fair enough," she says. "Go ahead."

"She needs to keep her pretty, pouty mouth shut."

"Agreed."

"Or she might have another accident."

Amanda arches her left eyebrow. "Another?"

He puts his glass down. "She almost got killed in a so-called car accident yesterday, coming home from the airport. I thought that might have been you, removing any future embarrassment to your firm."

Amanda stares right at him, face showing no emotion. "And here I was, thinking it was you, removing any future embarrassment to your President."

Parker waits, and he slowly gets up to leave. "Guess we'll leave that one be."

Amanda says, "I guess we will."

# CHAPTER 41

MARSHA GRAY IS back at the front door of the sad-looking apartment complex where Sally Grissom lives. She's taking a gamble, but she's all right with that. Her whole life has been one big gamble, and sometimes it's almost exhilarating.

She takes about thirty seconds to use a small transmitter on the keypad, overriding the signal and disabling the lock.

Done.

Into the entryway, up three flights of stairs. There's a smell here, of being poor and desperate, and it's a mixture of urine, cooking grease, and moist trash. It brings back a load of memories of growing up in rural Wyoming. The night wind that would cut through the cracks and fissures in their mobile home. The blocks of government-issued cheese. Having one pair of much-patched dungarees to wear, day in and day out.

Now she has on a Comcast jacket and baseball cap, pulled down low, with a heavy utility belt hanging around her slim waist. Like wearing a burka in some areas of the world makes you invisible, wearing a working-class outfit like this accomplishes the same thing.

On the third floor now, moving quietly and rapidly to the target door. A quick untraceable phone call to the apartment management—identifying herself as a credit union rep doing a background check on Sally Grissom—had gotten her the correct apartment.

There. Marsha scoots down, notices the Block doorknob and lock. Impressive stuff. That Secret Service agent knows her way around home protection.

"But this mama's no meth head," she whispers, and after a few moments of tugging and pulling with locksmith's tools, the door is unlocked. Marsha slowly opens it, and she notes a chain lock up near the top.

Well, there you go.

Looks heavy and functional, but Marsha knows better.

From her supposed Comcast workbag, she quickly removes a rubber band and a length of adhesive tape. She eyeballs the door opening and sees a kitchen, nothing else. Good. She slides her right hand into the gap and wraps the rubber band around the chain, draws it back out to the hallway, and securely fastens the other end to the tape.

Marsha carefully extends her hand back into the apartment, stretches the rubber band as far as she can, and tapes it to the door. With that done, she brings her hand in, slowly closes the door, and—

Hears a slight tinkle. With the door closing, the stretched rubber band—held in place by the tape—slides the chain free. Marsha opens the door slightly, tugs the taped chain loose, and takes two steps into the kitchen, closing the door behind her.

Not bad.

She's just successfully broken into the apartment of a senior Secret Service agent.

Time to get to work.

In the kitchen she smells cooked bacon, and there's a twinge of envy there, of being part of a family that would actually get together to share a breakfast, that actually cared about one another. Marsha shakes off that feeling and notes a living room to the left, and a hallway in front of her. The television is on, the volume turned up.

With the chain lock in place and a television playing, it's clear someone's home.

Marsha pauses, waiting to see if anyone is going to appear, demanding to know why and how she got in. If she's very lucky, she'll explain that the door was unlocked and as an eager Comcast employee, she had knocked and then let herself in upon hearing someone say enter.

Nobody appears.

She slowly makes her way to the living room.

Someone's on the ratty-looking brown couch.

Marsha takes a slow, quiet, deep breath to calm everything down.

A young girl is stretched out on the couch, watching the screen. About ten or eleven, slim, very pretty, with long blond hair, a light-blue comforter over her. Despite the fact she's watching television, she's also plugged in to a video game on her iPad, and the girl—no doubt the daughter of the senior Secret Service agent—has earbuds in.

Which explains why Marsha's entry has gone unnoticed.

Then a thought punches into her.

What's her overriding goal?

To keep an eye on the Secret Service agent and disrupt where necessary, causing an opportunity to take care of the First Lady.

The young girl on the couch is moving her gaze from the television to her iPad, back and forth. She takes the earbuds out and examines them, like they've suddenly stopped working.

Instead of leaving the surveillance devices behind as planned...well, here's an opportunity, stretched out on the couch, where Marsha could take direct and violent action and truly disrupt the Secret Service agent's investigation.

Why not?

The girl shifts her position on the couch, and her head moves in Marsha's direction.

# CHAPTER 42

SCOTTY IS DOING his best to get me home as quickly as possible, but his fast driving and judicious use of lights and siren aren't easing the tightness in my gut. Three calls to Amelia have gone unanswered, straight to voicemail, and I even swallow my pride and call her dad, and even Ben's damn cell phone isn't answered.

Scotty spares me a glance. "What's wrong?"

"Scotty..."

"Boss, I mean, what's wrong besides that mess we're still dealing with?" Then he says, "No answer from Amelia, right?"

"Right," I say, putting my useless iPhone on my lap.

"I'm sure she's all right," he says. "I mean, kids."

We force our way through a red light, traffic screeching to a halt, horns blaring. He whips the steering wheel in a blur, left-right, left-right, leading me to think of him driving an armored-up Humvee somewhere, dodging small arms fire or RPGs.

"Scotty."

"Yeah, boss?"

"Back at the waterfalls...did you see anything out of place? Anything odd?"

Scotty's a smart fellow and knows I wouldn't be asking this just to pass the time. "No, it looked...well, it was a circus, but a well-managed one. I didn't see anything that shouldn't have been there. What got your attention?"

"Just for a moment, across the river, I thought I saw a flicker of light. And movement. Like someone was checking us out."

"Anything more than that?"

"No, not a thing."

Scotty says, "Maybe it was a birdwatcher, wondering what was going on. And when he or she saw all the fuss, decided to get the hell out."

"Perhaps," I say, very much unconvinced, and I try my iPhone again.

No answer. My insides are a mix of anger at Amelia for doing something to get me so upset and scared, along with a real fear that something bad has happened to her. And my veteran cop mind has too many dark examples of what "bad" could turn out to be.

Scotty says, "Sorry she's not answering."

I just look out the windshield, as the traffic slowly pulls to the side.

He says, "Maybe she's taking a nap. Or maybe a shower. Or maybe she turned her phone off. Kids, am I right?"

I wait as long as I can, one hand nervously fingering the red wool scarf my daughter made me.

"Scotty?"

"Yes, boss?"

I say, "The minute you marry, have a child, watch over him or her, see him or her grow up, suffer inside every time you see them cry or fall down or be scared...then you can lecture me on what you think might be going on with Amelia."

His jaw tightens, and I know I've gone too far, but I'm afraid if I say any more, the tears of wondering what the hell is going on with Amelia will start flowing, and I don't want to do that in front of my subordinate.

"Coming up now," he says with ice in his voice, as we race through the run-down area my daughter and I call home. "About another block."

"Thanks, Scotty," I say, but he doesn't answer me.

# CHAPTER 43

SEEING THE YOUNG girl's head move, Marsha quietly takes two steps back, the rear of the couch now blocking the girl's view. Fine. Marsha hears a siren from outside and thinks, *No, the plan, the plan is a good one, let's stick with the plan.*

She goes back into the kitchen, sees a wall-mounted phone, and in a few seconds, a surveillance device is placed within the handset.

Next?

The bedroom, for whatever pillow talk this old lady might share.

Marsha goes down the hallway, opens one door, sees a neat and well-made bed with stuffed animals on the colorful bed-spread, a bookshelf made of concrete cinder blocks and rough wood planks, packed with kids' books, and there's a sharp tug, for without the stuffed animals—her parents never had any money for toys—this could have been her bedroom, back there in desolate Wyoming.

She closes the door.

Stop thinking so much, she nags herself, and now, here's the old woman's bedroom.

Plain and simple.

Just like her.

That makes her smile. There's a phone by the nightstand, and that'll be a good place and she works quickly, another device deposited, and then she thinks, well, maybe behind the bureau.

Marsha walks to the bureau and freezes.

A muffled adult voice, coming from the kitchen: "Honey, I'm here!"

Damn it!

Marsha whirls around—there's no television here, no home computer, hard to explain why she's here and what she's doing, and that damn Secret Service agent, already suspicious and wired up by what she's been doing—

Marsha sincerely doubts she's going to give Marsha a friendly hello and usher her out of the apartment.

Then—

A figure comes into the bedroom, and Marsha throws herself at the shape, thinking of her old training—*overwhelming and sudden force will win, nine times out of ten*—and there's a struggle and Marsha's right hand touches a heavy scarf and she works hard, getting a superior position, her strong arms and hands around the slim neck, and a hard twist and *crunch* and it's over.

Marsha drops the body to the floor.

Time to leave.

She bursts out of the dark bedroom, races back down the hallway, heading to the lights of the kitchen, and the young girl is in front of her, screaming and screaming, and for the briefest second, Marsha wonders if she should take her down as well...

A split-second decision.

No, to eliminate her would raise too much of a ruckus.

Marsha slams the young girl aside as she bursts through the apartment door.

Marsha reverses course—never go out the way you came in—by taking a rear set of stairs and going out a fire door. In a minute she's out on the street, calmly walking along and stripping off her Comcast clothing, dumping it in a storm drain, hearing the sirens get louder as she gets closer to her parked Odyssey minivan.

Earlier, back at the waterfalls, Marsha had been oh so eager to speak to Parker Hoyt.

Now, not so much.

# CHAPTER 44

UP AHEAD AT my apartment building there are blue and red flashing lights, and Scotty swears and passes through a police line, driving through the yellow-and-black police tape and getting us as close as he can. He nearly sideswipes a police cruiser and I'm out, no longer an ex-cop, no longer a Secret Service agent, no longer anything except one very frightened and alone mother.

"Amelia!" I yell, and I punch and push my way past a couple of cops holding back the local neighbors, and I fish out my Secret Service credentials and yell, "Who's in charge! Where's my daughter! Who's in charge!"

Besides the fear there's the clammy coldness of guilt covering me, guilt about being a single mom, leaving her alone in this rough neighborhood, being so stubborn I wouldn't give Ben a second chance so that we'd be safe at our previous home, and if it wasn't for the fact I'm running so hard and fast, I'm sure I'd be throwing up in this packed parking lot.

"Mom!"

I can't help myself—that single word makes me burst into tears, and there's an opening along the police line, and there's my sweet and terrified Amelia, sitting in the open rear of an ambulance, a gray blanket over her shoulders, two EMTs with blue latex gloves gently poking and probing.

"Mom!" she yells again, and she joins me in bawling.

I hug her and kiss her, and the EMTs stand aside. Amelia's blubbering about a bad man getting into the apartment and a fight, and I whirl at the touch of someone behind me.

"Ma'am?" comes the soft male voice. Before me is an African-American male, early thirties, gray suit and raincoat, brown eyes filled with concern. He has a closely trimmed beard and around his thick neck, dangling from a chain, is a detective's shield.

"Detective Gus Bannon," he says, "Fairfax County Police Department." He looks to his notebook and says, "This young girl...Amelia Miller. She's your daughter?"

"Yes...can you tell me what happened? Is she okay?"

He gestures for the two of us to move away from the ambulance, and Amelia is still sobbing, so I kiss her forehead and something else stabs at me: the presence of a stuffed panda bear she had gotten some years back at the National Zoo.

I haven't seen it in her hands for at least two years.

I follow Detective Bannon around to the side of the ambulance, and he says, "About thirty minutes ago, someone broke into your apartment. Your daughter is fine. She's scared and she might have a bruise on her wrist and—"

"How did she get bruised?"

"From the intruder," he softly explains, and I want him to hurry up and tell me what happened, who did it, how it can be made better, and with a shock I realize that for the first time ever,

I'm the one answering questions, I'm the one being impatient with the police, I'm—

I'm the victim.

He goes on. "The intruder ran out through the kitchen, pushed Amelia away."

"Male?"

He nods. "We think so. It happened very fast, your daughter says. A short man, dark-skinned, wearing some sort of uniform."

"Uniform? Like a firefighter? Or cop?"

The detective shakes his head. "More like a utility worker. Or a technician. Maybe a cable TV worker. That's all we've got for now."

I just nod, realize my hands are clenched, and right now, both hands want to be around the intruder's throat. I'm so angry and focused and relieved that Amelia is safe that I don't hear what the detective says next.

"Excuse me?" I ask. "I'm so sorry, I was drifting there for a moment."

He looks embarrassed, staring down at his notebook. "That's all right, it happens. I was asking, Mrs. Miller, if—"

"Grissom," I automatically say. "I've always kept my name."

"But you're married to Ben Miller. Who works for the Department of the Interior."

I feel like a huge storm is coming right at me, and I can't do a thing but close my eyes and pretend it's not out there, heading my way.

"I am, but we're currently going through a divorce," I say. "Detective, please. What's going on?"

"It seems like your husband, Ben Miller, he came into your apartment and surprised the intruder. There was an altercation in your bedroom."

Everything seems so loud now, the voices, the sound of sirens, the engines idling from the parked emergency response vehicles.

He looks down at his notebook. "I'm sorry to tell you this, ma'am, but your husband, Ben Miller, he's dead."

# CHAPTER 45

THE ROUTINE IS always the routine, and I go through it like one of those smiling robots at Disney World, just nodding and looking around and following the lead of Detective Bannon. We go to the open entryway into the apartment building, ducking under the police tape, and he thoughtfully holds up the tape for me. We go upstairs and the detective talks aimlessly to me—the weather, the ongoing World Series—all in an effort to distract me from what I'm about to see.

It doesn't work.

At the open door to our apartment, a uniformed police officer with a clipboard takes our names and checks the time of our entry, a good way of controlling access to a—

Crime scene.

My apartment is no longer the refuge for an angry mom and scared daughter, trying to make sense of a crumbling marriage and family, but is now the scene of violence and death.

Toward a man I once vowed to spend the rest of my life with.

"Here," Detective Bannon says. "We need to put these on. And I know you live here, but—"

"I know," I say. "Don't touch anything."

We both slide on light-blue paper booties over our footwear, and then I take that first step into a place that is no longer a home.

The first thing I notice is the smell of cooked bacon, from that morning, and I turn away from the detective and wipe at my teary eyes. This morning I had been in this very kitchen, with my daughter and my husband, and did I take an opportunity to be nice? To thank Ben for making breakfast? To thank him for trying to make amends?

No.

The remembered voice of my daughter slices through me like a razor: *If you weren't so mean, we'd still be a family! Why do you have to be so mean?*

"Ma'am?" Detective Bannon asks quietly.

"Ah . . . just give me a sec, okay?"

"Sure."

I take a deep breath, feel like bawling out loud, but no, I've got to see this through. I wipe at my eyes again and turn and say, "It's all right. Let's do it."

He briefly touches my upper arm. "We don't have to do this. We don't."

"It's all right. Where . . . where's Ben?"

"In your bedroom."

We walk past two forensics techs taking photos, dusting for prints, and I go with Detective Bannon, and the oddest thing happens—my muscle memory comes back. I remember the times I've gone into crime scenes over the years, the chatter of the police radios, the murmur among the forensics techs, the smell of the chemicals . . . it's all familiar to me.

It's almost comforting.

Detective Bannon stands at the open door and I stand next to him.

*Oh, Ben,* I think. *Oh, Ben.*

My husband, the man I had loved, the man who wooed me after we had met when I was in the Virginia State Police, investigating a complaint at the Green Springs National Park, my Ben is on his back, legs splayed wide, one arm across his chest, the other one stretched above his head. Another forensics tech—this one a chubby woman—is taking photographs, and Bannon says, "Sandy, give us a moment, will you?"

"Sure," she says, stepping past us and out to the hallway. I step closer, look down at my dead husband. His face has grayed out and his head is turned at an odd angle, and he's wearing a waist-length leather coat and he has a blue knitted scarf tucked around his neck. The detective looks at my scarf and says, "They look similar."

I say, "My . . . our daughter made them. Red for me, blue for him. She hoped that, well, I think she hoped that the two of us sharing the same kind of scarf would soothe things between us."

Bannon just nods.

Poor Amelia.

I ask, "Cause of death?"

"Not official, but it looks like his neck was snapped."

"Jesus Christ," I say. "Any idea how it happened?"

Bannon says, "Your daughter . . . she heard the door being unlocked and then your husband yelling out a greeting, like—"

"'Honey, I'm here,'" I say dully. "That's a code phrase we both used, if we're coming home . . . I mean, well, coming in. That way, Amelia won't be startled or scared."

"Okay," he says. "Your daughter says she had called Mister Miller earlier, because the neighbor who usually watched her after school couldn't make it, and you were running late."

My throat is so thick it feels like it's choking me. Detective Bannon says, "Your daughter says Mister Miller came in, there was a brief greeting, and then he saw your bedroom door was open, and there was a shadow back there. He...he told your daughter to be still, to call nine-one-one if something happened, and he went to investigate. There was a struggle, then the intruder ran past, knocking your daughter over, and she got up, called nine-one-one."

I say, "Did she see Ben dead?"

"Wi ll, I, well    "

"Detective, did my daughter see her dead Miller?"

He sighs. "I'm afraid so. After she made the call...she ran back. She tells me that she thought he was unconscious, that he had been knocked out while trying to protect her. Your daughter...a brave girl."

"She has a brave father," I say, and then the memories and the good times Ben and I shared, from our first dates to our marriage to our Alaskan honeymoon and that magic night when a small and squealing baby girl was placed in my arms, just overwhelm me, and I kneel down next to him and I kiss his cold forehead.

Back in the kitchen I'm answering more questions from Detective Bannon, and then I say, "Hold on."

"Yes?"

"You said...you said that Amelia heard Ben come through the door, right?"

He looks to his notes. "That's correct."

"She didn't say anything about her undoing the chain?"

"No, she didn't."

"Are you sure?"

"Ma'am, what are you getting at?"

I walk to the door, see the chain dangling free. "When I last talked to her, when I said I was...running late." Another sob avoided and I go on. "I told her to make sure the door was locked and the chain was secured."

Detective Bannon says, "Maybe she forgot."

I shake my head. "No. I told her to do it...I was on the phone when Amelia said she was at the door, putting the chain in."

He says something, and my fingers gently touch the dangling chain. Halfway up the chain is the sticky residue of an adhesive.

Like an adhesive tape.

I say, "He broke in. He picked the lock, and when the door opened, he saw the chain was fastened. Then he used...oh, I don't know, a string, a cord, a length of rubber band, and some tape...and he got the chain off."

Detective Bannon touches the chain as well. "Ma'am, you're on the third floor. To get entry, the intruder had to have had a key, or picked the lock. And then he had to work to get this chain off."

My mind is racing. I don't say a word back to the detective. He says, "Which tells me this wasn't a random burglary. Or some crack head or meth head breaking in to steal some jewelry or electronics. You...this apartment was targeted."

"Yes," I say.

He steps closer, lowers his voice. "Your daughter says you're a secret agent. I thought she was just being a kid, you know? But ma'am, what is your job?"

"I work for the Secret Service."

Bannon absorbs that for a moment. "What do you do for the Secret Service?"

I answer automatically, like I always do. "I'm the special agent in charge, Presidential Protective Division at the White House."

"The White House . . ." he starts, and then stops. He takes another step closer. "Special Agent Grissom, I need to ask you this."

"Yes?"

"All of the evidence here is leading me to think that the break-in was deliberate, was planned. Is there anything going on with your job, Agent Grissom, that would cause someone to...take action against you?"

Where do I begin?

"No," I lie. "Not a thing."

# CHAPTER 46

TAMMY DOYLE IS curled up in her bed, the television set on low, lights off in her bedroom. A long, long day and she's happy to be home, but she's also missing being at work. It's strange, but at work she could focus on the phone calls, checking the invoices, calling her clients across the globe, and just getting things checked off her never-ending task list. Except for the Secret Service agent's visit and a couple of odd looks and comments, she was able to temporarily put the whole Atlanta disaster behind her.

But now, at home, the loneliness is gnawing at her. For the past eight months she's been able to thrive, knowing that she would meet up with Harry at some point, and that anticipation had always kept her in a good mood.

But now?

What anticipation?

Another day of ducking out of her condo, ducking into her office . . . waiting for Harry to call her?

And suppose . . .

She's a big girl. She knows the pressure Harry must be under.

If it would mean him winning re-election, mean him getting ahead...he would dump her. Publicly, if it would serve him.

Tammy feels a good cry coming on. All those whispered promises, all the times together...

She picks up the remote, starts changing the channels, looking for something, anything that isn't related to the upcoming election and the "Ambush in Atlanta," and then she's on the History Channel, some program about tanks and—

That tickles a memory.

Moving tanks moving around in the North African desert. World War II, Germans versus the British and fighting in sandstorms.

Tammy gets off the bed, goes to her small office. Starts going through the piles of receipts and business cards that she always collects during the week.

There.

The business card from Jamal, the Ethiopian cabdriver who took her home yesterday.

She scrambles and finds her iPhone, ignores all the missed calls screaming at her with their bright letters and numbers, and punches in the number.

It rings.

It rings.

It rings and—a burst of static.

"Hello?"

In her dark living room, she sits down in a chair. "Jamal? Is this you?"

"Yes," comes the suspicious voice. "Who is this, please?"

"This is Tammy Doyle," she replies. "I'm the woman who was in the car accident yesterday, with your cousin...I'm sorry, I didn't get his name."

"Ah, yes, Caleb. A good man."

"I need to speak to him. Do you know where he is?"

He laughs. "Oh, yes, I do. He's here with me . . . we're watching the football match, Ethiopia against Ghana. Hold on."

Some rustling and tumbling, and Caleb comes on and says, "Missy? Are you all right? Did you forget some luggage, then?"

"No, I'm doing well, thank you. And I have all of my luggage. It's just . . . can I ask you a question?"

"Yes, missy, but please, make it quick. We've waited two months to watch this."

She shifts in the darkness. Outside there are lights from the tribe of reporters, still eager for her to come out and confess all. Tammy says, "The accident . . . you said it made you remember when you served in the army in Ethiopia. Driving through the desert, in sandstorms, dodging armored vehicles."

"Yes, yes, very true."

Tammy grips her iPhone hard. "What did you mean by that? I mean, the pickup truck that struck us . . . was it . . . armored in some way?"

Caleb says, "It was, it was. That's what I told the police agents. The pickup truck . . . it was black, very heavy-looking, and there was something on the front . . . a big piece of black metal, welded on." Caleb gives an amused giggle, like this sort of thing was always spotted on the Virginia highways. "It looked like somebody had fixed the pickup truck so it would cause bad damage, very bad damage, to my taxicab. Lucky for the both of us, it hit the trunk and not the center. Eh?"

Some shouting in the background, and Caleb says something in Amharic, and to Tammy says, "Please, I must go. The match, it's very important."

"Thank you, Caleb," says Tammy, and he hangs up before she even has a chance to ask him how he's feeling.

In the darkness now, for at least ten minutes, and another memory has come forth, one that's screaming for attention.

When she had come home yesterday, her boss, Amanda Price, had been here waiting for her.

Supposedly just to talk.

But maybe she was here for another reason. To search her place, to find something her firm could use against Harry, something embarrassing or humiliating like photos on her home laptop, showing them in a compromising position. Or an email. Or something worse.

And why would she be confident in coming to her condo unit without thinking she'd be caught?

Because . . .

Because Amanda knew she was going to be in a traffic accident.

She knew.

Remember what her boss had said when she had told Amanda of the car accident?

*"Interstate Sixty-six . . . what a horror show that can be."*

How did she know that?

How did Amanda know the accident took place on I-66?

Tammy sure as hell hadn't told her.

She moves around her condo, making sure the windows and the door are locked. In her kitchen, feeling panicked, she takes a carving knife and goes back to bed.

Never has she felt so alone.

# CHAPTER 47

THE PRESIDENT OF the United States is hanging up his Oval Office phone—after a disappointing conversation with his campaign's lead pollster—when there's a knock on the near curved door and Parker Hoyt comes in, looking troubled.

"Yes?" he asks.

Parker comes over, sits down in front of him. "No news."

"No good news, you mean," he says sharply. "So far the investigation has turned up her untriggered panic button, a partial note we know Grace wrote that isn't helpful at all, and the remains of a poor unidentified woman. Am I missing anything?"

"No, sir."

"Now what?"

"Well, it—"

Harrison interrupts him. "I just got off the phone with Taylor Smith. She says the overnights have shown a two-point drop nationally in the polling. Two points! Can you imagine what it's going to be by this weekend?"

"Sir, trust me—"

The President leans over his desk. "That's what you told me on Air Force One. 'Trust me, trust me.' Well, I've trusted you so far and what has that gotten me? A drop in the polls, and the whispers out there that are going to start turning into shouts about the First Lady. Where's the First Lady? Where's the First Lady? Well?"

Parker has his hands folded in his lap. "We've done an extensive search up and down the river by the horse farm, using her Secret Service detail and elements of Homeland Security under the guise of a training mission."

"And?"

"It's time to change the approach."

"In what?"

Parker says, "Sir, the First Lady...has gone rogue. She must be up to something...what, I don't know. But we don't have to play her game. We need to be a step ahead of her."

"By doing what?"

"Sometime tomorrow, we leak the story to the press that she's gone missing, following a ride at the horse farm she frequents. We believe she's lost, injured, or perhaps even...drowned. We get the story out that way, we get the general public looking for her. A woman so prominent can't hide forever."

"But suppose... I mean, suppose she's found?"

Parker smiles. "Then it works in our favor. She'll have to explain why she went missing, why she frightened you and the other members of the administration, and that story will be on the front page and on the cable networks. Not the story about you and Tammy Doyle. And speaking of Miss Doyle, you haven't been in contact with her, have you? Remember what I said coming back from Atlanta. No phone calls, no contacts, nothing."

Harrison recalls the not-so-happy conversation he had yesterday with Tammy and decides to leave it be. He's not in the mood for a lecture.

"I listened very carefully to you, Parker." The President leans back in his chair and stares at his chief of staff, and there's something else going on there, something he can't quite figure out.

"Parker?"

"Sir?"

"You've got something else going on," he says. "Spill."

Parker nods. "Agent Sally Grissom."

"She all right? She still keeping her mouth shut?"

"Ah . . ."

"What the hell is it, Parker?"

"Sir, Agent Grissom's husband was murdered at her apartment about two hours ago."

It was like one of the bullet-proof French doors behind him had opened up a crack, for it felt like a cool breeze was tickling the back of Harrison's neck.

"Go on."

"It seems that there was a break-in, or a burglary attempt, and Ben Miller, her husband, caught whoever was there. A fight ensued . . . and he was killed."

He shakes his head. "Was anything valuable stolen? Was it a burglary?"

"We don't know that yet."

Harrison stares and stares at the man most responsible—besides himself—for getting him into the White House.

"So you're telling me that less than two days after we tasked Agent Grissom to find my wife, her husband is murdered."

"Yes, sir."

"Hell of a coincidence."

"Yes, sir."

"Parker . . . you've got to tell me, right now, if you or I or anybody in this administration, however distant, was responsible for his death."

Parker says, "Sir, I'm…Harry, that's a damn insulting question, and you know it."

"Parker, answer the damn question!"

Parker stares right back at him. "Mister President…we bear no responsibility for that man's death. And if you think otherwise, you'll have my resignation on your desk within the hour."

Harrison thinks maybe he's pushing him too far, and says, "Parker, please, you're overreacting. I just need to know and—"

Parker interrupts him again, a record. "Harry, when I first met you at the State House in Columbus, you were like a dedicated and eager puppy stumbling over your own paws. You had lots of raw talent, and you needed somebody to mold and direct that talent. That's what I did, and defending you and your administration has been the key part of my life. No time for a wife, no time for a family. Don't you dare insult me like that again."

Harrison slowly shakes his head. "No insult was meant, Parker. I…it's a tough time for all of us."

"It certainly is," Parker says, standing up. "Is that all, sir?"

"For now," Harrison says. "Do keep me informed…and make sure Agent Grissom gets a card or flowers or something similar from me."

"Yes, sir," Parker says, heading to the door, and when he reaches the handle, Harrison calls out, "Parker?"

He turns. "Sir?"

"Usually I'm relaxed about such things, but don't ever call me Harry again in this office. Do I make myself clear?"

Parker just nods, exits the Oval Office, and like before, the President of the United States is alone.

Still wondering whom he can trust.

# CHAPTER 48

MARSHA GRAY IS in her out-of-the-way apartment outside of Silver Spring, Maryland, watching a Discovery Channel special about snipers and having fun picking out the errors, when her iPhone rings. She checks the incoming call and sees it's Parker Hoyt, for the third time in the last ten minutes. The previous two times she's hung up on him after the call deteriorated into insults and name-calling, and she's deciding to give him a third try.

"Yes?"

She hears his heavy breathing. "Don't you ever hang up on me, ever again."

"What, you expect me to keep a line open with you, twenty-four/seven?" Marsha asks. "I always hang up on you when our conversation is complete."

"You know what the hell I mean."

"Perhaps, but I'll say it for the third time, Mister Hoyt. Just because you're paying me doesn't mean you have a blank check to scream at me or insult me. You want to have a serious, employer-to-employee conversation, I'm open to that. Otherwise, the minute the insults fly, I'm off to do something more productive. Like watching television or trimming my toenails."

More heavy breathing. "Did you have to kill him?"

Marsha says, "Of course I did. I was there in the apartment, pretending to be a Comcast employee, with very illegal and technical surveillance equipment on my body. What, you think I should have given up? Let myself get arrested? That would have been a fun police interrogation later, don't you think?"

"Answer the damn question! Did you have to kill him?"

"Sorry to shatter any illusions you might have, Mister Hoyt, but when I'm in a hand-to-hand combat situation, my goal isn't to leave them with a lump on the skull. He's dead, I'm alive, and that's the way I wanted it."

"And what the hell were you doing there in the first place?"

On the television, the program depicts a sniper who is supposedly in camouflage, and Marsha thinks a Cub Scout wearing corrective lenses could spot him from fifty meters away. "I was trying to gather something missing from this little op, which is actionable intelligence. You've given me scraps and pieces, always late, and I've done the best I could with those scraps. Well, I was tired of doing the best I could. I wanted to try excellence for a change, by placing surveillance equipment in her apartment, and her vehicle, if I got lucky."

"You should have told me beforehand."

"I tried, but for some reason, Mister Hoyt, you weren't answering your phone. And you told me earlier that if need be, I should act on my own. So I did. So unless you have anything else to tell me, give it a rest."

More breathing. He says, "By this time tomorrow, we're going to leak out that she's missing. Get the news media and the public involved."

"Ah," she says. "Try to flush her out of whatever hole she might be hiding in."

"That's right."

"And my job?"

"Same as before…but to be clear…we're looking for a final solution."

"How German-like of you. Okay."

"Are we done?"

"For now."

"What do you mean by that?" he asks.

She wonders for a moment, and then decides to make it all clear. "I just want you to make sure that you remember I'm a professional. And you don't last in this business by being an amateur. And a professional has something in hand to guarantee one's safety. So if there's a funeral next week for the First Lady, there better not be an FBI contingent breaking into my apartment with an arrest warrant the day after. Clear?"

A long, long delay, and she's sure he's trying to keep control of his temper. "You're threatening me."

"No, I'm setting expectations. Pay me, keep your end quiet, and my end will be quiet as well."

Then he loses it, calls her a number of names, and then hangs up.

Marsha shrugs, sees that once more, she's successfully recorded this call from the chief of staff, and happily goes back to watching the documentary on snipers, which makes her smile in amusement for the next forty minutes.

# CHAPTER 49

ON THIS DAY, the worst of days, I'm like an actress in some play, not knowing my lines or responsibilities, just being gently pushed along by those in the know. The day has been a jumble of images and sights, and now, I'm in the final act of this performance, a cloudy and cold day in a Jewish cemetery near Capitol Heights, Maryland, holding Amelia's frigid hand in my own as the rabbi speaks over Ben's open grave.

It's been just a day since I last saw my husband, dead in my bedroom, but because of my in-laws' religion, he's being buried this afternoon. Esther and Ron Miller are standing on the other side of the dirt pile, holding each other. Both are wearing black, and Ron is wearing a yarmulke. My father-in-law just stares and stares at the plain pinewood casket, but every now and then my mother-in-law looks at me with her eyes full of restrained fury and pure hate.

I make no excuse for that look, for I can see that from her point of view, it's fully deserved. Ben wasn't particularly observant and he never pressured me to convert, but his mom would drop hints the size of boulders whenever we came to visit, especially after Amelia was born. Now she's staring at me, a Gentile with a Gentile daughter, and with her familial line cut off with the remains in that casket.

Other members of Ben's family are lined up in solidarity, and there are coworkers of his from the Department of the Interior. I spend a few dreary seconds trying to decide whichever interns over there might have slept with my husband. My side—God, the horror of having sides at a graveyard ceremony—consists of me; Amelia; my deputy, Scotty; and one of my two sisters, Gwen, who works for the NSA and is standing at my left. She's five years younger than me and about five times as smart. My other sister, Kate, is flying home from a GAO conference in Seattle, and my parents—last I knew—were trying to get flights north from Florida in the middle of a tropical storm.

I squeeze Amelia's hand, but she doesn't squeeze back. I haven't slept. I've been consumed with making the necessary phone calls; watching the coroner's office remove that heavy black plastic bag containing a man I had loved, lived, and laughed with; and above all, being with my daughter once I told her that her daddy was dead and that she would never, ever see him again.

The long wails, sobs, and cries from Amelia yesterday cut at me and cut at me, like somebody coming after me with a large knife for hours, until finally she fell into a slumber. By then we were in a motel room, and I was on the bed with her, not sleeping, watching the sun eventually rise and trying so desperately not to think of anything.

For the past hours, from the motel room to the synagogue and to here, Amelia's been quiet, as if being a good little girl will somehow bring her daddy back. Her face quivers and her eyes are wide and red-rimmed, and I glance at her every now and then, seeing she's no longer my daughter from the day before. Oh, she is and will forever be my Amelia, but something deep inside of her has broken, and when it does heal, it will heal crookedly, with bumps and ridges and memories, and she will be a different daughter.

The rabbi continues his prayers. He's one of the most gracious and generous men I've ever met, and I'm ashamed to say that I've forgotten his name. But he knows the family status and tensions, and does his best with his soothing and reassuring voice, to bring some sort of closure and completeness to this horrid day.

*Oh, Ben, I think, I never . . .*

I never what?

I . . . never.

Just that.

The rabbi—dressed in a baggy gray suit and holding a small leather-bound book, with a yarmulke on his head—makes some sort of gesture and my husband's casket is lowered into the ground by two tired-looking cemetery workers dressed in jeans and gray sweatshirts, and Esther, Ben's mother, cries out and her husband squeezes her shoulder.

When the casket is finally lowered into the ground, the rabbi steps forward and speaks to us all. Near him are two battered cardboard boxes filled with old books, and he explains that these old Jewish books are going to be buried with Ben as a sign of respect and honor. There is also a mound of dirt with a shovel, and the rabbi explains that those who wish to can come up and deposit a book into the open grave and then toss dirt in with the shovel.

"But to mark our mourning," he says quietly, "we are to use the reverse side of the shovel to show that what once was is now turned upside down."

There are sobs and some whispered conversations, and one by one, Ben's friends and relatives come up, and when there's a pause, I lead Amelia to the pile of old volumes. She picks one up and carefully places it into the open grave, and then I take the shovel—and following the lead of others—toss in three shovelfuls of dirt, the blade upside down.

I then bring Amelia's hands up, and with a sharp whisper she says, "I can do it by myself," which breaks my heart again, and clumsily, but with strength I didn't know she had, she matches my three shovelfuls of dirt with her own.

Then we step aside.

A dual line forms and mourners pass through, and most ignore me, although Amelia does come in for some special attention. I'm dreading going back to the synagogue, for a large meal has been prepared, and I must continue to play my part as the evil grieving widow. My sister Gwen, as loyal as ever, sticks with me as the mourners dribble away, and then Scotty comes up to me with a grim look on his face.

"Boss... I hate to do this to you, but we need to head back to the White House."

"But... Amelia, I sure as hell can't."

Gwen steps forward, arm around me, hugging me. My younger sister, whose hair is graying out and who has fine lines around her bright blue eyes, all from her job at the Puzzle Palace over at Fort Meade, deciphering and interpreting horrible secrets that should forever remain secret.

"I'll take care of Amelia," she says.

"Gwen... I don't know when I'll be back."

"Don't fret," she says. "I got some time coming to me. It'll be just me and your little firecracker, until parental units and sister Kate show up. I'll host 'em until things get straightened out."

My throat thickens and the tears come, and in the middle of this cemetery with the gravestones with Hebrew lettering and the Star of David, I give her a long, long hug. She whispers to me, "Always got your back, big sis, remember that. Always."

I pull away and we exchange cheek kisses, and Gwen says to my daughter, "Hey, Amelia, how about spending some time with your nutty Aunt Gwen?"

Amelia looks up to her. "You live where there's an indoor pool, right?"

Gwen says, "That's right, sport."

"I'd like to go swimming. But I don't have a suit."

Gwen takes her hand. "We'll get you a suit, I promise."

The two of them start walking away, and I realize I haven't even said good-bye to Amelia, when Scotty gets my attention.

"What the hell's going on?" I ask. "Have they found . . ."

He shakes his head. "Nope. Take a look."

He flips his large iPhone on its side so I can read the screaming headline from the *Washington Post*:

## FIRST LADY REPORTED MISSING; MAY HAVE DROWNED AT HORSE FARM

I swear and Scotty grabs my arm, and we start to run out of the cemetery as dirt continues to be shoveled over my husband's grave.

# CHAPTER 50

PARKER HOYT HEARS a burst of loud voices outside of his office, with Mrs. Glynn coming in loud and clear with, "You can't go in there!" and sure enough, Special Agent Sally Grissom slams the door open, pushes her way through, and slams the door behind her.

"Agent Grissom," he says, "what a not-so-pleasant surprise. Sorry to hear about the death of your husband... shouldn't you be with your daughter?"

She strolls forward, face twisted with fury, and Parker has a momentary lapse into fear—after all, this crazed woman is armed—but she stops at his clean desk and slaps down a sheet of paper.

"I just got this off the wire downstairs," she says. "News flash from a 'highly placed administration source,' about the First Lady being missing and presumed drowned. That source was you, you son of a bitch."

Parker doesn't even acknowledge the paper before him. "Why are you here, Agent Grissom? You should be taking the rest of the week off."

"Why? Why the news leak?"

"Sit down."

"I like standing."

"My office, my rules," he says. "Park it."

She slowly takes an empty chair, and Parker feels once more that little thrill again, of bending someone else's will to his own. He says, "Is there anything inaccurate in that news flash?"

"Anything? The whole damn thing is inaccurate. You don't know if she's drowned or not."

"And neither do you," he says. "Your agency, which managed to lose the First Lady two days ago, has come up with exactly nothing. Zero. Zip. Even when you somehow bribed Homeland Security to come in and help, all you did was find some poor drowned homeless woman a couple of miles downstream."

Her teeth are clenched as she says, "That's not true. We found the note, we found the panic button, and—"

"The note and panic button? A groom from the horse farm could have found that. Or some birdwatcher. Or fisherman. No, the great and mighty Secret Service, upon losing their protectee, haven't been able to do squat these past two days. Zero. So now it's time to change the playing field and players."

Grissom picks up the sheet of paper with the printed news bulletin on it and crumples it in her hand. "By leaking this crap?"

"Exactly," he says. "Before, it was you and your agents, and Homeland Security, trying to keep it secret, trying to keep it low-key. That approach didn't work."

"That was your approach, not mine," she protests.

"And it didn't work," he says. "FDR once had a process of trying something, and if it didn't work out, he dumped it and tried something new. That's what I did. The quiet approach didn't work. Now, in a few hours, the FBI will be all over this, along with thousands upon thousands of concerned citizens who will join the hunt—without even being asked—for their beloved First Lady."

Grissom says, "You still think she's in hiding, trying to humiliate the President. And if you make it a big production and find her hiding someplace, then all of the bad news from Atlanta will go away."

Parker thinks Grissom is way too smart to stay within the Secret Service, but she's not dark enough where it counts—in her soul—to truly figure out what's going on. "If that happens, the President and I will be thrilled. She will be found, safe. And if she isn't in hiding...if something else is going on, well, again, besides the full force and fury of federal investigative agencies, the American public will be helping us as well."

Grissom says, "And what about the Secret Service?"

Parker smiles. "Come now, Agent Grissom, you've had your forty-eight hours and a chance to shine. It's time for competent adults to step forward."

She says, "You...if you're so damn competent, did you know the First Lady was..."

The Secret Service agent stops talking. Parker waits. "Go on," he says. "Finish your sentence. Did I know what about the First Lady?"

Grissom sits there, stubbornly, and for God's sake, again there are raised voices outside and Mrs. Glynn says, "You can't go in there, he's in a very important meeting," and sure enough the door opens up and a man in uniform steps in, eyes wide, face pale. He has on black trousers, a white dress shirt with gold badge, and black necktie, and Parker recognizes him as one of the many faceless members of the uniformed Secret Service, out there on the perimeter of the White House grounds manning the gate booths and kiosks.

There's something in his hand.

Parker says, "What's going on? Who are you and what do you want?"

The man ignores Parker and goes right to Grissom.

"Supervisor Grissom," he says, voice strained. "You need to see this."

She stands up and says, "What is it?"

"You need to take a look," he says, handing over the package. Parker sees it's a large, clear plastic bag containing a standard business-size manila envelope. "This was dropped off at the South Gate about ten minutes ago."

Grissom says, "Gloves?"

"Right here, ma'am," and from a rear pants pocket, he passes over a pair of light-blue latex gloves and she snaps them on, and the agent passes over the package.

"What is it?"

The agent swallows, his voice tight with anxiety. "It's a human finger."

# CHAPTER 51

I'M TIRED, EXHAUSTED, fighting tears in front of this confident and horrible man, and I realize I've slipped up in almost asking him if he knew what I knew—namely, that the First Lady had expressed her love to another man.

Parker looks like he wants to fight me over that incomplete sentence, and while I'm not saved by the bell, I'm saved by the arrival of one of my Uniformed Division guys, an ex-Marine named Stephenson.

I can barely hear what he's saying, but I'm staring at the plastic bag marked EVIDENCE with black-and-red letters and those four words—*It's a human finger*—bore into my skull like four separate high-speed drills. On the top of the envelope is a row of lines, and on the first line is Agent Stephenson's name, and I ink in my own name below his, keeping the chain of evidence.

Parker says, "Holy God, do you think that's—"

"Shut up," I tell him. "I'm working."

I slowly open the adhesive flap to the plastic bag. "Who dropped it off at the South Gate?"

"One of the homeless guys that hangs out in Lafayette Park, a character called Gregory. He's been there for years, a regular, but we're still interrogating him."

"How did he get it?"

"Another homeless guy passed it on to Gregory, with a twenty-dollar bill, and told him to bring it to us. Gregory didn't recognize the other guy. It was a cut-out operation."

"Sure was," I say, removing the manila envelope from the plastic evidence bag. There's the slightest lump about midway down the envelope. "Who else knows about this?"

"Just me, ma'am," he says. "I... opened it up and saw what was inside, and then I came straight here, looking for you."

Parker says, "What are you waiting for? Open the damn thing up!"

Luckily his desk is clear. I put the evidence bag down and re-open the nine-by-twelve envelope. The adhesive hasn't been used, which means whoever prepared this was at least smart enough not to lick it shut and leave DNA evidence behind.

I peer into the envelope, maneuvering it so one of Parker's office lamps is illuminating the interior. Inside there's a single sheet of paper and there appears to be block typesetting on it.

I ignore that for now.

There's a small plastic sandwich bag, and there's something pink contained within. I take a breath and reach in and pull out the bag, rest it on top of Parker's clean desk.

It's the last joint of a finger, perhaps the pinky finger. The nail is colored a light red, and there's a bloody piece of gauze wrapped around the severed end.

Parker seems frozen in his chair, hand held up to his mouth.

"See, ma'am?" Stephenson says. "That's what I saw."

The skin is still pink, which means the joint was severed not too long ago. I say, "Stephenson, whatever happened at the South Gate never happened. Understand?"

"Yes, ma'am."

"Good," I say. "You have another bag or container with you?"

He fumbles in his pocket, takes out a small plastic bag with a pill in it. "My antacid pill," he says with a touch of an apology in his voice. "Haven't taken it yet."

"Yeah, well, we're all pretty busy, aren't we," I say. With my latex-covered fingers, I pick up the severed finger, and after Stephenson swallows his pill dry, I put the joint into his bag. I dig into my handbag, pull out my business card, then scribble my name, date, and the time on it, and slip it into the bag.

I say, "You're to leave here, not talk to anyone, and take that to Gil Foster, over at the Technical Security Division. Not particularly in his wheelhouse, but tell him what's going on, he'll get it to the right person, and he'll confirm what we suspect through our fingerprint records."

"Yes, ma'am," and he's out of Parker Hoyt's office as fast as he came in. When he's gone, Parker says, "What else is in the envelope?"

I slide out the sheet of paper, and Parker gets up from his chair and walks around, and we both read the note with its ink-printed letters:

WE HAVE THE FIRST LADY. SHE HASN'T DROWNED.

FOR HER SAFE RELEASE

A. DEPOSIT $100 MILLION IN CENTRAL BANK OF CARACAS, ACCOUNT HPL 0691959, ACCESS CODE B14789, WITHIN THE NEXT TWELVE HOURS

B. HARRISON TUCKER TO MAKE PUBLIC SPEECH IN 24 HOURS TO APOLOGIZE FOR WHAT HE DID TO HER

C. SHE WILL THEN BE RELEASED ALIVE. ANYTHING ELSE OCCURS, HER BODY WILL BE RELEASED SO THAT SHE CAN BE BURIED WITH HER FINGER.

I sense Parker is trembling from looking at the note, and I say, "Guess she's not in hiding, Mister Hoyt."

# CHAPTER 52

HOYT GOES AROUND the desk and sits down, and damn the man, he seems to pull it all together in those five seconds and once more is in charge. "Very well, Agent Grissom, I'll take it from here."

If the cold bastard had told me I had just been appointed ambassador to Iceland, I wouldn't have been more surprised. "Take what from here? What are you talking about? We need to work this!"

"What do you mean by *we*, Agent Grissom?" he says smugly. "This is a kidnapping, pure and simple. That falls under the jurisdiction of the FBI. I'll be contacting them presently to start the investigative process."

"It'll take them at least a day to get brought up to speed," I say. "We can't afford to wait that long. You know it, I know it...the First Lady is in extreme danger."

"And that's why the FBI is going to handle the investigation. Not a handful of bumbling Secret Service agents."

My heart is pounding so hard with anger that I can feel it in my neck. "You slimy son-of-a-bitch—two days ago we weren't bumbling. Two days ago you and the President ordered me to investigate the First Lady's disappearance, and you made it quite explicit what we were to do."

He leans back in his chair, hands folded quietly over his belly. "I don't quite understand what you're saying, Agent Grissom."

The hot fear that's been coursing through me has been dizzyingly replaced with cold horror. "Don't even say that, Mister Hoyt."

He shrugs. "I seem to recall a brief meeting in the Oval Office two days ago, when you expressed concern about the First Lady's whereabouts. I also recall you saying that you knew where she was, that it would all turn out fine, and that was that."

"You ordered me to look for her! You ordered me to do it quietly and without public attention!"

He says with a cool, smooth voice, "Do you have any of that in writing, Agent Grissom? A memo? An email? A little handwritten note from the President on a slip of paper?"

I clench my fists. "You can't get away with this. You won't."

"Let's recap," he says. "The past several years haven't been good for the Secret Service, now, have they? Drunken agents. Prostitution scandals. The White House being shot up and no one noticing for a couple of days. Now we have an incompetent trio of agents who've lost track of the most important woman in the United States. A trio who've been supervised by a flighty, emotional woman who's going through a bitter divorce...and whose husband has just been murdered."

I'm biting the inside of my cheek, trying to keep it under control, and Mister Hoyt says, "And that's the narrative, Agent Grissom. Reporters don't do news stories anymore. They report on details that reinforce the narrative. And which narrative are they going to believe? The President's or yours?"

It's so quiet and empty in this large office that I feel like I've entered into some kind of tomb or mausoleum.

"The President's narrative might not work," I point out. "He's had a few rough days lately."

"And so have you, Agent Grissom. Do you really want the extra attention you and your daughter would receive by going public?"

*Bastard,* I think, *cold, cold bastard.*

I say, "Are you going to pay the ransom?"

"Up to the FBI and the President."

"And the televised apology?"

"Up to me . . . and the President."

With that chilly phrase, I know there's no way that Parker Hoyt is going to allow the President to grovel like that on national television.

Which means the First Lady is a dead woman.

And . . .

From Parker Hoyt's calm gaze, I have a sharp blow of understanding.

A dead First Lady is an outcome that Parker Hoyt is hoping for, to take away from the "Ambush in Atlanta," weeks before the election.

He says, "I have a lot of work to do, Agent Grissom. So please show yourself out."

I've been dismissed. With Ben's death and burial, and with this meeting, and seeing the severed finger of the First Lady, it feels like I'm slowly being filled with hydrogen, about to float away, one spark away from total destruction.

I get up.

I can't think, can't plan, can only move.

Can only listen.

He calls out, "Agent Grissom, a suggestion? Cash in your life insurance policy or your retirement savings and hire the best lawyer you can find. You're going to need it."

I get to the door, open it, and then a thought comes to me.

I turn and say, "Mister Hoyt? A suggestion. Get the best Kevlar protective vest you can afford and start wearing it. You're going to need it."

Then I leave.

# CHAPTER 53

GRACE FULLER TUCKER, former First Lady of Ohio, daughter of a prominent family from the Midwest and current First Lady of the United States, is resting on her side on a creaky bed with a thin mattress inside an old, rural building, her left hand throbbing from the pain of her severed pinky.

She doesn't dare move.

Not at all.

She takes a deep breath, feels tears trickling down her cheeks. She's cold, hungry, and thirsty. She's still wearing her riding gear from two days ago—black stretch jodhpurs with stirrups, tan turtleneck sweater, and short black cotton jacket. Her boots have been stripped off and her helmet tossed aside.

Grace looks at her thick-bandaged left hand, again feeling the horror of seeing her arm stretched out, fastened so she couldn't move, hearing the *clink-clink* of the instruments, looking away and thankful that at least some anesthesia had been administered. There had been that dull sensation, feeling the sawing movement, still looking away, her stomach cold and empty, and even throwing up and not being able to move.

So here she is.

Why is she here?

She thinks back and knows it's because of the choices she's made, even all those years ago, when she had attended a charity event at the Cleveland Clinic, where her family had been the primary sponsor, and a newly elected state senator called Harrison Tucker had caught her eye.

Decision.

She could have turned away from that smiling and charming face, gone somewhere else, but she had stayed.

Even with the Extra Strength Tylenol trying to do its work, the painful throbbing continues in her left small finger.

She had stayed.

Grace thinks that if she were to die in the next twenty-four hours, the inscription on her tombstone could read:

SHE STAYED.

Stayed with Harrison while he rose through the ranks of the Ohio State Senate, when he became a two-term governor, got his party's nomination to be President, and then was the winner-takes-all, getting the keys nearly four years ago to 1600 Pennsylvania Avenue.

Oh, yes, she stayed, while he made promises, compromised, and made more promises. She had come along with him, her burgeoning career in education and early childhood development dying along the way, until she found herself in a place that always had horrified her—being a politician's wife. The type of woman who laughed at bad jokes, who kept a smile on her face while slicing through yet another chicken dinner, and who would make small talk with thick men with smelly breath who had the ability to write huge checks to campaigns and PACs.

Then…her own illness. When, some years back, the annual

mammogram—at the same Cleveland Clinic her father and now deceased mother were prominent in, ironically—had shown something suspicious, and then a follow-up had done the same, and then a needle biopsy had shown cancer cells, well, Governor Harrison Tucker, running in the primaries, had said all the right words, had made all the right gestures.

But that damn black slug Parker Hoyt, she had caught him meeting with Harrison, about the sympathy vote Harrison could count on when the news came out about her illness.

And that had been that. A nasty argument had ensued, and for once in her life, she had won a victory against Harrison and against being the perfect political wife, and she had suffered in silence during those months of surgery and chemo and the ultimate realization that she could never, ever bear children.

Grace hears footsteps outside of her cold and plain room.

Then there was the presidency, with the thoughts that she could circle around to where her life had once been, to really make a contribution to the health and safety of children—especially the ones who were homeless through no fault of their own—and that had been a four-year struggle of budget compromises, setbacks, and defeats.

Because she had stayed.

The door to her room creaks open.

A gruff male voice says, "I want to look at that hand."

Grace doesn't say a word, doesn't move.

As she always has done, she stays.

# CHAPTER 54

IT'S THREE A.M. and I'm at a McDonald's in Forestville, Maryland, waiting. I've finished off two cups of coffee and two Sausage McGriddles sandwiches. I was hungry earlier, which I suppose is a good sign, but I'm still not conscious of having tasted anything.

So much going on.

I'm sharing this common eating area with a number of folks that you would expect to see in an urban McDonald's at three a.m.—bundles of young men and women, laughing and chatting, working women staring at their breakfasts, and two long-haul truckers, sitting in their booths, just shoveling fuel into themselves so they can keep on truckin'.

A door opens up. Scotty comes in, glances around, and then spots me, slides into the booth.

"Boss."

"Hey," I say.

"How's Amelia?"

"With her Aunt Gwen."

"Boss, I'm so sorry that—"

I hold up a hand. "It's done. And I'm not going to talk about it. Let's wait, all right?"

We don't have to wait long. The door swings open, and two members of CANARY's protective team come in, looking like they just spent the past hour holding up a sign and begging passing motorists for coins. The lead agent, Pamela Smithson, comes by, accompanied by Tanya Glenn. They skip the food counter and push in next to Scotty.

"Where's Brian?" I ask. Pamela yawns and Tanya says, "I saw him out in the parking lot. Looks like he was making a phone call."

Scotty says, "At three in the morning?"

Tanya says, "Maybe he was telling his mommy what he wants for breakfast."

Pamela slightly smiles and then the door swings open, and the young male agent hustles in, saying, "Sorry, didn't mean to be late."

He sits next to me, and I say, "That's all right. I haven't started yet."

And before I start, Pamela says, "Sally, I know I speak for Tanya and Brian by saying how sorry we were to hear about Ben. Is there . . . is there any news? About the investigation?"

"No," I say.

Next to me, Brian says, "Do the local police have any leads?"

"None that I know of," I say, and Tanya speaks up: "Sally, I can't believe your daughter was there when—"

I hold up my hand once more and say, "No offense, guys, but shut your traps."

Their faces flush or freeze. I've gotten their attention.

Good.

"There's a lot going on and I don't have much time," I say.

"Just tell me this to start: what have you been doing the past few hours?"

Scotty and the three other agents give quick glances to one another, as if they're wondering if this senior Secret Service agent has finally gone off the rails, and one by one, the answers come.

"Having a beer, watching HBO."

"Asleep."

"In bed, trying to sleep."

"I was sleeping, too."

I say, "Any of you get any phone calls from the FBI?"

No verbal answers, just quick shakes of the head.

"I thought so," I say.

I check, just to make sure we're relatively alone in this large McDonald's, and I say, "CANARY's been kidnapped. About nine hours ago, a ransom message was delivered to the White House."

Their faces show various stages of shock and disbelief, and CANARY's lead agent is the first to respond.

Pamela says forcefully, "How do we know it's not a fake? Ever since the news got leaked about her supposed drowning, every freak and nutcase has crawled out of their mom's basement and started posting conspiracy theories on the Internet. Maybe this note's just part of it."

"This note came with a severed finger joint," I say. "The fingerprint matches."

Whispered obscenities and wide eyes, and Scotty says, "Boss . . . what's going on?"

"Nothing's going on," I say. "That's the problem. I was with Parker Hoyt when the ransom note and the finger arrived. He said he was going to contact the FBI and tell them what happened."

Silence. Out in the kitchen, there's some arguing going on in Spanish.

I say, "None of you have been contacted by the FBI, you . . . the shift working with CANARY when she disappeared. You should have been the first ones interviewed."

Scotty says, "What did the ransom note say, boss?"

"A hundred-million-dollar payout by six o'clock this morning. At six p.m. today, the President goes on national television to apologize for his affair."

Tanya Glenn's eyes are moist but sharp, like knives coming out of a dishwasher. "What are you telling us, Sally?"

I say, "The money may be paid. But there's no way the chief of staff is going to have that speech delivered."

Out in the kitchen, there's a loud noise as something crashes to the floor.

"Parker Hoyt wants CANARY dead," I say. "And it's up to us to stop him."

# CHAPTER 55

SAVE FOR SCOTTY, everybody else is looking at me with cold skepticism. The youngest agent, Brian Zahn, says, "With all due respect, Agent Grissom—"

His boss, Pamela, interrupts him. "Sally...you've been under a lot of stress, and God knows that—"

My turn.

"Parker Hoyt also told me that my role in looking for CANARY, along with this detail, was unauthorized and illegal, and violated the wishes and orders of the President. Which meant that according to the law, you were accomplices to me while we illegally searched for the First Lady."

Tanya says, "The bastard..."

Scotty says, "Why does he want CANARY dead?"

I say, "Have you seen the news? CANAL's poll numbers are collapsing like an avalanche. Something has to save him. And what's that something? A dead First Lady, someone for the nation to mourn, so the voters can show their sympathy for CANAL when they go into the voting booth in a few weeks."

"Ma'am," Brian says, "that's...cold."

Pamela says, "That's DC. So what are you thinking?"

*All right,* I think, *this is where it's going to get interesting.*

"Folks...it's time to face facts, as ugly as they are. All of us, our careers are destroyed. Ruined. Months or years from now, when this is finally settled, we'll be very lucky if we can get hired as mall cops. That is, if we're not serving time in prison."

I let that sink in and say, "We can do one of two things. We can sit back, let Parker Hoyt do whatever he's doing, and let CANARY get killed."

Brian says, "We could go to the FBI."

With a tight tone in his voice, Scotty says, "It's three a.m. That means we'll get a duty officer, who'll have to contact her senior officer, and if you think she's going to act on her own, no. It'll have to go up the chain of command...that is, if anybody would believe us."

Tanya says, "And what's the other thing we can do?"

"Find her on our own," I say.

Pamela says, "Boss, no offense—our track record right now sucks. We haven't found a damn thing."

"Which means we don't have to retrace our steps. Pamela...tell us again what you found from the horse farm's security force and its surveillance cameras."

She says, "Surveillance cameras along the property fence line showed nothing unusual. Security personnel said the same thing. And no aircraft overhead—if somebody had an idea of swooping in with a helicopter to grab her. The gate cameras also showed us coming in with CANARY that morning...and nobody, I mean nobody, left the grounds until you and Scotty showed up."

I say, "So we go back."

"What?" Scotty says.

"We've trusted the horse farm staff to tell us that all was well.

236

But that means the buildings weren't searched intensively. Just a quick walk-through. But this time . . . we make it thorough."

"Now?" Tanya says.

"No time to waste."

"They won't like being woken up," Tanya says.

"I'll order them breakfast when we're done. Anything else?"

Brian speaks up. "There's another—"

Pamela says, "Stow it, Brian. We're going to follow Sally's lead."

She catches my look "Back to the horse farm. Before we all get arrested.

Scotty laughs. "Yeah, as Benjamin Franklin once said, well, we must all hang together, or we're all going to hang separately. Or something like that."

A Hispanic male dressed in dirty black slacks, a black striped dress shirt, and a red necktie with a McDonald's logo on it comes over and says, "Please. If you're going to stay here, you must order something more to eat."

I get out of the booth. "We were just leaving."

# CHAPTER 56

SINCE I WAS there last, the Westbrook Horse Farm has certainly gotten busier. Cars and trucks are parked on either side of the access road, even though it's still a couple of hours before sunrise. We're crowded in a Secret Service Suburban, and it takes the judicious use of flashing lights and sirens before we can get any farther.

Pamela is driving, and once she nudges the car into the parking lot, we all step out and take in the madhouse. There are at least a half-dozen television satellite trucks, with news correspondents doing stand-ups in halos of bright lights. There are bands of men and women, going out on the trails, with flashlights, wearing knapsacks and using walking sticks. There's even what looks to be a troop of Boy Scouts, forming up and ready to join the search, and there's a mass of law enforcement personnel, from the Virginia State Police to the county Sheriff's Department to local police, plus a smattering of volunteer firefighters just to round things out. The thick woods with the riding trails are being lit up by bands of searchers, all heading to the river where some hours ago Parker Hoyt had told the *Washington Post* the First Lady had apparently drowned.

Standing next to me, Scotty says, "Talk about the circus coming to town."

Next to him is Tanya, who just shakes her head. "What a mess, what a mess."

"Forget it," I say. "That's not where we're going."

I lead my group of renegade investigators toward the stables and farm buildings, and within a few seconds, two security officers come out of the shadows and stop us.

"Sorry, folks, nobody's allowed to come over here," the first one says, and the second one says, "Bad enough to have all those crazies out tromping through the grounds."

I hold out my identification. "We're not nobody, and we're not crazies. We're the Secret Service, and we're coming in."

My folks line up behind me, and maybe the two security officers are tired or overwhelmed, but the near one unhitches the gate and we walk through, while he mutters something about not getting paid enough to handle this mess.

"All right," I say. "Make it happen." I start pointing to buildings, one after another, assigning them to the agents. I say, "Be thorough, but haul ass. We don't have much time."

For about thirty minutes I'm in one of the large barns, taking in the scent of horse, grain, and hay, and with flashlight in hand, I make my way across the cobblestoned floor, pointing the light into each stall. Most of the horses avoid me and ignore me, and some make grumbling noises and slight whinnies.

One horse stands out, the beautiful black Morgan named Arapahoe belonging to the missing First Lady.

I carefully flash the light around his enclosure, making sure the First Lady isn't tied up in the corner with a bloody hand.

I say to the horse, "You know what happened, pal. Wish I could make you talk."

He blinks his sad brown eyes.

I wonder if horses can mourn.

I resume walking and find a ladder at one end, and climb up, the small flashlight in my teeth.

The upper part of the barn has boxes, piles of leather gear, some old saddles and boots, and clumps of hay. I move around and twice bump my head on an overhead beam—painful but not limiting—and when I move my way back down the ladder, about ninety pounds and seventy years of Virginia womanhood is angrily waiting for me.

"I'm Connie Westbrook," she announces. "Who the hell are you?"

She has steel gray hair bundled at the back of her head in a tight bun, and she's wearing a tan robe over a nightgown and knee-high wellingtons. One wrinkled hand is holding the robe closed against her chest, and the other is holding a flashlight.

When I get to the bottom of the ladder, I do her the courtesy of showing her my identification. "I'm Sally Grissom of the Secret Service," I say. "I'm the special agent in charge of the Presidential Protective Division."

Connie seems to be one of those old Commonwealth of Virginia matrons who can trace their lineage back to the original founding of Richmond, and who still calls the Civil War the "Late Great Unpleasantness."

"So?" she asks. "Why are you here?"

I start out of the barn, and she keeps up with my brisk pace. "You know why."

"And where's your warrant, Agent Grissom?"

I go out into the cool air and see the sky is lightening over in the east. "Really, ma'am? The First Lady has gone missing at your facility and you're concerned about a warrant?"

She purses her lips. "You're here illegally."

"I'm here to find the First Lady."

"She's not here," she snaps at me. "I've already told your... personnel that very same fact. And now my fields and trails are being trampled, torn up, and my horses are panicking. And I want you to leave... and just as soon as I can, I'm getting those other... people off my property."

"Well, we're looking again," I say. "Just to be sure."

"I forbid it."

I give her a grind stare, up and down, up and down, and I say, "Ma'am, you can forbid it all you want, and while you're at it, you can forbid the sun to rise over there. Both will be equally effective. Now—"

A voice crackles in my earpiece. "Boss, Scotty."

I lift up my wrist, trigger the microphone. "Sally here, Scotty. Go."

"Small outbuilding, about fifty meters to the east, in a grove of oak trees," he says. "There's something going on."

"Like what?"

"Like a locked door," he says. "And a trash bag outside."

A slight crackle of static "With bloody bandages inside."

# CHAPTER 57

IN A MATTER of seconds, I'm at the building, and Scotty is standing outside, his flashlight illuminating a white plastic trash bag outside of a locked wooden door, painted green. Oak trees are nearby and overhead, and there's a dirt path leading back to where we were. Unlike the other buildings we've been searching, this one is worn, with a sagging roof. It's one story and there are small windows set up near the roofline.

I turn, and Connie Westbrook has managed to keep up with me.

I flash my light over at the building. "What's in here?"

"Nothing," she says.

Scotty says, "Over here, boss."

I check the torn top of the white trash bag. Inside are crumpled fast food bags, McDonald's and Burger King, and I nudge the top, where there's a couple of crumpled white gauze bandages, stained brown with old blood. There's also bits of string— used sutures?—and cotton swabs.

Back to Connie I say, "Care to change your mind?"

She folds her arms, says not a word. Pamela and Tanya appear, breathing hard, running from wherever they've been. Scotty doesn't say anything, just illuminates the open plastic bag with the used bandages.

Pamela turns and says, "Who's this?"

"The farm's owner."

Pamela's on her, both strong hands on her robe, and she yells, "Is she in there? Is she in there, you old bat?"

Tanya pulls her off and the woman nearly falls, but she's still there, not backing away, eyes filled with hate, staring at us. Scotty says, "I might be hearing things, boss, but I thought I heard a voice from inside."

I step up to Mrs. Westbrook. "The key. Get the key to that door and right now."

She says, "Go to hell," in a grandmotherly tone of voice, if one's grandmother had once been a prison matron.

I turn. "Scotty. Get that door open. I don't care what you do . . . get the damn thing open. And where the hell is Brian Zahn?"

Tanya says, "No idea."

"Hold on, boss," Scotty says, and he races to a near barn, smaller than the one I was exploring, and comes back in under a minute. There's the sound of honking horns out by the parking area, with a few whoop-whoops of sirens, and the hum of power generators— I wish I had one right now, turning this pre-dawn slice of Virginia farmland into noon—but there's no time, and Scotty is back, carrying a sledgehammer at port arms, as if it were a Colt M4.

He goes right up to the door with no hesitation, and with one hard blow, the solid doorknob flies off. Scotty drops the sledgehammer, takes out his service weapon—as do the rest of us— and with pistols and flashlights in hand, we move forward.

Scotty elbows the door open, yells, "Freeze! Secret Service!"

And I'm right behind him, and the first thing I see is the anguished and scared face of a woman.

# CHAPTER 58

IN THE LIVING quarters of the White House, on the second floor, Parker Hoyt nods to a male Secret Service agent standing guard outside the plain door. He knocks on the door twice, enters, and from years of practice, flips a switch on the inside wall that turns on just a few subdued lights in the master bedroom.

The room is lit up, and the President of the United States is curled on his left side, sleeping, wearing light-blue cotton pajamas. Parker feels a flash of jealousy that Harrison could be sleeping with all that's been going on. Parker's been limited to catching naps on an old Army-style cot in a storage closet adjacent to his large office.

"Mister President? Sir?"

The President snaps wide awake, looks to Parker, and says, "Any news?"

"No, sir, I'm afraid she's still missing."

The room is well-furnished, with old oil paintings and some landscapes of Lake Erie, but Parker and scores of other people in the White House know it's been a very long time since the First Lady shared this bed with this man.

Parker has an envelope in one hand, and with a free hand, he pulls over a chair, sitting next to the President.

He rubs at his eyes, says, "Good God, Parker, it's not even five in the morning."

"I know, sir, and I hate to disturb you, but we need to make a decision."

Harrison runs a hand over his head. "What decision is that?"

"This one," he says, removing a single sheet of paper from the envelope. "It's a Presidential Directive from you, ordering the Treasury Department to transfer one hundred million dollars from its Judgment Fund to that bank account in Lebanon."

Parker glances at his watch. "I've spent all night preparing for this transfer, and we have just over an hour to make it happen."

Harrison takes the single sheet of paper, and then a pen that Parker offers. "What the hell is the Treasury Department's Judgment Fund?"

He says, "It's the fund the Treasury Department maintains to pay out lawsuits or settlements. Also, truth be told…it's your emergency slush fund. That's how, when the Iranian deal got settled a few years back, we were able to deliver pallets full of hundred-dollar bills to the mullahs the next day."

The President reads the sheet, nods, and then looks to his chief of staff.

"When can I see the draft of the speech?"

*Here we go,* Parker thinks. Aloud, he says, "What speech is that, sir?"

Harrison says frostily, "It's too early in the morning to jerk me around, Parker. You know what speech. The one where I go on live television and apologize for the way I've mistreated Grace." He twists in his bed and looks at the nearby clock. "It looks like I need to be delivering that in just about thirteen hours."

Parker says, "Mister President, there isn't going to be any speech."

His eyebrows lift up. "The kidnappers...they've adjusted their demands?"

"No, sir," Parker says, "we're not going to meet their demand."

"The hell we're not."

"Sir, I—"

"I better have a draft of that speech by midmorning, or I will personally—personally!—call the heads of all three networks and the cable news channels, requesting airtime for six p.m. later today. And then I'll make the remarks by myself."

"I'm afraid I can't let you do that, sir."

"Parker—"

"Sir, please hear me out."

The fingers clenching the pen seem as tight as a lock, and Parker is sure the President is fantasizing about shoving that pen down Parker's throat.

"Sir," he goes on, "if you were to make that speech, what does it gain the country?"

"What does it...hell, Parker, it gets the First Lady free!"

"Perhaps it does, perhaps it doesn't," Parker says. "But hear what I said. 'What does it gain the country?' For you, personally, it means your wife is freed. For the First Lady, she's free, and her friends, family, and followers will be thrilled. And with all the news coverage, and investigative reports, and everything else, in three weeks, you will be smiling on national television, congratulating the governor of California on his success. And less than three months later, that bumbling boob will be sworn in."

The President keeps quiet. Parker says, "But let's say we pay the ransom. That gains us another twelve hours. Perhaps she's found. Perhaps she's freed. The news will be of her successful return...without the added burden of you apologizing to more than three hundred million of your fellow citizens that you couldn't keep your presidential dick in your pants."

"You . . ." and the President can't say anything more.

Parker says, "If we're fortunate, she might be dumped on a street corner somewhere, and we can keep the news quiet until after the election."

"The press will crucify us if we try that."

"They might," Parker says. "And we'll just say . . . after you've been successfully re-elected . . . that we didn't want to toss anything into the last few weeks of election coverage that might impact the election. The people will eventually respect that. So what if the press doesn't?"

Harrison says bleakly, "Suppose they follow through with their threat. And harm comes to her. . . . What then?"

"Then the nation will rally around a President suffering the grievous loss of his wife. Your affair will be overlooked. Your margin of victory will even be larger."

Harrison shakes his head. "That . . . the cynicism . . . I mean . . ."

"Mister President, excuse me for being blunt. When it comes to kidnappings, chances are that the First Lady is already dead. Once they get their money, the kidnappers will want to rid themselves of her. They know the entire federal government will be chasing after them . . . and they will want to leave no witnesses behind. With the added thrill of humiliating the leader of the free world in the process."

There's a pause. Parker says, "Remember what I said. How does your speech, how will it serve the country? It won't. It will ensure the election of a granola-crunching fool who will roll back all of the progress you've made — both domestic and foreign — and your legacy will be a bungled affair and a kidnapped First Lady."

Another pause. Parker thinks, *We're close. Let's go in for the kill.*

"Or...you make the necessary sacrifice on behalf of the nation. You get re-elected, with an enormous mandate, and you have four more years to build on the previous four years. For the benefit of the American people and for a safer world."

He waits.

Waits.

The President of the United States looks at his hand, the one grasping the pen, like he's wondering how it got there.

With a savage motion, he scrawls his signature on the presidential directive, and shoves both the paper and pen back at his chief of staff.

"Get out of my sight," he snaps.

Parker stands up. "Yes, sir."

# CHAPTER 59

I PUSH PAST Scotty, using my flashlight, and besides the frightened woman in front of me, there are other people as well, men and women, boys and girls. They blink and hold up their hands against the flashlight beams, and they all appear to be Hispanic.

I quickly count off eight, and there's no First Lady back there, just cots, a few buckets with dishes and soiled clothes, a hot plate and laundry hanging from a clothesline in the rear. There are two men, two women, and four boys and girls from toddlers to pre-teens.

Tanya grabs Mrs. Westbrook by the scruff of her robe and pushes her in. "Is this what you're hiding, you bitch? Cheap migrant labor? Paying them next to nothing for the privilege of shoveling out the shit from your million-dollar horses?"

For a small woman she's pretty tough, and she easily breaks free. "No, it's not that, not at all."

"Then what is it?" Tanya demands.

Mrs. Westbrook ignores her and speaks in soft Spanish to the two families, and they nod and a couple try to smile as they settle back on their cots. One of the men has a bandage wrapped around his left wrist. It comes to me that this is what they're used to, being in rough quarters and knowing that at any moment of the day or night, armed men and women from the government could break in.

"There," she says, looking back at me. "You're in charge here, are you not?"

"I am."

"Then let these people be."

"I want an explanation," I say.

"You'll get it...just as soon as you give these people their privacy."

I gesture to Scotty, Pamela, and Tanya, and we step out, and with the rising sun, everything is becoming more visible. Not more clear, no, not that, but definitely more visible. Scotty closes the door and picks up the broken doorknob, looks around with some embarrassment, and drops it to the ground.

"You...people," she begins, with her old and strong voice. "You think you know everything."

She bundles her robe tighter about her slim frame. "For more than three hundred years my family has lived here, and raised generations here, and yes, for a while, kept slaves. That's our enduring shame, that my family, at one point, owned human beings. You can read the old journals and old stories about my ancestors, and how proud they were that they treated their property well. But it was still an abomination. No matter how many years have passed, it was still an abomination."

I say, "You're making penance."

"For once, miss, you're making sense." A fierce nod. "Yes...this farm, this place, was never an Underground Railroad back in the day. But it is now. Those two families...they have jobs, a new life waiting for them up north. All we do is make sure they get there, without being harassed or arrested."

She stares at me. "Are they going to be arrested?"

"No," I say, holstering my pistol. The others follow.

"Am I going to be arrested?"

Tanya mutters something about what she'd do if she were in charge, and I say, "No, Mrs. Westbrook, you're not going to be arrested."

"Are you and your . . . people, are you done here?"

Then it hits me like a slow moving yet large and wide tidal wave, an overwhelming sensation of being utterly exhausted, bone-tired, and worthless. The sun is coming up. The ransom will probably be paid, and we're through here. A few minutes ago, it seemed like success was within reach, just past that wooden door, just past that trash bag with bloody bandages.

So damn close and yet so damn far.

Scotty looks around and says, "Where the hell is Brian?"

"Good question," I say. "Pamela? He belongs to you. Where did you last see him?"

"I didn't," she replies, rubbing at her cold hands.

Tanya says, "I saw the kid go back and grab his laptop from the Suburban. He said he wanted to check something out."

"And you let him do that?" I demand. "This was a hands-on search, not a—"

There's shouting coming from the direction of the parking lot. As one, our little group turns, and in the better light, I see Brian running in our direction, carrying a laptop under his arm.

More yells and then I make out his words:

"I know where she is! I know where she is!"

# CHAPTER 60

I HEAR WORDS from the other agents, and instantly I cut them off at their throats.

"Shut your mouths, all of you, right now," I say.

Brian races up to me, nearly slipping to the ground as he passes through a patch of mud, and nearly out of breath, he gasps out, "She's here . . . she's here . . . I just know it."

In seconds we're around Brian, and he opens up his laptop and says, "When we started searching I thought about how we lost CANARY, and how her horse Arapahoe came back by himself."

Pamela says, "So?"

"Damn it, you know how that horse loved her," Brian said, trying to hold the laptop open with one hand while working on the keyboard with another. "But the horse came back alone. If CANARY had tried to sneak back through the woods and ended up here somewhere, no way Arapahoe would have left her alone. He would have gone through the woods and brush with her."

"All right, so what do you have?" I asked. "Where is she?"

He moves the laptop around and says, "Damn it, I had a good signal earlier..."

"To hell with showing me something on the laptop," I say. "What did you find?"

He nods, tries to catch his breath, and then says, "I went back to the river."

Tanya says, "The river was a bust. You know it, I know it, Homeland Security knows it."

"But everyone assumed she had fallen off the horse," Brian said, slowly walking backward, gazing at his keyboard, looking for that elusive carrier signal. "Or had slipped in. Or hinted on that note, maybe had committed suicide. So everybody was looking downstream. Who was looking upstream?"

Scotty says, "Some of the Homeland Security units went upstream, I know that for a fact."

"But did they search the buildings?"

Scotty says, "Yes, they did. At least two miles upstream."

Brian smiles. "But they didn't go far enough...okay, here we go."

I say, "Brian, I don't care if the Death Star is beaming you down instructions. Tell me—right now!—what's going on."

He nods, takes another breath, and says, "Real estate records. I got into the local tax assessor's office, started looking up and down the river, looking to see if there was someone out there, a friend or somebody, a place where she might have sought refuge."

Tanya says, "Wait a minute, the ransom note and the severed finger, how can—"

I hold up my hand. "Go on."

Brian says, "None of the names looked familiar, and none were connected to the First Lady...but I saw that one little remote farmhouse, about three miles upstream, it belonged to something called the Friends of Lake Erie Association...it's a charitable group. Based in Ohio."

"Ohio . . ." I whisper.

"Ah, here we go," he says, turning the screen around. "Look! Look who's the chairman of the Friends of Lake Erie Association."

I note the name, the photograph, and with as much quiet authority as I can muster, I say, "Brian, you take the lead. Find the quickest route between here and that farmhouse, and let's haul ass."

As we start moving, Mrs. Westbrook yells out, "Hey, who's going to pay for this broken doorknob?"

I yell back. "Send the bill to Homeland Security."

Then we all start running.

# CHAPTER 61

PARKER HOYT IS leaning back in his office chair, dozing, when a ringing phone wakes him up.

He lurches forward, automatically picks up his standard office phone, says, "Hoyt," and realizes he's talking to a dial tone.

The phone keeps on ringing.

It's his other phone.

He tries to put his standard phone back into the cradle, misses, and it clatters across his clean desktop. Parker lunges for the other phone, grabs it.

"Yes?"

"We're checking out a small farmhouse, about three miles upstream from the horse farm. She might be there. It's within walking distance."

"Wait—you're still working the case? Grissom was told to stand down!"

"Yeah, well, she doesn't listen well. We're out freezing our asses off, ready to get moving."

"Give me the address," he says, and he fumbles for a pen, grabs it, doesn't see anything to write on, picks up a crumpled poll report from last night—Harrison Tucker's polling collapse is deep and widespread—and he flattens it out, says, "Go."

"Fourteen, that's one-four, East Dominion Road, Walton."

He scribbles the numbers and words and says, "Why do you think she's there? What's the evidence? Could it be a safe house for terrorists?"

The voice laughs. "Only if the terrorists are environmentalists. It belongs to a conservation group from Ohio."

"Ohio . . . why in hell does that matter?"

"Gotta go."

Parker sits up straight, like every bone in his spine has just fused together in one hard column. "No! Damnit, tell me why it matters!"

"Because of the guy who's the chairman of the conservation group."

And he mentions the name, and before Parker can react, his hired contact hangs up the phone.

# CHAPTER 62

WHEN HER PHONE rings, Marsha Gray answers it before the second tone chimes through.

"Yes," she says, flipping on the recording function on her phone.

"You know who this is," comes the voice of the President's chief of staff.

She yawns. "We've shared so many intimate moments, how can I forget?"

"Stow it," he says. "I've got information—what you call actionable intelligence."

She swings her legs out of her bed, grabs a pencil and notepad from the nightstand. Pencils always write, they never run out of ink, and they never freeze in cold weather.

Marsha says, "Parker, I love it when you try to talk macho and all, but get on with it."

She senses he's trying to contain his temper, and that makes her smile. He says, "East Dominion Road, number fourteen. A rural farmhouse. It's in a town next to where the horse farm is located. Walton."

Marsha quickly writes it down. "Good intelligence?"

"Excellent intelligence."

"Nice change of pace," she says. "What do you want?"

"I think you know."

Marsha checks the time. "Remind me, sir. I need to have clear and crisp orders."

"Whoever's in that house...they don't get out."

"All right," she says. "And Grissom?"

"If that gets the job done, then do it."

She looks at the time again. "I'll get there as soon as I can."

"Just get there," he says. "And report when you do so."

Parker hangs up and so does Marsha. She yawns, gets out of bed, and goes to her closet. It seems this particular weird and important job is about to come to an end, and that's when things can get hairy indeed. It's one thing to get to a point and make the shot.

Getting out in one piece is just as important.

Marsha opens the closet, switches on the light, notes the various bits and pieces of gear she's accumulated during her career in the Corps and then her freelance life.

*Time,* she thinks, *to go full battle rattle.*

# CHAPTER 63

WHEN HE GETS off the phone with Marsha Gray, Parker paces around the office for a moment. Lots of pieces are starting to fall together, but he's concerned about Marsha saying it might take some time to get to that remote farmhouse.

He sits down, looks at the overhead maps and detailed information about the house in Virginia on his computer screen.

Well.

He picks up his private phone, makes another call.

This morning is too important to rely on one person, as good as she is.

At the offices of Global Strategic Services at Crystal City in Arlington, Virginia, Rupert Munson, an executive vice president of internal operations, is skimming the morning news headlines on his office computer when his phone rings. Rupert likes to get a feel of what's going on out there in the world, but he never depends on what he calls the "dinosaur media," like the *Post* or the *Times* or any of the cable channels. He reads those out-of-the-way reporters and commentators, people he trusts because they believe the same things he does, and right now the news is whether or not the busty lobbyist found with President Tucker wasn't in fact the former girlfriend of the President of Russia.

There are some blurry photos posted on the Internet that seem to make the case, and as Rupert picks up his phone, he sourly thinks that in his lifetime, not once has there been a President he has respected or admired. Maybe Reagan—although Reagan was too liberal for Rupert's tastes—but that was before his time.

He answers the phone with, "Munson," and one of the corporation's operators says, "Mister Munson, I have the White House on the line for you."

Earlier he had been a bit sleepy from having stayed up too late last night, surfing his usual Internet bookmarks, but those few words have just snapped him wide awake.

"Who is it?" he asks.

The operator replies, "He didn't identify himself, but he did provide a code phrase that indicates that he is at the White House. Before the call proceeds, on your phone, you need to press the E-one switch."

On the mess of buttons on his phone console is a green switch marked E-1—meaning Encryption One—and when he presses the switch, the call between here and the White House is now encrypted. Rupert doesn't like the E-1 channel because more often than not, the call is filled with static and has odd echoes, as if he were talking to someone at the bottom of a well, but this call is clear and sharp.

The nameless operator says, "Your party is now on the line," and there's a *click* as the operator signs off, and he says, "Rupert Munson here."

"Rupert? Parker Hoyt, chief of staff for the President."

Holy crap. Rupert switches the phone from one hand to another. "Mister Hoyt, what can I do for you?"

Hoyt's voice is clear and sounds exactly like him, although the voice is also troubled. "We have a situation that's developed here...and I need the corporation's assistance."

Rupert knows of Parker Hoyt's tenure at the corporation and instantly realizes he wouldn't be calling if it wasn't something important.

"Go ahead, sir, what is it?"

Hoyt says, "The scandal in Atlanta...it's impacting our operations here, and it's impacting the President's decision making process. We have actionable and detailed intelligence that a terrorist cell from ISIS has infiltrated the country and is set to start a series of terrorist attacks, perhaps as early as this afternoon."

*Good God,* Rupert thinks. "Go on, Mister Hoyt."

"The President has been notified that this ISIS cell is located at a remote farmhouse in rural Virginia. Despite all of the briefings, the pleadings, and meetings, the President is refusing to take action from federal forces. He won't even contact the Virginia State Police or local authorities. He just wants to wait it out."

Rupert says, "I understand, Mister Hoyt."

"I think you and I both know what waiting it out will mean. It will mean putting hundreds of innocent civilians at risk because the federal government won't take prompt, severe, and necessary action. And that's where you and the corporation come in."

Rupert is starting to feel the initial thrill of being part of something confidential and important, something so necessary in the fight against terrorism. "We're here to help, Mister Hoyt."

Parker seems to breathe a sigh of relief.

"I knew I could count on you and my company," he says.

# CHAPTER 64

OUR QUIET BLACK Chevrolet Suburban pulls to a halt in the early morning mist on East Dominion Road. The lane is one-vehicle wide, cracked and bumpy, and on either side, it's bordered by high grass, stone walls, and distant lines of woods. For the past several minutes, we haven't seen a single passing vehicle. A mailbox, dented and rusting, is leaning over toward the dirt driveway. Black-and-white stick-on numerals denote 14.

Scotty is driving and says, "Why don't we just roar right up?"

"Because it's not going to happen," I say. "You folks are going to stay right here while I wander up and see what's what. We roar in, we make a big appearance, a loud show, who the hell knows what might happen."

From the rear Pamela says, "For God's sake, Sally, that place could be filled with terrorists, or the KKK, or anybody else that has a grudge against CANARY and cut off her damn finger. You're really going up there alone?"

I open the door. "I am. But I'll have my Motorola up and running, and I'll call if I need backup. But let me make this clear—all of you are staying right here until I contact you. Or if you don't hear from me in fifteen minutes."

Tanya says, "What happens in sixteen minutes?"

I nod to the big man behind the steering wheel. "Then you can assume that Scotty is now acting special agent in charge of the Presidential Protective Division, and you'll follow his orders."

I step out, take a cool breath, and rearrange Amelia's thick red scarf around my neck.

My Amelia, I think, as I go up the dirt road. My poor little girl.

I'm grateful my sister is taking care of my sweet Amelia, and I would give anything to stop this walk so I could phone and talk to my little girl, but I stay with my job.

It's quite the cool morning, and I'm glad for Amelia's scarf. I unbutton my black wool coat so I can get easy access to my SIG Sauer, but I'm gambling I won't need it this morning.

Birds flitter overhead, going into the brush and trees. I have a pang of memory, of being in the Girl Scouts, and I wish I had remembered the identification of all those birds I had studied back then.

I wish I remembered lots of things.

Like that giddiness and pure joy that came from those first years with my Ben. Once, those memories would take my breath away, but now that's gone.

My poor murdered Ben.

The dirt driveway rises up and swings to the left. Here the brush has been trimmed back, and a one-story cabin is before me. In front of the cabin is dirt and gravel. Two vehicles are parked to the left, under a grove of pine trees. One is a black Mercedes-Benz S-class with red-white-and-blue Ohio license plates. The other is a black heavy-duty Ford pickup truck, with one hell of a dented front area. It looks like someone has welded lengths of black steel beams to the front of the truck.

I shake my head.

Not my concern.

I step closer to the cabin. There's a simple door in the center, and next to the door is a carefully stacked pyramid of firewood. There are two light-brown wicker chairs, and one of them is occupied by a man.

He's in his late sixties or early seventies, thick white hair, wearing a plain blue Oxford button-down shirt, khaki slacks, and polished brown loafers. He may be old, but his face is set and his brown eyes are staring right at me.

Across his lap is a shotgun. I can't tell the manufacturer at this distance, but it looks clean and well maintained.

"Good morning," I call out to him.

He nods, says nothing.

I get closer.

"This is a very pretty area of Virginia," I say. "Nice and remote, out of the way, with no noisy neighbors. Even has a river out in the rear of this house."

The man doesn't even nod. By now I'm looking at his hands. They are loosely clasped over the shotgun. I hate to think of it, but if his hands start moving, I'm going to have to react.

I won't like it, but I'll do it.

"How are you today, sir?"

Finally, his head looks to me. "Who are you?"

I say, "Sally Grissom, special agent in charge of the Presidential Protective Division."

The expression on his face doesn't change. "What do you want?"

I can't believe I'm saying the words that I'm saying, but I go ahead.

"Mister Fuller," I say. "I need to see your daughter, Grace."

# CHAPTER 65

OUTSIDE A REMOTE contractor hangar at Andrews Air Force Base, Paul Moody is seated in the pilot's seat of a heavily modified OH-58H Kiowa helicopter, going through his pre-flight checklist, ready for his sudden and important morning mission. For years he has flown in the service of his country for the US Army, flying helicopters similar to this one in Iraq, Afghanistan, Nigeria, and on two very classified occasions, in northern Iran.

It's a clear day, and the checklist is going smoothly. For the past sixteen months, he's been flying for Global Strategic Solutions and has loved every minute of it. He gets to fly in-country, for one, which means no matter where he lands, there will always be clean water and good toilets. He knows that doesn't sound like much, but after years of flying in those barren moonscapes on the other side of the globe, where a hole in the ground is considered a toilet and the water is always warm and heavily chlorinated, it's sheer luxury to close out a mission and still be in the States.

Not to mention the dating opportunities with women who

don't have husbands or brothers around to cut your head off if you try to hold their hand.

Most of the missions he's done for the corporation have been providing air security for VIPs coming for a visit in the States— more often than not, classified visits, where, if noticed, a certain VIP would have been arrested by the FBI on war crimes charges. And twice he has gone "weapons hot" in supporting a law-enforcement mission—he never asked too many questions— which ended up with tractor trailer trucks on remote highways in the west being shot up at night and crashing into remote ravines.

Still, some days, he missed flying those missions overseas, a lot of time flying solo, providing close-in air support for guys on the ground who needed help, and needed help fast. His job was to put him and his bird between the enemy and the good guys, and one thing he learned early on was that if he wasn't getting shot at, he wasn't doing his job.

The engine is now running smoothly and he toggles his radio. After getting clearance for takeoff, and with his left hand on the collective lever and his right on the cyclic stick, he slowly takes off and makes course to Walton. There's a farmhouse in that town that is hiding an ISIS cell, and Paul is about to pay them a very quick and violent visit.

He changes the radio frequency, contacts the support office for his company's internal operations division.

"This is GSS Tango Four," he announces. "Outbound."

Somewhere in Crystal City, a woman's voice replies via his earphones. "Copy that, Tango Four."

He's quickly gaining altitude in the clear blue sky. The side of his helicopter is flanked by two weapons pylons, each carrying a classified modification of the AGM-114 Hellfire. These particular missiles are made of a specially compressed cellulose material and exotic false-positive explosive compounds, meaning that when they reduce the farmhouse to rubble, forensics investigators will find traces of what will appear to be an exploded propane gas tank.

And no evidence he was ever there.

# CHAPTER 66

MARSHA GRAY NEARLY bursts out laughing as she drives by the black Chevrolet Suburban pulled over to the side on East Dominion Road, all of the Secret Service agents inside looking up the dirt driveway. Talk about being blind to threats. If she was carrying something heavier than her usual sniper rifle, like an M249 Squad Automatic Weapon, she could have easily ventilated that Suburban and its passengers in two full sweeps.

But nobody inside pays her Odyssey minivan any notice as she glides by. No wonder these clowns lost the First Lady.

She travels a number of meters until the road curves and she loses sight of the Secret Service vehicle in the minivan's rearview mirror. Good. And even better ... a dirt driveway to the left. Marsha pulls in, and after ten meters or so, there's a grassy section to the right between two maple trees. She backs in the minivan and switches off the engine, leaves the keys in the ignition. If she needs to move quickly, there'll be no time to fumble around for the keys.

Marsha gets out and retrieves her duffel bag from the rear seat, holding her sniper rifle and other equipment and gear. She quickly changes, putting on her familiar battle rattle—save for the helmet, no need to carry three-plus pounds of unnecessary weight on your noggin—and starts to slip through the woods. Marsha has always had the ability to navigate with the minimum of gear, and she uses the map and compass application on her iPhone to move her through the woods and small fields.

A flash of history comes to her: perhaps this same territory was once trod by Union and Confederate troops, duking it out more than a century ago.

If so, then history is about to be made here again.

She climbs up a slight hill that dips down into a muddy ravine, and then easily climbs up and . . . there you go.

A nice view of the side of the cabin, and there are two people talking, a man sitting down in a chair, and a woman standing in front of him.

From her duffel bag, she pulls out her binoculars. She crawls through the brush and gets a proper view. Binoculars up and a brief focus. Old man comes into view. Looks like he's got a shot-gun across his lap. *What the hell?* she thinks. Does he have a moonshine still in the rear?

Marsha shifts her view.

Ah, there you go.

That Secret Service agent, dressed in a black coat and wearing that stupid red scarf from before.

Talk, talk, talk.

She lowers her right hand, finds her iPhone, slides through the screens, and her outgoing phone call is picked up after one ring.

"Hoyt," he says.

"Gray," she whispers. "I'm on station. I'm near the house, and I see Grissom chatting it up with some old buck. What now?"

Hoyt sounds like he's in a good mood. "Everything's all set. You're just backup, all right? And backup only if I call you. You understand?"

"That I do," she says.

It looks like the discussion over there is getting more heated. Marsha says, "What's your backup going to be? A lightning bolt from the heavens?"

Damn, Hoyt even laughs. "You could say that."

And he hangs up.

In the distance, Marsha hears the familiar *thump-thump* of an approaching helicopter. She wiggles back and unzips her duffel bag further, taking out the same rifle she used overseas, which will be just as good here.

The only difference is the type of ammunition she will be using, and when it comes right down to it, that won't make any difference at all.

# CHAPTER 67

THE OLD MAN doesn't even blink. "I don't know what you're talking about, Agent Grissom."

"Mister Fuller," I say, "I'm not sure how or why the First Lady ended up here, or how she injured her finger, but I can tell you that she's in danger, and we need to get her out of here as soon as possible."

He stays quiet, and I'm going to move past him but I'm still concerned about that shotgun. He's older than me by thirty or so years, but he still looks to be in pretty good shape, and if he were to move fast and sure, he and that shotgun could easily cut me in half.

Leaving my Amelia an orphan.

I'm beginning to regret my decision to come up here alone.

He stares at me with contempt. "What do you know about my daughter?"

"I know a lot," I say. "I know of her service at the side of Harrison Tucker in Ohio and here. Her charity efforts. Her devotion to—"

"You know crap," he says. "Grace...she was our only child. Maureen and I, we gave her what we could, but we made sure she fought and earned her own way. And she did. Grace had a head for numbers, for business, and she had the compassion and heart to take care of the forgotten ones. Grace could have joined my company as a young lady...be president of it now, running our hospitals and our medical device companies. But she tossed it all away to stand by that...slug."

"Mister Fuller, I appreciate—"

"My daughter! The First Lady, strong, pretty, a cancer survivor and fighter...and what does her idiot husband do? Does he remember his marriage vows? Does he fight to make their marriage work? Does he behave like an honorable man? No...not on your life. Not only does he toss her aside, he humiliates her. Publicly. And for what? Some younger tramp..." He shifts in his seat, wincing as if he's in pain somewhere in his upper torso. "I...I even tried something to hurt that woman, I did. To make her feel some of the pain she and Harry had given to my daughter. To make it right. To make it all right."

I step closer, thinking if I get a bit nearer, I can tug that shotgun away from him and get into that house.

"Mister Fuller, please, is she here?"

"Go away."

"Mister Fuller, your daughter's in terrible danger. We've got to get her out of here."

He makes to speak and there's a *creak* as the door to the small farmhouse opens up.

Mister Fuller doesn't turn, or take notice.

But I take notice.

Grace Fuller Tucker, First Lady of the United States, Secret Service code name CANARY, steps out onto the porch. She looks tired. She has on black stretch riding slacks and a gray, shapeless sweatshirt, and her left hand is heavily bandaged.

"Agent Grissom," she says, voice tired. "What kind of danger am I in?"

# CHAPTER 68

PAUL MOODY LOVES flying, loves being in control, and especially loves hugging the terrain as he roars over the Virginia farmland, heading to the target farmhouse. To fly an aircraft or a helicopter several thousand feet above the ground takes little talent, about as much as driving a truck. But this... being alert, getting that adrenaline rush, sensitive to changes in the landscape and elevation, that takes skill.

He follows his instrumentation, looks up through the windshield, and—

Yep, there it is.

One practice swoop and then he'll be back, scorching the farmhouse and sending the ISIS terrorists inside to whatever hellish afterlife awaits them.

He and his Kiowa sweep over the farmhouse and then he goes into a wide curve, turns on the switches arming the two Hellfire missiles, and, remembering his job, he toggles the microphone once more and says, "This is GSS Tango Four, on target, weapons hot."

The nice female says, "GSS Tango Four, acknowledged."

His thumb gently caresses the button on top of his cyclic handle that—once armed—will send the two appropriately named Hellfire missiles on their way.

Not long now.

# CHAPTER 69

PARKER HOYT STARES and stares at his special phone, waiting to hear back from Munson at Global Strategic Solutions, who quickly agreed to cooperate with his earlier request. In his mind's eye he can see how this morning will unfold. First, that black ops helicopter from his past company will attack the farmhouse where, almost certainly, the First Lady is hiding out with her father.

*Boom.*

When that's done, he'll leak to the news the report of her missing finger and the ransom demand, conveniently leaving out the second part of the demand, a national weep-fest on television by the President, apologizing for his sins against his frigid wife.

With that whipping up the news media to a froth, eventually some fire department is going to respond to that burning farmhouse and extinguish the blaze. At some point they will find two bodies in the rubble, along with evidence that a propane tank— used to heat the building—had unexpectedly exploded.

Time for them to identify the bodies? Not too long, especially since one will be a female of a certain age, missing part of the pinky on her left hand.

And with more leaks coming from a shocked White House, the narrative will be established: Grace Fuller Tucker, First Lady of the United States, had been kidnapped and held for ransom at this remote farmhouse, owned by her father, and her father had been kidnapped as well.

For who would expect the FBI—in searching for the First Lady, a kidnap victim—to go to a property owned by her father?

And after the payment was made, no doubt the kidnappers went to some place with public Internet access to verify the transfer of funds, just as the house exploded.

What a horrible, terrible thing to have happened to the President of the United States.

And as for Munson and the helicopter pilot, well, of course they'll keep their mouths shut. They were expecting to eliminate a terrorist cell. Mistakes were made. Happens all the time.

There will be a funeral—the First Lady and her poor, dead father, interred together, either back home in Ohio, or if Parker Hoyt has his way, in Arlington National Cemetery. Parker is sure there are rules for who gets interred at Arlington, and he's also confident he can find a way to either break the rules or get around them.

And a few weeks after the funeral, the big-hearted and gracious voters of the United States will send Harrison Tucker back to the White House for a second term.

That's what Parker Hoyt is imagining.

That's what Parker Hoyt is anticipating.

If only the damn phone would ring.

# CHAPTER 70

THE FIRST LADY looks exhausted and it's apparent she's in pain from her severed finger, but I have no doubt she's still in control. She takes one more step onto the porch and says, "I know you. You're Agent Grissom."

"Yes, thank you, ma'am," I reply, "but we don't have time for this. I need to get you out of here as soon as possible. You're in terrible danger."

She looks over me and says, "Are you alone?"

"I have an SUV waiting for us at the bottom of the road." I step one more time closer to the porch and say, "Ma'am, I really must insist. The chief of staff, he—"

"The chief of staff is a pimp," she says. "Did he send you here? Does he know where I am?"

"Ma'am, my agents and I, we're here by ourselves," I say. "As far as I know, Mister Hoyt doesn't know you're here. But he means to do you harm. He's agreed to make the ransom payment, but he won't allow the President to make a national statement on his...indiscretions. And if that means causing you harm, I don't doubt he'll do it."

She looks to her father and says, "Dad, I told you that was too much."

"Don't care," her father says. "I wanted to hurt the son-of-a-bitch as much as he hurt you."

Enough is enough. I jump up on the porch, nearly stumble, and I grab the shotgun by the barrel and fling it onto the gravel behind me. Mister Fuller is so surprised he just sits there, and I grab the First Lady by her good arm and say, "Ma'am, we're leaving. I'm responsible for your safety, and I don't know how he's going to do it, but I know the chief of staff doesn't want you around. He sees you as an embarrassment."

I manage to propel her down the wooden steps, and she tries to wriggle out of my grasp. "Dad! Come along! Please!"

He shakes his head, stands up. "No politician or lackey is going to run me off my own property. You two get along. If somebody shows up, well, I won't be defenseless. I intend to get my shotgun back."

"Please, ma'am," I say, and I half-shove, half-drag her down the driveway. I swivel around, and true to his word, Mister Fuller is easing his way down the porch steps to retrieve his shotgun.

The First Lady doesn't put up much resistance and I bring my left arm up to my mouth, toggle the radio. "Scotty, Scotty, this is Grissom. Can you hear me?"

I push and drag. I repeat myself. "Scotty, Scotty, this is Grissom. I need you up here, with the Suburban. Now."

Still no answer.

We move about six or eight meters when I hear the sound of an engine, and I think, good, Scotty's heard me and he's on his way.

The First Lady says, "What's that over there?"

I look and see it's a helicopter, a Kiowa by the looks of it, and it's armed with a weapons pod on each side.

"Scotty, Scotty, this is Grissom! I need you now!"

Still no answer.

I look up at the approaching military-style helicopter and think, damn, too late.

# CHAPTER 71

PAUL MOODY NOTES the closing distance to the target farm-house when he spots something else: two figures racing down a dirt driveway.

Damn.

Members of the ISIS cell escaping?

His priority is striking the house, but he wants to get a good view of these two figures so he can supply a description later, help the Feds or whatever law enforcement agency is in charge, so these two can be scooped up later and maybe be sent to the tropical prison paradise that's GTMO.

There's a small video screen in his instrument dashboard, and with the onboard surveillance equipment pod stored over the rotors, he instantly gets a good view of the two figures.

Women, he thinks.

How about that.

It doesn't make much difference, for he has had sharp experience with old women, young women, girls who weren't even into their teens yet, and all of them were capable of firing off an RPG-7 or an AK-47, or coming at you, smiling and holding up a cold bottle of Coca-Cola while hiding a suicide bomb vest under their robes.

But these women . . .

They're no longer running.

They don't look armed.

They're waving at him.

Like they're happy to see him!

He slows his approach to the farmhouse, part of him thinking it's a trap, that they want him to hover so that somebody in the woods can fire off a rocket-propelled grenade and take out his main rotor, but the woman on the left . . . she looks,

Familiar?

He toggles another switch.

Zooms in the camera.

The military-grade technology is about a year or so out of date, but it's still good enough that he can make out the facial features of both women, and the one to the right, the taller of them, is waving frantically and—

He recognizes the woman on the left.

Recognizes her really well.

Good God, what has he gotten himself into?

# CHAPTER 72

MARSHA GRAY SEES the Kiowa swoop in over the house and knows from experience what the pilot is doing—just prepping a dry run so there's no surprises when he circles back to turn that farmhouse into charcoal and cinders.

Good ol' Parker Hoyt sure is escalating things. She has no doubt the flying death machine up there is operating under his direction, and if it looks like he's taking a Gatling gun to a knife fight, so be it.

She feels some satisfaction that this job is coming to a conclusion, but she's not pleased that she isn't the one wrapping things up. In some jobs you're the lead, and in others, you're backup, and if playing second fiddle was going to be her destiny today, well, she and her bank account will be all right with it.

The helicopter is coming back, racing along, just above the treetops, and with her binoculars up to her face, Marsha is admiring the man flying that Kiowa. Those guys are legendary for being nuts and loving a good fly and a good fight, and she's sure this job is going to be packed away in just under a minute.

The Kiowa gets larger, larger, and then—

It flares up, stops.

Just like that.

What the hell?

For a brief moment Marsha thinks the pilot is going to get up close and personal. She knows at least twice over in Afghanistan that crazy Kiowa pilots and crews would go up in the air with M4s across their laps, so they could shoot at the Taliban from inside their cockpits, very face-to-face—and very forbidden!— but she can't believe this pilot would be doing this.

What's he doing?

A few seconds pass.

Then the Kiowa...it wiggles back and forth, like it's waving, and then it roars off.

Damn it!

Marsha tosses her binoculars aside, grabs her Remington rifle and iPhone, and starts running.

The Kiowa pilot broke off for some reason, and now Marsha is no longer the backup, she's the primary. Parker Hoyt earlier said not to move unless she got a call from him, but there's no time. From here she can see the Secret Service agent and the First Lady are running down the driveway, but she doesn't have a clear shot.

She needs to haul ass and cut them off.

Marsha starts to run.

She's on the hunt.

She loves it.

# CHAPTER 73

AFTER CONFIRMING WITH his own mind that the First Lady is actually standing there in front of his Kiowa, Paul Moody is done for the day. He gives the women a good-luck wave by going side-to-side with the rotors, and with that, he's outta there.

With the target farmhouse and the two women behind him, now it's time to pass on the news. His finger hits the radio switch and he says, "This is GSS Tango Four, GSS Tango Four."

The cool and professional woman replies, "GSS Tango Four, go."

"GSS Tango Four, mission aborted. Repeat . . . mission aborted. Coming home."

His faceless contact is not impressed. "GSS Tango Four, return to target area. Complete your mission."

God, what a beautiful morning. "Sorry, darlin', ain't gonna happen."

"Those are your orders!"

"Ma'am, I'm no longer in the employ of Uncle Sam. I'm under contract to you-know-who, and I've just ended my contract."

She continues to sputter, and he switches the radio to another frequency.

Women.

He checks the fuel gauges, sees he has a number of hours of flying time available to him, but knowing how pissy Global Strategic Solutions can be, he better put this bird on the ground before his former employer sends up a couple of other birds to take him down. Unofficially, he'd die with a missile up the exhaust port or a close-in strafing with a thirty-caliber chain gun, but officially, he would die in a training accident, and that would be that.

Paul steers his Kiowa northwest. Up there outside of Rockville, Maryland, is a strip belonging to one of Global Strategic Solutions' competitors, Tyson International Services.

He wonders if they're hiring.

Only one way to find out.

# CHAPTER 74

SO ONCE AGAIN I'm running away from danger with a protectee at my side, like the hundreds of drills and training ex-
ercises I've participated in, except this one is no drill, and I'm
running, panting, so scared that I'm going to lose it all in the next
sixty seconds or so.

I wish I had taken a couple of agents along with me, so we
could be running with a protective screen around CANARY, but
it's too late for regrets or recriminations. I just want to run and
drag her down the driveway, get her into the relative safety of our
Suburban, and then get the hell out of here. Get someplace safe.
Like Pennsylvania or Delaware, anyplace miles away from here
and the District of Columbia.

"Agent . . . please . . . not so fast . . . please . . . not so fast . . ."

Fast? I feel like we're running in sloppy mud up to our
knees, and I swerve around, looking for that military helicopter,
knowing deep in my bones that it hadn't been out here for a
sightseeing trip.

But the helicopter has sped off.

Ordered off?

Or sent away because something else is coming in our direction?

I move as fast as I can dare, not wanting the First Lady to stumble and fall, wasting precious seconds in our fast exit. So many questions I want answered—from how did she end up here, to who had kidnapped her and severed her finger, and did she write that possible suicide note but—

Not enough time!

Not enough time!

I think of wasting five seconds or so, trying to raise Scotty again over my damn radio, but instead I push on, thinking that in those five seconds, I'll be that much closer to the armored Suburban and the four armed Secret Service agents within, and—

"Agent! Please!"

"Ma'am, I—"

Up ahead a small man emerges from the bush-covered slope, dressed in camo gear, carrying a long rifle with a telescopic sight, and the muscle memory from years of training kicks in.

"Gun!" I scream, and I whirl around, grabbing CANARY, protecting her with my body, enveloping her, just like the training, just like the training, just like—

The sound of the rifle shot and the hammer blow to my back happen in a brief second.

I fall into blackness.

Amelia, I think, poor, orphaned Amelia.

# CHAPTER 75

MARSHA GRAY RAISES her scoped Remington, nodding with satisfaction. Dead center to the back, and the bonus is that she isn't using a standard .308 cartridge, but rather what's known as a frangible round, something designed to break up easily upon striking, like the cartridges the air marshals use, so any gunfire in an airliner won't puncture the hull and cause a sudden depressurization.

Plus, this round is carrying the same type of poison that she used the other day against that poor kid Carl, back at the Hay-Adams Hotel. Any forensics testing will show that this over-worked and pressured government employee had died from sudden heart failure.

She works the bolt of the rifle, ejecting the spent cartridge, and then grabs the brass and runs up the dirt road, her battle-rattle gear jostling along, not wanting to leave any evidence behind. Marsha knows she only has a handful of seconds before those Secret Service clowns back there figure something is amiss after hearing a rifle shot blast through the morning air.

Marsha gets closer. The dead agent is sprawled over the First

Lady, who's struggling to get out from underneath the taller and heavier dead woman. She brings up her rifle, doesn't even bother using the scope, because at this range, she can't miss. She'll make the shot and then get the hell out, and leave behind the mystery of how a Secret Service agent and the First Lady both died of apparent heart attacks at the same time in the same place.

So what, she thinks. Folks still can't figure out how and why Jack Ruby nailed Lee Harvey Oswald back in the day, and this will just be one more mystery for the ages.

The First Lady is talking, pleading, mouth moving, and Marsha just ignores the sounds, starts squeezing the trigger —

As the agent rolls over, brings up an automatic pistol, and shoots Marsha three times in the chest.

# CHAPTER 76

I'M CONSCIOUS AND my back is hurting like hell, and I hear the rattle of someone's camo gear as he approaches, and when I think he's close enough to take the shot, I roll over and quickly squeeze the trigger of my SIG Sauer three times, hitting the gunman right in the center chest, three times in the 10-ring mark at a shooting range, and he flips right onto his back, even though he's probably wearing a vest.

I stand up and go over to him, pick up his rifle, toss it down the road, as four agents come racing up, all of them with their service weapons out, all of them moving like sprinters, and I say, "Clear!" and get back to CANARY.

She's trembling, eyes wide.

"Ma'am, are you all right?" I ask. "Are you injured?"

The First Lady shakes her head, starts to get up. I lift her up with one arm and a weeping Pamela Smithson, her detail lead, helps her up on the other side.

"No, I'm fine, I'm fine…just had the wind knocked out of me…but Agent, that man, he shot you. Are you all right?"

"I think so," I say. I look over and see Tanya, Scotty, and Brian examining the gunman, and I take off my scarf, and then my wool coat. I wince. I feel like there's going to be one hell of a bruise back there by this time tomorrow morning, if I'm still alive.

Pamela looks with me as I examine my coat. There's a tear in Amelia's scarf, and another, smaller tear in my coat, and what appear to be fragments of some ceramic that is dissolving before my eyes.

Pamela whistles. "Boss, you should buy a lottery ticket when this day is done, 'cause you're the luckiest woman alive. That looks like a round the air marshals use, to break up on impact. It broke up, all right, on that damn thick scarf and coat of yours."

"Not lucky yet," I say, putting my coat and scarf back on. The other three agents are still standing over the body of the gunman, and I say, "What do you got? Does he have any ID on him?"

Scotty calls back. "He's a she, boss, and she's still alive, though barely. Underneath all this camouflage, she had on a Kevlar vest."

Tanya says, "Too goddamn bad, I say."

Smithson is now talking to the First Lady, and I go over, look down at the gunman, a slight frame that is dark-skinned, in uniform, and I think—

I have no real evidence, but I'm certain Ben's killer is on the ground before me, unconscious.

I have to take a deep breath, focus, and restrain myself, so I don't put a fourth round in her head.

I say, "Any ID?"

"Nothing," Tanya says.

"Any radio, or cell phone, or anything?"

Brian says, "Nothing, ma'am. Looks like she's clean."

*Focus*, I think, *focus*.

"Tanya, get back down to the road, get the Suburban up here right away."

"You got it, Sally."

She runs back down the driveway, and I reach around to my belt, tug out my handcuffs, toss them to Brian. "Secure the prisoner," I say, "and tight."

"On it," he says.

There's the roar of the Suburban as it comes bouncing up the trail, skids to a halt. Tanya jumps out from the driver's side, leaving the engine running.

"Pamela! Get CANARY in the rear."

She doesn't answer, but she pushes and propels the First Lady into the Suburban and slams the door. A constricting feeling in my chest has just lightened up some. In the Suburban, she's not perfectly safe, but she's a hell of a lot safer than she was five minutes ago.

"What the hell is going on down there?" comes a voice, and Mister Fuller is limping his way down the road, and Tanya and Scotty react as if he's another threat, until I say, "Stand down, stand down. That's CANARY's father."

No time for explanations, or questions, or anything else.

Now it makes sense. This remote cabin was the other place where a stressed First Lady could be happy and relaxed.

"Scotty and I are leaving with CANARY," I say. "Pamela, you, Tanya, and Brian stay behind, guard the prisoner, start calling law enforcement, and make sure the prisoner gets to the hospital alive, got it? I don't want any accidents between here and the hospital. That shooter is to stay alive, and I don't care who you guys have to kill to make it happen."

Like the good agent she is, Pamela nods in agreement. "What should we tell the locals when they get here?"

"Anything you like," I say. "No one will believe you anyway. Scotty, let's go."

In a few seconds we're in the Suburban. Scotty makes a sloppy U-turn, and we're bouncing back down the dirt road. I look out the rear and see Mister Fuller is trying to talk to Pamela, who's on her cell phone, and Brian is kneeling right next to the shooter, putting on the handcuffs, while Tanya stands, aiming her pistol down.

"Where to, boss?" Scotty says as we hit the pavement of East Dominion Road.

"No idea," I say. "Just drive until I think of something."

# CHAPTER 77

PARKER HOYT IS again pacing in his office when his special phone rings, and he nearly trips over his own feet, rushing to get to it.

He grabs it, noting his hand is moist from worry.

"Yes?"

Hiss, pop, crackle of static.

"Hello?" he asks again.

Another burst of static, and a voice says, "It's over."

He collapses in his chair with relief. "Thank God."

The voice says, "You should get out of town. Like, now."

"Why?" he asks. "You told me it was over."

"Well, the phone must have dropped the first part," the voice says. "It's over because CANARY's been recovered and she's safe."

Parker closes his eyes, willing that the voice on the other end of the line will say something else, hoping he is pulling some sort of stunt to get more pay, more prestige, more anything.

"What happened?" Parker asks.

"A female shooter ambushed CANARY and Grissom as they were leaving a property in Virginia that belonged to CANARY's dad. Grissom did her job, and CANARY's still alive."

*Damn, damn, damn,* he thinks.

The shooter.

Marsha Gray, of course. Good lord.

"Is the shooter dead?"

"Not at the moment," the caller says. "She took three nine-millimeter rounds to the chest, broke her sternum and a few ribs. She's unconscious at the moment."

Marsha Gray, alive.

*All right,* he thinks. *Her word against his. It'll mean—*

"Another thing," the caller says. "She had an iPhone with her. Could only open it with her thumbprint, but I managed to do so. Found lots of interesting recordings there . . . taped conversations between you and her."

A long pause and Parker feels like he's about five seconds away from having a coronary event.

"Name your price," he says. "I need to have that iPhone."

"We'll deal later," the voice says. "In the meantime, I gotta go."

Parker sits up in his chair. "Wait, wait, please . . . don't hang up."

"Make it quick."

Parker rubs his head. "You . . . are you in a position . . . I mean, can you . . ."

"Can I what?"

Parker takes a deep breath that makes him feel like knives are being dug into his lungs. "Can you . . . finish the shooter's mission?"

No reply.

The hiss of static.

More crackling and popping noises.

Is his caller still there?

The voice speaks up, tone firm.

"I'll think about it."

And hangs up.

# CHAPTER 78

WHILE SCOTTY IS trying to find someplace to park our Suburban, I'm at the door of a pretty yet not-too-fancy townhouse in a wooded section of Laurel, Maryland, which is about eight miles away from my sister's place of employment at Fort Meade.

I ring the doorbell, wait, arm around CANARY. We're both exhausted, woozy on our feet, and her face winces from the pain that's no doubt coursing up her left arm, while my own lower back is throbbing like it's getting punched over and over again.

I ask, "How are you doing, ma'am?"

"Please, call me Grace."

"Not going to happen, ma'am," I say.

I ring the doorbell again, a dark thought coming to me—suppose something has happened to Gwen, to get at Amelia? That could work, grabbing my daughter...

"This is your sister's place? Are you sure she's going to let us stay?"

"She has to," I say. "She's family."

And thank God I can see movement through a curtain-covered window, and the door opens, and it's my sister Gwen all right, wearing an apron, her hands dusted with white flour, and also bearing one surprised and confused look on her face.

"Sally, I mean—Mrs. Tucker, uh, come in, come in," she says, and we go in and I close the door behind us and lock it.

From the kitchen I hear Amelia call out, "Who's there, Aunt Gwen?" and I have to fight so hard not to run into the kitchen and scoop up Amelia and quit the Secret Service right here and now, and leave and take her with me.

I say, "Gwen, the rear door to this place. Is it locked?"

Gwen, bless her, snaps to and says, "I think so, but I'll double-check. Be right back."

As she hustles out I move the First Lady into the living room on the right, then draw the curtains. The doorbell rings, and I slide out my SIG Sauer and gently pull one of the curtains aside.

It's Scotty.

I unlock the door and let him in.

"Took you long enough," I say.

"I wanted to give the parking lot a quick look-see," he says, putting his own pistol away in its holster. "Didn't see any un-marked vans or single guys sitting in cars, watching the place."

By now my little girl has heard all the voices and comes run-ning in, wearing an apron three times her size, her hands covered with flour as well, and she screeches, "Mommy!" and that's it, I'm no longer a Secret Service agent, just one tired and frightened mother.

"Oh, honey," I call out, and I hug her and kiss her, and hug her some more, and she complains, "Mommy, not so tight!" and I can't speak back because my eyes are full and my throat feels like it's stuffed with cotton.

After some minutes pass, Amelia is gently banished into the spare bedroom that's temporarily hers, and when she says,

"Will you have some chocolate chip cookies later? Me and Aunt Gwen made them!"—and of course we all say yes, including the First Lady—for the first time today there's actually a slight smile on her face.

Gwen brings us all coffee in the living room, and I have my pistol out on the coffee table, and I recall something, then pop out the magazine and put a fresh one in. Three rounds have already been expended, and I want fourteen full rounds available if need be.

My sister watches me and says, "I wouldn't worry too much. My house is scrubbed."

The First Lady speaks up. "What does that mean?"

Scotty's pistol is in his lap, and he's maneuvered his chair so that it's facing the door. "It means, ma'am, that this house, the utility bills, and everything else are under a different name. Not her own, so she can't be traced."

CANARY says, "Are you a spy?"

"Not brave enough," she says. "Just read and think a lot."

I finish reloading my pistol and say, "I imagine you're wondering why I'm here, along with . . . Mrs. Tucker."

"Good guess."

"Best you don't know much," I say.

Gwen smirks. "Like need-to-know? You know how many times I've heard that?"

"Still," I say, "it might help out if this all goes to a congressional investigation one of these days."

She nods. "I see. What can I do?"

"We need to spend the night," I say.

"Deal."

"Among other things," I say.

Gwen nods. "Deal again. Anything else?"

Not being on the run and being in my sister's warm and comfortable and so far safe home, makes me feel like I'm about to fall asleep in the chair.

"We need to get the First Lady someplace safe, which isn't the White House. Or the Eisenhower Executive Office Building. Or any other government place."

CANARY speaks up. "I may have a thought or two about that."

I slowly nod. "I thought you might."

# CHAPTER 79

AFTER SOME HOT tomato soup and French bread, followed by chocolate chip cookies—and Amelia is so proud of how good they are that I have to turn my head to hide my tears—I clean up and find my way, along with Amelia, to her bedroom. CANARY is going to sleep in Gwen's room, Gwen is going to make do with a pullout couch, and Scotty has a blanket and a foam mattress on the kitchen floor.

Gwen lets me borrow a pair of sweatpants and an old T-shirt, and I say, "Sis . . . I owe you so much."

She gives the two of us a quick hug and kiss and says, "Not another word. Get to sleep, all right?"

She leaves and closes the bedroom door. A small nightlight illuminates part of the bedroom. I snuggle in and move around, and Amelia is there, and I spoon with her and have sweet flashbacks of the many, many times we slept together when she had a nightmare or was scared of thunder or something else. Ben would grumble (poor Ben!) but secretly I just liked the scent and warmth of my little girl. Even the pain in my lower back seems better.

"Mom?" she whispers.

"Yes, hon."

"I miss Daddy."

The words just slip out, like truth often does. "Me, too, honey. Me too."

Her shoulders start to shudder and I know she's crying, and I let it be. She rustles around, and I sense her wiping her nose with a bedsheet.

"He was brave, Mommy, wasn't he?"

"Your daddy was very, very brave," I say. "One of the bravest men I know."

"And he didn't even have a gun. He went after that bad man, and he didn't even have a gun."

"That's right. He wanted to protect you, like a brave daddy does, and that's what he did."

She snuggles up against me and I can't quite believe it, but I'm drifting off. So much to think about, so much to do, but after the last forty-eight hours, my body is surrendering.

"You're brave, too, Mom."

"No, no I'm not."

"That nice lady downstairs. The one with the hurt hand. She told me you were brave."

I rest there, thinking, and say, "Are you sure?"

"Uh-huh," Amelia says. "That nice lady told me…that I should be proud. That my mother was the bravest woman that lady ever knew." And Amelia raises her voice just a bit. "And who is she, Mom? She looks familiar. And how did she hurt her hand?"

I brush her hair with my hand. "Go to sleep, hon. Go to sleep. We'll talk more in the morning."

No pushback from my little girl.

Thank God for small miracles.

\*　　\*　　\*

At some point during the night the bedroom door slides open, and someone comes into the bedroom, and from underneath my pillow I grab my pistol and roll over to cover Amelia's body, and Gwen whispers, "Boy, always on the job, huh?"

I get off Amelia so as not to wake her, and my younger sister comes around the foot of the bed and kneels on the carpeted floor next to me. "You doing all right?"

"I think I am," I say, yawning. "What's up?"

I see she has some sheets of paper in her hand. "Sorry to say this, Sally, but you guys need to leave. Now."

# CHAPTER 80

THERE'S HUSTLE AND bustle, and soon enough, I'm in the living room with Scotty and the First Lady, and we're dressed and ready to go. Gwen passes over a lumpy envelope to me that I slide into my coat while no one is looking, and while we're all yawning and rubbing our eyes, Scotty is as sharp as ever.

My lower back still aches.

"Are you sure we need to do this?" he asks.

"Very sure," I say, looking to my sister, who says, "Amelia's still sleeping."

I choke up. "You tell her ... you tell her ..."

Gwen comes to me, squeezes my hand.

"I'm going to tell her that she can have scrambled eggs or pancakes. That's what I'm going to tell her."

I squeeze her hand back. "That sounds fine."

Scotty is next to CANARY, who says, "Why are we going so early? And where are we going?"

"I'll tell you in a moment, ma'am," I say. "But first things first ... Scotty. Will you do a sweep of the parking lot and come back with the Suburban?"

"On it, boss," he says, and he unlocks the door, and then slips out. I give him a few seconds, and motioning to the First Lady, we follow him.

We step outside on the small sidewalk. The sun is up, but it's still damn early. The First Lady is dressed, and she holds her bandaged left hand awkwardly, but I'm not in the mood for interrogating her.

I'm in the mood for my primary job.

Off in the distance among the parked cars I see the form of Scotty, looking around, making sure that there's no one out there with bad intent, waiting.

I can't help myself. I yawn. The First Lady smiles and says, "Still pretty tired."

I say, "Some days my only goal in life is to be someplace where I never have to set an alarm, ever again, so I only wake up when my body tells me."

A car suddenly starts up, and I reach for my pistol, then relax. It's a woman in a silver Lexus, slowly going by, drinking from a travel mug of coffee. She waves at us both, and we wave back, and she drives on, ignorant of whom she's just passed.

I say, "Earlier you said you had an idea of a safe place where we might go."

"I did," CANARY replies.

I slide my hand into my coat, to the lumpy envelope that my sister has just given me.

"Now's a good time to let me know," I say.

# CHAPTER 81

TAMMY DOYLE IS in her office at Pearson, Pearson, and Price, pleased that she was brave enough to pass through the front doors of her firm this morning. With the news about the missing First Lady, the stakeout has thinned, with most reporters and TV crews heading out to the newer and juicier story in Virginia.

She knows the equations of news very well.

What gets more attention?

A live mistress or a dead First Lady?

A slight knock on the door and Ralph Moren, the group's admin aide, comes in, bearing a cup of coffee, and he says, "You're looking pretty fine this morning."

"Thanks, Ralph."

He passes the cup of coffee to her, and before she can take a sip, he says confidentially, "There's a phone call for you."

"Who is it?"

"You won't believe it," he says, smiling.

"Try me."

"Lucian Crockett."

Tammy is stunned, remembering the last time she heard that name, back at her condo. "There's a mistake. Amanda's been trying for months to reel him in as a client."

Her assistant smiles and shakes his head. "No mistake. He asked for you directly and specifically." Ralph gestures to her phone. "Line three, Tammy. Don't keep him waiting."

Ralph leaves, but Tammy does keep Lucian waiting because she's trying to process what's going on. Lucian Crockett is the CEO of the nation's largest fracking and gas recovery corporation in the American Southwest, and the lobbying firm of Pearson, Pearson, and Price—and especially Amanda—have been trying to get him and his billions of dollars of assets under the firm's lobbying umbrella.

Tammy stops hesitating. She picks up the receiver, punches in the switch for line three, and says, "Tammy Doyle here."

"Miss Doyle?" comes a gravelly and self-assured voice. "Lucian Crockett here. Thanks for taking my call."

"My pleasure, Mister Crockett. Thanks for calling. What can I do for you?"

He laughs. "I always love doing things informally. Drives my accountants crazy. May I call you Tammy, Miss Doyle?"

"Certainly."

There are voices raised out in the common office area, but Tammy ignores the commotion. "Then you can call me Lucian," he replies. "Look, I know you're a busy woman, and you've been in the news lately, so I'll make this quick and to the point. I want your company to represent me and my folks, the sooner the better. We need to get a jump on a lot of permitting and zoning issues, and your company has just the kind of folks we need to push things along."

Tammy says, "Well, that's wonderful news indeed, Mister, er,

Lucian. But I know you've been in discussions with my boss, Amanda Price, and—"

His cheerful voice quickly turns to ice. "Amanda? Well... 'tween you and me, Tammy, that bitch has been playin' with me for months, like a cheerleader dating a star football player, taggin' and taggin' him along, and I'm tired of it."

"Well—"

"My wife and my mother, bless 'em both, well, they've seen you on the TV. They like how you hold your head high. They don't like the way Tucker has treated you. And I told 'em that you worked for Pearson, Pearson and Price..., well, they advised me..."—and he chuckles, like he and Tammy both know what the word *advised* means—"that I should go with your company, but deal only with you. And not Amanda Price."

Tammy's heart is thumping with joy, thinking of the millions of dollars that will be coming into the firm, and all thanks to her. "Well, Lucian, that's highly irregular, and—"

"Here's the deal," Lucian says. "Yes or no, don't have time to keep on dickin' around... last time Amanda and I chatted, she said her last offer was the best she could do, take it or leave it. Seems she felt like she had to charge me more in case she loses some of her nature-loving clients 'cause of what we do. Bitch. Okay, I'm gonna take the offer, but it's gonna be with you and only you. Make myself clear?"

Tammy's thoughts are racing. Amanda will say this is impossible, that she won't allow it to happen, but the other partners in the firm... they'll smile and make it happen.

"Lucian, you've got yourself a deal," Tammy says, smiling.

When she's done, she goes out to the common area and sees what the fuss is all about. There's a television set on in the corner, and she pushes her way through to see—

Grace Fuller Tucker, First Lady of the United States.

She's smiling, laughing, and there are small children around her, hugging and giggling, and on the walls are finger paintings and drawings, and in the crowd near the First Lady, Tammy spots the Secret Service agent who had earlier interviewed her.

"What's going on?" Tammy asks.

One of her coworkers says, "The First Lady's alive. Seems like she fell in the river while riding her horse, got knocked out, hurt her hand... managed to crawl to a barn... Secret Service found her this morning."

Tammy watches the First Lady smile and smile, sees the joy and pleasure in her eyes, standing alone and strong, and proud and defiant, and someone says, "She looks awful."

"No," Tammy says. "She looks wonderful."

# CHAPTER 82

EARLIER GRACE FULLER TUCKER had been chilled, hungry, and her left hand had been throbbing with slow pangs of pain, but now she's warm, happy, and feels oh so safe.

She's back at A Happy Place Forever, the homeless shelter in Anacostia she had visited before leaving the East Wing on the day the scandal broke, and with the children, her staff, and Agent Grissom around her and television crews coming in one after another, she feels invulnerable.

The questions are now coming at her, like fast-pitch softballs back when she was on the softball team at OSU, and like she did back in the day, she's hammering them.

"Mrs. Tucker, what happened to your hand?"

She holds up her left hand. "I'm not sure. I think when I fell in the stream, I crushed my little finger somehow. It's doing better, thanks."

"Mrs. Tucker, who treated it?"

"The Secret Service...they gave me initial care. I'll be off to George Washington later this morning to have a medical professional look at it."

"And your head?"

She widens her smile, takes her good hand, rubs the back of her neck. "Despite the best efforts of the Taccanock River and of Arapahoe, it seems to be still attached."

Some laughter from the staff and even some members of the rapidly growing press corps.

"Mrs. Tucker, do you know there's been an extensive search for you these past few days?"

A little African-American boy is hugging her so tightly, and she just reaches down and squeezes a bony shoulder. "I know...and I'm most grateful for those who took part in the search. You have my deepest gratitude."

"Mrs. Fuller, why are you here and not at the White House? Or a hospital?"

She says, "I know it sounds odd, but I wanted a little pick-me-up before going to the hospital...and this is the perfect place to get that."

Another hug from the boy at her side, and she wonders if anyone out there is noticing that she's not saying anything about returning to the White House.

The cameras are flashing, microphones are being extended to her, and the bright lights from the television cameras make the interior of this homeless shelter for children look like it's in Phoenix at high noon.

But she's waiting, waiting for that question that's going to come her way, and sure enough, here it comes.

"Mrs. Fuller...if I may...and I'm sorry to bring this up, but do you have any comment about the apparent relationship your husband is having with a K Street lobbyist?"

One more wide smile, one more squeeze of the homeless boy's shoulders.

"No, I don't," she says.

# CHAPTER 83

FOUR DAYS AGO, when I came into the Oval Office, the President and the chief of staff had been sitting on a couch, asking me to sit across from them in an inviting and open manner.

Not today.

The President is sitting behind his desk, and Parker Hoyt is standing by his side. They both have grim looks on their faces, like attorneys who've just learned the governor has turned down the last chance for clemency for their death-row client.

That's all right.

This will be my last visit to this office, and if I'm lucky, the last time I talk to either of them.

Parker Hoyt looks to the Man, and I jump right in.

"Mister President, I know the news has reached you already, but I'm pleased to report that the First Lady has been recovered," I say. "Save for her little finger and some bumps and scrapes, she's doing fine."

President Tucker looks to his chief of staff, as if he's seeking some reassurance, and I say, "I'm sure you're pleased, no matter the status of your...marriage, that Grace Tucker is alive and reasonably well. But as to Mister Hoyt...I feel you should know that he has been working behind your back to hinder this investigation."

Parker Hoyt's face flushes, and he says, "Agent Grissom, you are way the hell out of line. Leave. Now."

"Not until I finish my briefing to the President."

"Out!" Parker shouts, pointing to the near Oval Office door. "Now!"

I stride right up and get into his face, give it right back. "I don't work for you, Mister Hoyt! I serve in this White House at the pleasure of the President, and only him! If he wants me to depart, I'll do so, but not one goddamn second earlier!"

We lock eyes, and without shifting my head, I say, "Mister President?"

Oh my, this pause only goes on for a few seconds, but it seems like hours.

Then the President, in a soft voice, says, "Agent Grissom, please continue."

I smile at Hoyt, back away.

"Sir," I say, "in the course of my investigation, I've learned that your chief of staff, Parker Hoyt, has been in contact with his former employer, Global Strategic Solutions, and an independent contractor, Marsha Gray, a former Marine sniper. This woman was in constant contact with Mister Hoyt and was working under Mister Hoyt's direction."

The President's hands are clenched, and he stands up behind his desk.

"Parker?"

The chief of staff's eyes flicker, and I can sense his reptilian, political mind racing along, almost at light speed. "Mister President, that's not true. And you know it. Agent Grissom...you know she's been under tremendous pressure, and with the death of her husband—"

I keep my suspicions about Ben's killer to myself, and say, "Mister President, your chief of staff wasn't interested in rescuing the First Lady. He was interested in having her killed."

Face flushed, Parker says, "Harry... don't listen to her. She doesn't know what she's talking about. Look, you've known me for years, long years. I've always had your best interests at heart. Don't listen to her."

"Mister President," I say, "did you know that Mister Hoyt has a secure phone in his office that bypasses the White House communications system?"

He pauses. "I seem to recall a slight mention of it... right after the inauguration."

"That's how Mister Hoyt communicated with his former company and the Marine sniper. The sniper who came close to murdering the First Lady yesterday."

Hoyt's face is so red it looks like he's just emerged from a tanning booth. "Prove it."

I reach inside my plain black jacket, unfold three sheets of paper. "Mister President... these are phone records, listing the time and location of phone calls made between Mister Hoyt, his former company, and the arrested Marine sniper."

I put them on the President's desk. Hoyt says, "A forgery. It's a forgery, Mister President."

I say, "No, it's not a forgery. And a call from the President to the director of the National Security Agency at Fort Meade can confirm it. This phone listing... it's not evidence that can be admitted in court, but Mister President... I know you'll find it useful."

CANAL reaches over, his hand trembling, picks up the papers. He starts to look at them.

Hoyt is staring at me with pure, unadulterated hate.

It feels good, being on the other side of his hate.

I say, "If you gentlemen will excuse me, I need to leave."

I turn and walk to the curved door, and I can't resist.

"Mister Hoyt, if you'll recall our last conversation," I say, "you advised me to hire the very best lawyer I could afford."

I open the door before stepping out. "I suggest you take your own advice."

# CHAPTER 84

SEVEN FEET BELOW the Oval Office—I'm morbidly curious about how that conversation up there is going—I go to my desk, sit down, and just put my head in my hands.

A few moments pass, and then I get to work.

No time to waste.

The other agents studiously ignore me, as I find an empty cardboard box and two plastic grocery bags and slowly and carefully start packing up my personal belongings, putting them in, hating each second, but knowing it has to be done.

The door to W-17 opens up and my deputy, Scotty, walks in, sees what I'm doing, and comes over and sits down next to my desk.

"Boss," he says.

"Scotty," I reply.

I reach over my desk, pick up one of my last mementos, the carved-wood sign made by Amelia, SALLY GRISSOM, AWESOME AGENT, though I don't feel very awesome at the moment.

"Pretty quiet there, Scotty."

He doesn't say a word.

"I'm wondering why you're not asking me why I left you behind at my sister's place and borrowed her car to take the First Lady over to that homeless shelter."

Scotty says quietly, "You probably had your reasons."

"Good reasons," I say. "Let's not play around, okay? Show me some respect. I've seen the phone records. Just tell me...what did Hoyt promise you?"

My deputy's jaw clenches, unclenches, and there's probably a little battle going on, about what to say next, and Scotty says, "Your job. Plus a great career down the road at his company."

I nod. "Not thirty pieces of silver, I guess, but it'll do. And now's the time for me to ask, why?"

A slight shrug. "Nothing personal, boss. I did three tours overseas. I'm ex-Ranger. I've done things that you could only have nightmares about...and I'm supposed to be bossed around by a former Metro and Virginia State Cop? A woman?" Another slight shrug. "Not acceptable."

I keep my anger and outrage under control. "All right, thanks for telling me that."

I open up my drawer, rummage around, don't see anything personal in there, and I say, "My sister also told me you were restless last night, getting up a few times, like you were trying to sneak through the living room and come upstairs to where CANARY was sleeping. But my sister sure is a light sleeper, isn't she?"

Scotty doesn't respond. I give the drawer one last look, close it, and look up. Scotty is still there.

"Well?" I say. "Is there anything else?"

Now he finally looks uncomfortable. "Um, well, what now?"

"Beats the hell out of me," I say. "I'm ending my employment with the Secret Service and Homeland Security, effective...in about ten minutes. Upstairs I believe the President is in the middle of dismissing his chief of staff. At some point there may or may not be a congressional investigation, depending how this election turns out. But I'm certain there'll be some sort of internal and confidential Secret Service review as to what the hell went on here during the past few days. If not, an anonymous phone call to Homeland Security's Office of the Inspector General will certainly get things moving."

He stays quiet.

In the meantime Scotty, you're going to get what you want, to be in charge of the Presidential Protective Division," I gently place Amelia's sign into the top of the crowded box.

I force myself to smile. "Enjoy it while you can."

# CHAPTER 85

A SONG IN one's heart and a spring in one's step, that's how the saying goes, and Tammy Doyle is feeling it as she strides across the main office area—filled with rows of cubicles—now heading down a hallway and right up to the closed door of Amanda Price's corner office, quickly passing by her two administrative assistants, grabbing the doorknob, and walking right in.

A week ago she would have never considered doing something so rude and forward.

But a week is a lifetime ago.

Amanda Price, smoking a cigarette and on the phone with someone, looks up and says, "What the hell is going on, Tammy? Is the place on fire? Or has the President finally proposed marriage?"

The corner office has a great view of K Street and the surrounding buildings, the best in the company. "I need to talk to you, Amanda."

Phone in hand, Amanda puts her cigarette down in the crowded ashtray. "I can see you in an hour."

"Now."

Amanda's inked eyebrows lift up some. "Don't push me, Tammy."

"If I don't see you now," Tammy says, "you're going to be the one pushed. Out the front door."

Amanda speaks into the phone. "Jeb, sorry, something's come up. I'll call you back in sixty seconds. Promise."

Amanda slams the phone receiver down and starts in on Tammy, and Tammy yells back, "Enough! Amanda, I've been here some years and that's the last time you're ever going to raise your voice to me. Ever."

That gets her attention. She folds her hands before her, forming a slim and strong triangle. "I told Jeb I'd be calling him back in sixty seconds. You've got about thirty seconds left before I fire your ass and make that phone call."

Tammy says, "Lucian Crockett."

That puzzles her. "Go on."

"I just got off the phone with him. He's ready to do business with the company . . . but only through me."

Amanda clenches her fingers together into a fist. "You shouldn't have talked to him. When he called, you should have transferred the call to me. He and his company belong to me. I've been working to sign him up for months. Months!"

Tammy says, "Not my choice. He wanted to talk to me, and he made it quite clear: he and his company will do business with Pearson, Pearson, and Price, but only with me. Not you."

She reaches for her phone. "Get the hell out of here. Now."

"If you're thinking about calling Lucian, I wouldn't do it, Amanda. He doesn't like you. His wife and mother don't like you. The only reason they're coming here is via me." Tammy steps forward for emphasis. "If you go around me and try to mess this up, within the hour, the board of directors will hear from me on how you sabotaged a deal worth millions of dollars."

Amanda's finely manicured hand is still on her phone. "Are you testing me?"

"Not a test, Amanda. A statement of fact. Lucian Crockett is coming aboard, and I'm supplying the ticket."

She slowly draws her hand back. She looks at Tammy, looks out the windows, then back at Tammy.

Something resembling a smile creases her face. "Well...I suppose some arrangement can be made...for the good of the company."

"I agree, Amanda. For the good of the company. I'm glad you see it that way."

Silence, and Tammy decides to push it. "That's very understanding of you, Amanda. And I need to understand something else. Back when you...broke into my condo, and after I told you I had been in a car accident, you said traffic can be awful on Interstate Sixty-six. How did you know I was on Sixty-six? I didn't tell you. Did you arrange that accident?"

She shakes her head. "No...Tammy, there are corners I will cut, lines I will cross, but not something like...that. No."

Amanda glances with longing at her slowly burning cigarette. "Information. That's all. I always look to get information about our clients and our employees. Your name is on a list, that's all. And I got a phone call from a source of mine at the Virginia State Police, telling me about your accident. That's all."

Tammy says, "Fair enough." She turns and starts to the office door. "By the way, before you call Jeb back, make another call, will you? By the end of the week, I want a bigger office, with a better view."

The smile on that painted face disappears, but her voice is agreeable. "I don't see why not."

She leaves Amanda, and just before she gets to her soon-to-be former office, her cell phone rings and she notices the familiar incoming number.

Tammy feels it'll be the last time a call from this number will ever be received on her phone.

# CHAPTER 86

OUTSIDE OF THE Oval Office, it looks like it's going to rain. The President of the United States slowly sits down, and when his chief of staff makes to do the same, Harrison Tucker holds up a hand.

"You can keep standing," he says, so very tired and worn. "You won't be here long."

"Mister President, I—"

Tucker motions him to keep quiet. He says, "I blame myself, I guess, Parker. I got the first taste of power back in Ohio, loved it, and you just kept on feeding it and feeding it to me. Like an addict and his relationship with a pusher."

"Harry—"

Tucker shakes his head. "It's over. Get out and have your resignation on my desk within the hour. I'll be polite, I'll let you depart with my thanks and praise, but that's it, Parker. You're through."

His chief of staff walks around the front of his desk and leans over, both hands on the top of the Resolute desk. "You goddamn fool—put on your big-boy pants and listen to me. All right?

Listen to me! That bitch Secret Service agent...she's bluffing. She won't go public. She won't go to the press. We just need to get through the next four weeks and have you win the election. That's all. Just win the damn election."

Tucker feels like all he has accomplished, all he has built, all he's done since coming here to 1600 Pennsylvania Avenue is finished, done, spoiled because of this man standing in front of him.

"You wanted my wife dead. Get out."

"I wanted you re-elected. And if it meant losing that cold bitch—"

Tucker abruptly stands up, so he's practically nose-to-nose with his chief of staff. "All right, now you're out of here—I want your resignation, and I'm going to keep my mouth shut and let you twist in the wind. Get out!"

Hoyt says, "You're only here because I put you here, and this is how you pay me back?"

"You turn and start walking, or I'll have the Secret Service come in and drag you away. You want that on the front page of tomorrow's *Washington Post*?"

Hoyt turns and walks across the carpet, out of the curved door, not shutting it behind him.

Tucker slowly sits down.

He feels so terribly alone, isolated, even in this people's house with hundreds nearby.

Only one thing he can do.

He reaches for his phone.

# CHAPTER 87

AND TAMMY DOYLE gets inside her office door as her phone rings one more time, and she answers, and a woman says, "Miss Doyle?"

"Yes?"

"The White House calling," the woman says. "Please hold for the President."

For a long time that little greeting—"Please hold for the President"—had always thrilled her, making her feel oh so special and loved and cherished.

Now?

Tammy just feels dread.

"Oh, thank you," she says, and a quiet *click*, and that familiar voice comes on.

"Tammy?"

She walks to her small office window, thinking with anticipation of how much better her view will be by this time next week.

"Hello, Harry," she says.

She hears his sigh. "Damn...it's good to hear your voice. It really is. And I need to talk to you."

"Harry, glad to hear that Grace has been found. I didn't even know she was missing. Did you?"

Her lover seems startled by the question. "Well, there were indications…here and there…but look, Tammy, I know the past few days have been rough. I haven't been fair to you, or open. And I'm deeply sorry. In just a few weeks…the election will be over. And then we can start seeing each other again."

Tammy keeps on looking out at DC, such a faraway and fairy-tale place from the tenement building she had grown up in back in South Boston.

A fairy-tale place, she thinks. With evil kings and queens, with plots and betrayals, and the constant struggle for power.

"Tammy? I…love you, hon. I really do."

Those sweet words have now changed. They're just…words.

Below her small office, a taxicab honks its horn.

"Harry, I love you, too. But I'm going to miss you as well."

"Tammy…what are you saying?"

She earlier thought this call would be hard, or depressing, or upsetting, but no, she's finding it…

Empowering.

Liberating.

She says, "Harry, we had a grand time, with special memories. And I promise I'll never violate the confidence of what we shared. I'll keep those secrets forever. But I can't try to go back to what we had. It's impossible. It's time for the both of us to move on."

"Tammy, please, give us a chance, give us some time."

She says, "No, Harry, I'm sorry. My life is going to be mine, and mine alone. I'm not going to be connected to you in the future. I won't be a second First Lady, or the very first presidential girlfriend. I saw what happened to Grace. I'm not going to let it happen to me."

"Oh, Tammy . . ."

And for the first time in months, she uses that old, formal phrase.

"Good-bye, Mister President."

# CHAPTER 88

THE PRESIDENT OF the United States sits alone in the Oval Office.

The rain is coming down hard now, streaking and streaming down the French doors behind his desk and chair.

So it's over.

All over.

He broods, staring at his clean and empty desk, and at the photos of him and Grace that were there to fool visitors into thinking he had a wonderful and traditional marriage.

Now what does he have?

A sudden stab of fear, of acknowledgment.

He has nothing now.

Grace will never take him back.

Parker is gone.

And now Tammy wants nothing more from him.

The overcast sky makes it seem darker and more confined in the Oval Office.

The President of the United States stares at his phone.

He can pick it up and talk to the vice president, currently on a campaign swing through Georgia and Florida.

Or he could call his secretary, Mrs. Young, and have a wonderful gourmet meal delivered to him.

Or he could contact the famed White House switchboard, and in a matter of minutes, he could be talking to the president of Poland, the head of Columbia Pictures, the latest and most famous rap star, or the most beautiful movie star in Hollywood.

All that power, all that possibility, all within his reach.

But for what purpose?

Why?

The President of the United States is alone in his Oval Office.

He continues to stare at his silent phone.

# CHAPTER 89

ON THE FOURTH floor of the Waterford County Hospital, Deputy Sheriff Roy Bogart checks in on his VIP patient from the open doorway. She's rolled over in her bed, facing the wall, handcuffs still secured.

Good.

He steps out and walks to the nearby nurse's station. An empty chair is next to the patient's open door. Deputy Sheriff Nancy Cook is supposed to be working with him, but one of her kids is throwing up something awful, so she's running late.

No matter.

When he first checked in on the patient an hour ago, she wasn't moving or saying a thing, curled on her side, one wrist handcuffed to the Stryker bed. Roy is fine with that, having guarded lots of patients over the years. The ones that drove you nuts were the ones screaming about hospital brutality, about how they had to use a bedpan, or that they were about to hurl all over the floor.

This one, though, is perfect. Short, dark-skinned, kinda rough-looking, but from what he heard at the nurses' station, she was wearing a Kevlar vest when somebody shot her three times in the chest. Poor gal is all busted up, and the last time Roy tried to talk to her, she just looked away.

Okay, then.

At the nurses' station, he catches the eye of Rhonda Buell, the floor supervisor, who's a cute thing with a nice set of curves, and although he's old enough to be her father, he loves chatting her up.

She rolls over on her chair and says, "How are you doing, Roy?"

"Fine, hon, how about you?"

"Hanging in there," she says, smiling, and Roy fantasizes for a moment that she's one of those nurses that gets off on seeing a man in uniform. Maybe he could luck out when both their shifts end and set up a lunch date or something.

Roy says, "I'm about to swing down to the cafeteria, grab some coffee. Can I grab you a cup?"

Rhonda says, "Sure . . . but you sure you want to leave your patient alone?"

"Cripes," he says, "you said her chest is all messed up, she's handcuffed—I don't think she'll be breaking out anytime soon."

"Yeah, you're right," she says. "I hear word that there's a bunch of Feds, state cops, and local cops in a conference room on the first floor, fighting over who gets her."

Roy says, "I still don't know what she did, do you?"

Rhonda shakes her pretty little blond head just as the nearby elevator opens up, and a sweaty, red-faced Deputy Sheriff Nancy Cook comes out, a large woman in the sheriff's brown uniform, carrying a small cooler.

"Man—Roy—s-so sorry I'm late—" she stammers out. "You know how it is."

"Sure do," he says, and he thinks, *Perfect, she can sit and guard the prisoner, and I can make the cafeteria run.* "Let me get you set up."

He points to the patient's room and Nancy joins him, and they walk in and Roy calls out, "Hey, miss, this is the other deputy sheriff who'll be keeping an eye on you."

No reply, which isn't a surprise.

But a second later, there's a big surprise indeed.

There's no patient.

Just bunched-up pillows underneath the blankets, a dangling handcuff, and thick tufts of hair spread near the pillow that made it look like someone was sleeping. *Sweet Mary,* Roy thinks, she either tugged the hair out by herself or sliced it off.

Nancy is standing next to him, breathing hard.

"Christ, sorry to say this, Roy," she says, "but I sure am glad I'm late."

# CHAPTER 90

FOR PROBABLY THE last time in my life, I'm able to use my Secret Service identification to go past a police and agency cordon, and after some minutes of delay, I'm able to get to a special room at Blair House, which—irony of ironies—is within easy walking distance of the White House and is also the President's official guesthouse.

The door is opened up by one of the First Lady's "children" from the East Wing, and I'm ushered into a sitting room, where a refreshed-looking Grace Fuller Tucker is sitting at a round dining room table. There's a coffee setup spread before her, and she says, "Can I offer you a late-afternoon refreshment, Agent Grissom?"

Any other time, I would say no, but like I've thought many times over the past few days, this certainly isn't any other time.

"Sure," I say, "but I'll pour myself."

She nods, and I sit down across from her, get myself a cup of steaming hot coffee from a silver set, and add a few lumps of sugar. The First Lady has had her hair done, she's wearing black slacks and a plain white turtleneck shirt, and the bandage on her left hand is fresh.

"How's your hand doing?" I ask.

She holds it up and gives it a glance, like it's some foreign object that's been attached to her. "Doing much better," she says. "The ER doctors over at George Washington cleaned it up and re-stitched it, and I've got some very fine painkillers to take the edge off. They wanted me to spend the night, but you see how far that went."

The First Lady smiles, and it's nice to be the focus of her warmth and attention, despite what I'm going to say next.

"Was it hard," I ask, "having your father slice off that finger joint?"

Her smile never wavers. "He's spent many years at Cleveland Clinic, observing and evaluating. He did a perfectly fine job."

I take a sip of the coffee. "This had been in the works for a very long time."

"Not that long," she says. "Only when my suspicions about Harrison were confirmed."

"I did some additional checking in on Mister Fuller," I say. "It seems he's also on the board for the corporation that owns the *Cleveland Plain Dealer*. I can see if a reporter or an editor learned about your husband's affair, how that news might have gotten to him first."

Mrs. Tucker doesn't say anything, but there's the slightest of nods. I say, "With that information. . .he doesn't confront the President. You don't confront the President. Instead, he sets up that ambush in Atlanta. I was always puzzled by that. It's typical for a breaking news story for one outlet—television station or newspaper— to take the lead in getting the story. Very unusual to have an ambush consisting of a couple of network television crews and reporters from competing newspapers at the same place and the same time. Like they were all tipped off simultaneously."

Her smile widens. "It was an unusual story, was it not?"

"Not as unusual as your ... disappearance," I say. "So far, the cover story about your falling in the stream, striking your head, and injuring your finger, is still holding. How long do you think it'll stay that way?"

She picks up her own coffee cup. "May I ask why you're here, Agent Grissom?"

I say, "By the end of the day, it won't be Agent Grissom. It will be plain old Sally Grissom. Too much has happened over the past few days."

"I'm sorry about that."

"I'm glad you are," I say. "I had a nice career with the Agency, a nice record, and now ... it's gone."

The First Lady says, "Then come with me. I need someone with your experience."

"You'll always have Secret Service protection, even if you and the President eventually divorce."

"I know that," she says. "But I'm not saying I need someone to help with my protection."

Then it all clicks into place, like the times I've helped Amelia put together a puzzle. You struggle, struggle, and struggle some more, until one last piece makes everything clear.

"This was one well-thought-out operation, with the ransom note, the severed finger, everything else," I say.

She says, "I thought the note would be a puzzle and make you think I committed suicide. But from what I've learned, the suicide question was never really pursued. Why?"

"You didn't seem like someone bent on killing herself," I say. "No, you're the type of person who wanted to punish the President, destroy his chances for re-election, and along the way ... steal a hundred million dollars."

"I prefer to think of it as a reallocation," the First Lady says. "A hundred million dollars that I will be able to administer as I see fit, without strings or obligations attached, to help tens of thousands of children. For years I pled with my husband and Hoyt to make the necessary budget requests and allocations to do just that, and I was always laughed at, or ignored, or patronized. And then I decided to do something about it." She holds up her bandaged hand. "Not a bad exchange."

I sit there with Grace Fuller Tucker and just let the thoughts race through my mind. In my long years with the agency, I've always protected the office . . . the Office of the President, the Office of the Vice President, the Office of the First Lady, and so forth and so on. Who was there wasn't as important as the office itself.

But I'm not seeing an office or a protectee or a cipher in front of me. I'm seeing a strong woman—stronger than me—who has made compromises and suffered setbacks, who has regrets about never having children of her own, but who's going to set her own path and now make a difference.

Not as the First Lady.

But as a woman.

The First Lady says to me, "My father has already set up the charity I intend to lead. I'm going to need someone smart and tough enough to get those funds secretly removed from that numbered account and quietly distributed to my charity and others. It probably won't be as exciting as your previous position, but I guarantee, you'll be spending more time with your daughter from now on."

*Amelia,* I think. Poor, sweet Amelia, who saved me this morning with her love and her gift.

The First Lady says, "Will you join me?"

I don't even hesitate.

"You can count on it," I say.

# CHAPTER 91

AT HIS LUXURIOUS home in McLean, Virginia, Parker Hoyt is in his plain and clean kitchen. He finishes his morning cup of coffee before going out for his daily bit of fun.

He looks out the window over the sink and sees the crowd waiting for him at the end of the driveway. It's been like that every day since his surprise departure from the White House, and the reporters and photographers have camped out on the street, waiting for a comment, a bit of news, anything to feed the demanding maw of the nation's press corps.

*Well,* he thinks, putting the plain black mug in the kitchen sink, *they're going to have to wait a long, long time.*

He goes out to the entryway, slips on a jacket in preparation for picking up that morning's *Washington Post*, tossed on his front lawn. He has certainly kept himself busy these past few days, and there are plenty of opportunities out there beckoning him. For while he may be temporarily down, he will never, ever be out.

Parker opens the door, starts strolling down his driveway. The beast down there notices him, and there are murmurs and a couple of shouts, and the lights from the television cameras flare on.

He enjoys playing with them, teasing them, pleading ignorance and puzzlement over his sudden departure.

There's no way he'll tell those fools what he's been up to, the phone calls overseas to certain countries that want him to advise them on negotiating with what looks to be a new administration coming in, phone calls with his old employer, who's confident that there will be a position open for him in a couple of months, and even a New York book publisher who wants him to pen his memoirs for an obscene price.

Memoirs.

Why not?

But one thing is for sure, what won't appear in his memoirs are the recorded phone calls in that woman's iPhone, said iPhone being quietly delivered to him by the Secret Service agent in his employ, and then being torched in his fireplace.

Phone calls.

Funny that old crone Amanda Price hasn't called him back, but Parker doesn't care anymore. His future is bright, secure, and above all, safe.

"Mister Hoyt!"

"Can you tell us why you left the White House?"

"Have you talked to the President lately?"

"Who will win next Tuesday's election?"

He smiles the best he can at the group of people he loathes, and he says, "As I've said before, I really have no comment."

Hoyt looks to the lawn, and damn, his newspaper isn't there.

Where is it?

From the questioning crowd, a voice says, "Here's your newspaper, Mister Hoyt," and the paper is held out to him; he steps off his property to get it, and since he's not on his property, he's fair game for the baying crowd of reporters, who gather around him, press him with their questions, their demands, the *flash-flash-flash* of cameras, a sharp and quick sting to his neck—

His neck?

He staggers back to the driveway, puts his right hand to his neck, pulls the fingers away.

A spot of blood.

Now he's sitting on the driveway, feeling very tired, wondering how he got there.

And the last thing he sees, before the blackness descends upon him, is a slim, dark-skinned woman, who walks away from the chattering crowd and then turns.

Blowing a final last kiss in his direction.

# ABOUT THE AUTHORS

**JAMES PATTERSON** is one of the best-known and biggest-selling writers of all time. His books have sold in excess of 375 million copies worldwide. He is the author of some of the most popular series of the past two decades – the Alex Cross, Women's Murder Club, Detective Michael Bennett and Private novels – and he has written many other number one bestsellers including romance novels and stand-alone thrillers.

James is passionate about encouraging children to read. Inspired by his own son who was a reluctant reader, he also writes a range of books for young readers including the Middle School, I Funny, Treasure Hunters, Dog Diaries, and Max Einstein series. James has donated millions in grants to independent bookshops and has been the most borrowed author of adult fiction in UK libraries for the past eleven years in a row. He lives in Florida with his wife and son.

**BRENDAN DuBOIS** is the award-winning author of twenty-one novels and more than 160 short stories, garnering him three Shamus Awards from the Private Eye Writers of America. He is also a *Jeopardy!* game show champion.

Are you a fan of thrilling dramas that provide a glimpse
into the lives of the rich and famous?

# If so, you'll love . . .

### THE PRIVATE NOVELS

Jack Morgan has a powerful investigative mind, and is
trusted with the most high-profile cases across the globe.
As the lead detective for his private investigation firm, he
is privy to the scandalous secrets of the world's elite. From
thwarting murderous plots to protecting lives, Morgan is
relentless in his desire to get the job done. Featuring
high-octane action and thrilling twists and turns, the
Private novels will not disappoint.

**Discover the series with an extract from *Private Princess***

**Out now in paperback**

# Prologue

CRACKED LEATHER TOUCHED rich soil. Knee in the dirt, the man thought of what was to come, and smiled. A broken nose took in the smell of the damp earth, memories carried in its dank scent. Memories of digging spades, pleading eyes and shallow graves.

The owner of the gloves wiped them against his camouflage trousers, his memories cleansed as easily as the leather. To him, the image of those graves was as inert in his mind as the way a postman views the mail. It was his job to fill holes in the ground, and with pride – the man knew that he was good at it. Better than good. He had been born as just another shitbag on the estate, but now he was a hunter.

He was a killer.

He'd tracked in forests, stalked in deserts, kidnapped in jungles and killed in cities. He had done these things for service, for his country and for his brothers. Sometimes, he'd done it for money.

Today he did it for pride.

He did it for *justice*.

The hunter-killer turned his eyes up to the sky. Rain was beginning to fall, bouncing from the thick green leaves of summer. The hunter-killer welcomed it. It was his ally. It would cover him as he slid and crept his way closer to his target. Closer to justice.

He could see his prize now, and the proximity caused his heart to beat against his scarred chest, endorphins flooding his body as he pictured his kill and the satisfaction it would bring.

It had been a long stalk, but the prize would justify the suffering and the cost. This kill would come at a price – a great price – but he would not shirk it. The butcher's bill would be paid in full, and then there would be *justice*.

Fifty yards away now, and the hunter-killer begged his heart to still, despite the thrill of what was only moments away. Wet branches pulled at him as he moved forward, checking his pace. He forced himself to slow, too close now to fail.

He looked down at the pistol in his hand, checking it for dirt. There was none, as he knew there wouldn't be. Inside the weapon in his hand, a bullet rested snugly in the chamber, ready to shatter on impact, and to tear out a great chunk of flesh in the body of his prize.

The hunter-killer smiled as he pictured that carnage.

Then he brought the pistol up into the aim, and centred its sights on the back of his target. A target that had caused pain and misery and suffering.

With a smile on his face, the hunter-killer pulled the trigger.

# Chapter 1

**One day earlier**

JACK MORGAN WAS alive.

For a former US Marine turned leader of the world's foremost investigation agency, Private, that could mean a lot of things. It could mean that he had survived knife wounds, kidnap and helicopter crashes. It could mean that he had survived foiling a plot to unleash a virus on Rio, or that he had lived through halting a rampaging killer in London.

Right now, it meant that he was twenty thousand feet in the air, and flying.

Morgan sat in the co-pilot's position of a Gulfstream G650, the private jet cruising at altitude as it crossed the English Channel from Europe, the white cliffs of Dover

6

a smudged line on the horizon. To the east, the sun was slowly climbing its way to prominence, the sky matching the colour of Morgan's tired, red eyes.

He was exhausted, and it was only for this reason that he was a content passenger on the flight and not at the controls.

The pilot felt Morgan's hunger: 'You can take her in, if you'd like, sir,' the British man offered.

'All you, Phillip,' Morgan replied. 'Choppers were always more my thing.' He thought with fondness of the Blackhawks he had flown during combat missions as a Marine. Then, as it always did, the fondness soon slipped away, replaced by the gut-gripping sadness of loss – Morgan had walked away from the worst day of his life, but others hadn't.

*What is it the British say on their Remembrance Day? 'At the going down of the sun, and in the morning, we will remember them.'* Morgan liked that. Of course, he remembered those he had lost every minute *between* the rising and the setting as well. Every comrade of war, every agent of Private fallen in their mission. Morgan remembered them all.

He rubbed at his eyes. He was *really* tired.

But he was alive.

And so Morgan looked again at the printed email in his hand. The friendly message that he had read multiple times, trying to draw out a deeper meaning, for surely the simple words were the tip of a blade. As the sprawl of London appeared before him, he was trying to figure out if Private were intended to be the ones to shield against that weapon, or if it would instead be driven into the organisation's back.

He was trying to figure this out because the email had not come from a friend. It had come from Colonel Marcus De Villiers, a Coldstream Guards officer in the British Army. Though no enemy of Morgan's, he was certainly no ally, and when in doubt, Morgan looked for traps. *That* was why he was alive.

But De Villiers was more than just an aristocratic gentleman in an impressive uniform. He was the head of security for a very important family. Perhaps the greatest and most important family on earth.

And *that* was why Morgan was flying at full speed to London.

Because Jack Morgan had been invited to meet the powerful people under De Villiers' care.

He had been invited to meet the royal family.

# Chapter 2

MORGAN STEPPED FROM the jet into a balmy morning of English summer.

'Beautiful day, isn't it?' the man waiting on the tarmac beamed.

Morgan took in the uniformed figure – Colonel Marcus De Villiers was every inch the tall, impressive man that Morgan remembered from two years ago, when Private had rescued a young royal from the bloody clutches of her kidnappers. De Villiers had been a sneering critic of Morgan and his agents then, and Morgan was certain that, beneath the smile, the sentiment was still strong.

'It is a beautiful day, Colonel, but you weren't so keen to exchange pleasantries last time we met,' Morgan replied. 'After I refused to cover up the Duke of Aldershot's involvement in the kidnapping of his own daughter.'

'All's well that ends well.' De Villiers shrugged, trying hard to keep his smile in place.

'The Duke died before he got to trial and faced justice.' Morgan shook his head. 'I wouldn't call that ending well.'

'One could say that death is the most absolute form of justice, Mr Morgan, but that's beside the point. The whole business went away quietly, which was very well received where it matters.'

'If you've brought me here to boast that a royal scandal stayed out of the papers, Colonel, then you're wasting my time. I took this meeting out of respect for the people you represent, but I'm ready to step back onto this jet and head home if you don't tell me in the next ten seconds why I'm here.'

'Very well, Mr Morgan. I didn't bring you here to boast about avoiding a royal scandal. I brought you here to prevent the next one.'

# Chapter 3

MORGAN JOINED DE Villiers in the blacked-out Range Rover that waited beside the landed jet. The Colonel would divulge no more information, but he had said enough to get Morgan's attention.

The men were driven from London's outskirts into the lush green countryside of Surrey, where multimillion-pound properties nestled in woodlands. It was beautiful, and Morgan watched it roll by the tinted windows as he considered who he might be heading to meet, and why.

The British royal family was large, with Queen Elizabeth II at its head and dozens of members tied in by blood or marriage, but Morgan had some clue as to who they were driving to see in the English countryside. Colonel De Villiers had once told Morgan that the family's inner circle was his concern, so the American was either on his way to meet the Queen herself, or one of her closest family.

Morgan allowed himself a smile at the thought. Here he was, an American – and once an American service-man at that – driving to meet the monarchy that his nation had fought against for their independence. The fact that the bloodiest relationships could be repaired made him pause and look to De Villiers. There were enough people in the world that wished Morgan dead. Why not take a lesson from the United States and the United Kingdom?

'Thank you for inviting me here,' Morgan said to the Colonel. 'It really is a beautiful day, and a beautiful country.'

'It is.' The Colonel nodded. 'But don't let it fool you. At this time of year, you can get the four seasons in a day.'

The Range Rover left the main road and entered a long driveway flanked by woodland. It would have been hard for anyone to spot the two armed men camou-flaged amongst the trees, but Jack Morgan was not just anyone.

'Relax.' De Villiers smiled, seeing Morgan tense. 'They're ours.'

As the Range Rover came to a stop and crunched the gravel, Morgan took in the exquisite Georgian farmhouse of ivy-covered red brick that stood before him.

'It looks like something out of a fairy tale.' He smiled, allowing himself to relax.

But then, as the house's green door opened, Morgan's pulse began to quicken. It was not the sight of more armed men that caused it, but the figure that walked by them and into the dappled sunshine.

Morgan stood straight as he was approached by one of the most famous women in the world.

Her name was Princess Caroline.

# Chapter 4

THE PRINCESS PUT out her hand, offering it to Jack Morgan as he stepped away from the Range Rover.

'It's a pleasure to meet you, Mr Morgan,' she said.

'Please, call me Jack, Your Highness,' Morgan answered, feeling himself bow on instinct.

'Let's take a walk, Jack. De Villiers tells me that you're the person I need to speak to.'

Morgan looked to De Villiers, surprised that such praise would come from the Colonel. De Villiers' face gave nothing away, nor did he move to follow as Princess Caroline led Morgan away from the courtyard.

'It's too nice a day to be inside,' she explained as they entered a walled garden. Bright red strawberries clung to the planters. 'Try one,' she insisted.

Morgan raised his eyebrows as he bit down on the fruit and the juice hit his tongue. With food in his mouth, he had the excuse he needed to keep it shut – introductions to a mission always worked better when he let the client do the talking. Nothing brought out the little details as well as just keeping quiet and allowing the other person to fill the dead space.

'This place belongs to a friend of mine,' Caroline offered up against the silence. 'Aside from my security detail, there aren't many people who know that I come here. I like it. It's quiet and it's close enough to London that I can sneak off here for some peace without it being noticed. I hope you know how to keep a secret, Jack.'

Morgan nodded, but said nothing.

Princess Caroline smiled. 'You don't say much.'

'It's not every day I meet a princess, Your Highness.'

Her smile grew, but from insight, not flattery. 'I think it's more that you like to let your clients do the talking, to see what they may let slip.'

Morgan couldn't help but grin. She was smart.

'I like to read about crime, and detectives,' the Princess admitted, her smile then falling. 'I didn't ever think that I'd be needing one.'

Morgan held his tongue and waited. She gathered herself, and he noticed the briefest trace of sadness pass across her face, and something else: fear.

'I need you to find someone for me, Jack. A dear friend of mine. She's missing, and I need her found. Her name is Sophie Edwards.'

'Are the police looking for her?' Morgan asked, knowing the answer before her reply.

'No,' Caroline said.

Morgan knew that he would not be standing here if they were. More than that, he was certain that Princess Caroline's fear was an indication that this was more than a simple missing-person case. Where there are complications, people tend to want to avoid the shining beam of the law.

'De Villiers said there's a scandal to avoid,' he said bluntly. 'It's easier to avoid if I know what it is.'

'He shouldn't have told you that,' she whispered after a moment.

'I'd have been back on the jet if he hadn't.'

Princess Caroline nodded, but instead of talking, she walked towards the far door of the walled garden. Morgan followed, and they stepped out into the woodland that butted against the house. Shafts of warm sunlight cut their way through the canopy.

'Do you believe in second chances, Jack?' she asked, her eyes on the path that wound ahead through the trees.

'I do,' he answered, his eyes to the trail's flanks – some fifty metres away, armed men moved parallel to the royal who was third in line to the British throne. They were her deadly shadow. The guardians who protected her at all times.

'There are things in Sophie's past – things in her life – that should not be public knowledge,' she explained. 'I live life under a microscope, Jack, because I was born into it. I wouldn't change that. But for Sophie? She hasn't lived with it. She hasn't trained for it.'

'And what are these things in Sophie's past?' Morgan asked.

She walked on in silence for a few moments before giving her answer. 'Sophie is a young woman who's lived her life, and in doing so – like all people – she's made some bad decisions.'

Suddenly she stopped. She turned to face Morgan, her expression earnest. 'She doesn't deserve to have those bad decisions made public as a consequence of being *my* friend. Do you understand, Jack?'

Morgan did. He also understood that those under the closest scrutiny became guilty of the sins of their company, and guilt by association was never more magnified than in the scandal-hungry media of the twenty-first century. Morgan knew that Princess Caroline was a reflection of the time she had been born into – a people's royal who connected to the country on all levels, leading a life that seemed as close to their own as was possible, given her position – but the same machine that had built her reputation could savage her overnight.

Caroline read his thoughts. 'It's in the country's interest that the monarchy avoids scandal, Jack. We're the benchmark. The example. I should be someone whom people look up to.'

'And you're not?' Morgan asked directly.

It was a long time before she replied.

'I'm human, Mr Morgan. De Villiers will give you everything you need. I hope to see you again soon.'

She turned away from him then and continued to walk further into the woodland. Out in the trees, her armed shadows moved with her.

'I didn't say I'd take the job,' Morgan said to her back.

'You didn't need to,' Princess Caroline replied without breaking step. 'Your eyes did. You should learn to be a better liar, Jack.'

Morgan said nothing, because she was right.

He would take the job.

He would find Sophie Edwards.

'Clinton's insider secrets and Patterson's storytelling genius make this the political thriller of the decade.'
**Lee Child**

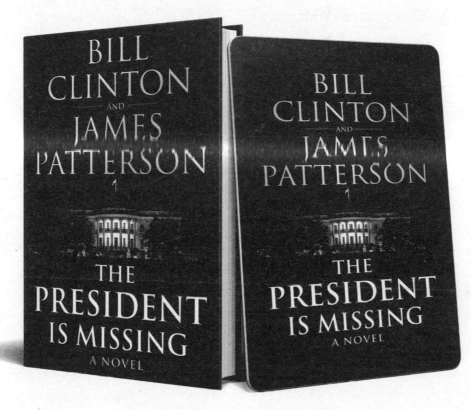

'A bullet train of a thriller. *The Day of the Jackal* for the twenty-first century.'

**A.J. Finn author of**
***The Woman in the Window***

'Relentless in its plotting and honest in its examination of issues that strike close to our hearts.'

**Jeffery Deaver**

# Also by James Patterson

## STAND-ALONE THRILLERS

The Thomas Berryman Number • Hide and Seek • Black
Market • The Midnight Club • Sail (*with Howard Roughan*) •
Swimsuit (*with Maxine Paetro*) • Don't Blink (*with Howard
Roughan*) • Postcard Killers (*with Liza Marklund*) • Toys (*with
Neil McMahon*) • Now You See Her (*with Michael Ledwidge*) • Kill
Me If You Can (*with Marshall Karp*) • Guilty Wives (*with David
Ellis*) • Zoo (*with Michael Ledwidge*) • Second Honeymoon (*with
Howard Roughan*) • Mistress (*with David Ellis*) • Invisible (*with
David Ellis*) • Truth or Die (*with Howard Roughan*) • Murder
House (*with David Ellis*) • Woman of God (*with Maxine Paetro*) • Humans,
Bow Down (*with Emily Raymond*) • The Black Book (*with David Ellis*) •
Murder Games (*with Howard Roughan*) • The Store (*with Richard DiLallo*) •
Texas Ranger (*with Andrew Bourelle*) • The President is Missing
(*with Bill Clinton*) • Revenge (*with Andrew Holmes*) •
Juror No. 3 (*with Nancy Allen*)

## ALEX CROSS NOVELS

Along Came a Spider • Kiss the Girls • Jack and Jill •
Cat and Mouse • Pop Goes the Weasel • Roses are Red •
Violets are Blue • Four Blind Mice • The Big Bad Wolf •
London Bridges • Mary, Mary • Cross • Double Cross •
Cross Country • Alex Cross's Trial (*with Richard DiLallo*) •
I, Alex Cross • Cross Fire • Kill Alex Cross • Merry
Christmas, Alex Cross • Alex Cross, Run • Cross My
Heart • Hope to Die • Cross Justice • Cross the Line •
The People vs. Alex Cross • Target: Alex Cross

## THE WOMEN'S MURDER CLUB SERIES

1st to Die • 2nd Chance (*with Andrew Gross*) • 3rd Degree
(*with Andrew Gross*) • 4th of July (*with Maxine Paetro*) •
The 5th Horseman (*with Maxine Paetro*) • The 6th Target
(*with Maxine Paetro*) • 7th Heaven (*with Maxine Paetro*) •
8th Confession (*with Maxine Paetro*) • 9th Judgement (*with
Maxine Paetro*) • 10th Anniversary (*with Maxine Paetro*) •
11th Hour (*with Maxine Paetro*) • 12th of Never (*with Maxine
Paetro*) • Unlucky 13 (*with Maxine Paetro*) • 14th Deadly Sin
(*with Maxine Paetro*) • 15th Affair (*with Maxine Paetro*) •
16th Seduction (*with Maxine Paetro*) • 17th Suspect
(*with Maxine Paetro*)

### DETECTIVE MICHAEL BENNETT SERIES

Step on a Crack (*with Michael Ledwidge*) • Run for Your Life
(*with Michael Ledwidge*) • Worst Case (*with Michael Ledwidge*) •
Tick Tock (*with Michael Ledwidge*) • I, Michael Bennett
(*with Michael Ledwidge*) • Gone (*with Michael Ledwidge*) •
Burn (*with Michael Ledwidge*) • Alert (*with Michael Ledwidge*) •
Bullseye (*with Michael Ledwidge*) • Haunted (*with James O. Born*) •
Ambush (*with James O. Born*)

### PRIVATE NOVELS

Private (*with Maxine Paetro*) • Private London (*with Mark
Pearson*) • Private Games (*with Mark Sullivan*) • Private: No. 1
Suspect (*with Maxine Paetro*) • Private Berlin (*with Mark
Sullivan*) • Private Down Under (*with Michael White*) • Private
L.A. (*with Mark Sullivan*) • Private India (*with Ashwin
Sanghi*) • Private Vegas (*with Maxine Paetro*) • Private Sydney
(*with Kathryn Fox*) • Private Paris (*with Mark Sullivan*) •
The Games (*with Mark Sullivan*) • Private Delhi (*with Ashwin
Sanghi*) • Private Princess (*with Rees Jones*)

### NYPD RED SERIES

NYPD Red (*with Marshall Karp*) • NYPD Red 2 (*with Marshall Karp*) •
NYPD Red 3 (*with Marshall Karp*) • NYPD Red 4 (*with Marshall Karp*) •
NYPD Red 5 (*with Marshall Karp*)

### DETECTIVE HARRIET BLUE SERIES

Never Never (*with Candice Fox*) • Fifty Fifty (*with Candice Fox*)
• Liar Liar (*with Candice Fox*)

### NON-FICTION

Torn Apart (*with Hal and Cory Friedman*) • The Murder of
King Tut (*with Martin Dugard*) • All-American Murder (*with
Alex Abramovich and Mike Harvkey*)

### MURDER IS FOREVER TRUE CRIME

Murder, Interrupted (*with Alex Abramovich and Christopher Charles*) •
Home Sweet Murder (*with Andrew Bourelle and Scott Slaven*) •
Murder Beyond the Grave (*with Andrew Bourelle and
Christopher Charles*)

### COLLECTIONS

Triple Threat (*with Max DiLallo and Andrew Bourelle*) •
Kill or Be Killed (*with Maxine Paetro, Rees Jones, Shan
Serafin and Emily Raymond*) • The Moores are Missing
(*with Loren D. Estleman, Sam Hawken and Ed Chatterton*) •

The Family Lawyer (*with Robert Rotstein, Christopher Charles and Rachel Howzell Hall*) • Murder in Paradise (*with Doug Allyn, Connor Hyde and Duane Swierczynski*)

For more information about James Patterson's novels, visit www.jamespatterson.co.uk